STONE WOMAN

ESSENTIAL PROSE SERIES 114

Canada Council for the Arts   Conseil des Arts du Canada

ONTARIO ARTS COUNCIL
CONSEIL DES ARTS DE L'ONTARIO
an Ontario government agency
un organisme du gouvernement de l'Ontario

Canada

Guernica Editions Inc. acknowledges the support of the Canada Council for the Arts and the Ontario Arts Council. The Ontario Arts Council is an agency of the Government of Ontario.

We acknowledge the financial support of the Government of Canada.

STONE WOMAN

BIANCA LAKOSELJAC

GUERNICA
EDITIONS
TORONTO • BUFFALO • LANCASTER (U.K.)
2016

Michael Mirolla, general editor
David Moratto, interior and cover design
Gabriel Quigley, author photo credit
Guernica Editions Inc.
1569 Heritage Way, Oakville, (ON), Canada L6M 2Z7
2250 Military Road, Tonawanda, N.Y. 14150-6000 U.S.A.
www.guernicaeditions.com

Distributors:
University of Toronto Press Distribution,
5201 Dufferin Street, Toronto (ON), Canada M3H 5T8
Gazelle Book Services, White Cross Mills,
High Town, Lancaster LA1 4XS U.K.

First edition.
Printed in Canada.

Legal Deposit—Third Quarter
Library of Congress Catalog Card Number: 2016935362
Library and Archives Canada Cataloguing in Publication
Lakoseljac, Bianca, 1952-, author
Stone woman / Bianca Lakoseljac.

(Essential prose ; 114)
Issued in print and electronic formats.
ISBN 978-1-55071-987-1 (paperback).--ISBN 978-1-55071-988-8 (epub).
--ISBN 978-1-55071-989-5 (mobi)

I. Title. II. Series: Essential prose series ; 114

PS8623.A424S76 2016   C813'.6   C2016-901525-4   C2016-901526-2

AUTHOR'S NOTE

Stone Woman begins in the summer of 1967, against the backdrop of tumultuous social and cultural changes. The Vietnam War rages on; the antiwar movement grows worldwide resulting in an unprecedented influx of American draft dodgers and military deserters to Canada; and Yorkville becomes the hub for the hippie movement not only in Toronto, but nationwide.

Although *Stone Woman* is a work of fiction, the inspiration for the novel stems primarily from two Toronto artistic achievements of the time. One is Frances Gage's *Woman*, a white Carrara marble sculpture commissioned by the Women's College Hospital and completed in 1971. The second one is the 1967 Art Symposium, as part of Canada's Centennial, which turns into a springboard for innovation in art and architecture in Toronto.

Commissioned by the City, twelve sculptors, selected through an international competition, are invited to design and construct modern artworks to be installed at High Park's Sculpture Hill. The first of its kind in Toronto, the Symposium is an interactive "gallery without walls," where visitors are invited to observe the artists at work, and in this way become involved in the project.

Ten sculptures were completed as part of the Symposium:

*Wessel Couzijn, Holland: *Midsummer Night's Dream*
*Hubert Dalwood, United Kingdom: *The Temple*
*Menashe Kadishman, Israel: *Three Disks*
Frank Gallo, United States: *Relief of Man Behind a Desk*
*Bernard Schottlander, United Kingdom: *November Pyramid*
*William Koochin, Canada (Vancouver): *The Hippy*
Pauta Saila, Canada (North West Territories): *Polar Bear*
Jason Seley, United States: *Hubcap Columns*
**Mark di Suvero, United States: *Flower Power* and *No Shoes*
Len Lye, United States, and Armand Vaillancourt, Canada (Montreal) did not complete their pieces.
Irving Burman's unfinished sculpture, consisting of two granite blocks, is displayed on a base near the north entrance to the park, on the east side of Colborne Lodge Drive.

This novel blends history, myth, memory, and fiction — and plays with the dates a little — as the magic in the story needed to have voice.

---

*Five sculptures still remain in High Park.
**Mark di Suvero's two sculptures were returned to the artist in 2010 for restoration, and have since been reinstalled at prominent places in Toronto.

For Sierra Sunrise,
Shellina, Aussie, Age
and
my mother Olga

PROLOGUE

Blossom
Winter, 2010

AMONG THE HILLS *and valleys of the ocean floor and colonies of coral, a white shadow of a woman shifts, then fades into the background. I hear my name called. Blossom! I slip behind a tall clump of coralline, peering through the transparency of the ocean vastness, then hop, weightless, over a mound, over a gorge. The shadow comes into focus, her limbs moving naturally as if she is a living being. But she has that white stone look — a sculpture of some kind. Where have I seen her?*

I pass my palm over my forehead, cold sweat transferring from one surface to another. I gaze at the mist sticking to the roadmap of my open hand.

If I were a palmist, would I be able to glimpse the future?

I am drenched in sweat, as if I surfaced out of the ocean in my dream. I try to recall the face of the figure. But all that comes to mind is her hair — cropped short, the same stone white as the rest of her, billowing gently with each stride as if she were a diver.

No, I did not see her face. I would recall it if I had.

Shivers pass through me, a cold silhouette of fear settles into my bones. I've been getting to know it, this lurking fear. What is the worst thing that could happen to me here, in this room, with sea-green walls hung with broken wings cast by a subdued light? The scent of antiseptic, the pitter-patter of the nurses' rubber soles is soothing in my twilight between sleep and consciousness.

Is forty-two an age to die?

No children of my own, no husband, no siblings, my parents long gone—just some distant relatives scattered all over the world. Except *him*. Chester. He is by my side day and night. But he is not even a fiancé, not that I'd want him to be, not now. What would be the point?

At times, I find more comfort among the dead than the living. I dream of my mother Liza who died when I was twenty-one. David's face from the faded photograph on my night table appears next to hers—the father I never met. I often think of Anna, my mother's friend, whose companionship got me through some tough times. Anna's recent passing left me feeling betrayed, as if she'd made a secret pact with the angel of death just so she could be close to Liza again.

Liza and Anna—how I long for those heart-to-heart talks.

My doctor is still looking for a donor. I am beginning to think that it's time to give up. My colleagues at the university have gone through the bone-marrow testing, as have my friends; neighbours from the High Park and the Bloor West Village area where I've lived most of my life; those I've nodded to on the streets; strangers I've never met. Toronto is a remarkable place. You may not know who lives next door, but if you need help, people flock from all walks of life to offer their bone-marrow.

Chester had insisted on being tested a second time. He thought there had to be a mistake, a miraculous chance that he would be the match the test somehow failed to reveal. He believes in miracles.

How could I tell him that our affections are but a life's trickster? For five generations, lovers in my family have lost their soulmate. He dies. Or she. Or vanishes without a trace.

Should I resign myself to replicating Liza's fate?

I envision his periwinkle eyes on me, burrowing as if they could heal by gazing into me. Has God sent him to make dying easier or harder? I sense his footsteps in the hallway getting closer. I close my eyes and wait for him to plant his lips on my cheek, gently, on my lips.

PART ONE

CHAPTER 1

April, 1967

SHE STANDS BY the edge of the reflecting pool at Nathan Phillips Square. She does not feel like going home, not just yet. Mirrored in the shallow water, the upturned arches of the new City Hall's twin towers are dipping into the pool as if it were bottomless. Framing the towers, the sky and the clouds mingle with the light ripples furled up by the wind.

A shadow of a man stretches over the ripples. It shifts closer to her own silhouette in the water, then joins it — the two effigies wobbling among the white clouds and patches of blue. She turns, and there he is again. Instead of a burger, he is now eating a sugar-dusted donut out of a paper bag.

"Oh, this?" he says, and points to the donut, as if continuing an ongoing conversation. He crumples up the bag noisily, turns on his heel and, swinging his arm behind his back, tosses the paper ball over his head and toward the garbage container. To her surprise, it hits its target.

He wipes his palms on his jeans and holds out a hand to her. "David."

"Just ... David?"

"That's it. David."

She pushes her sunglasses over her forehead, and sets them high enough to hold the long tresses away from her face. The tortoiseshell rim blends with her brown hair, a few unruly strands cling to her flushed cheeks, and she blows them away from the corner of her mouth.

She takes his outstretched hand. "Okay. Liza."

"Just Liza?"

"Yep."

He smiles and nods. His round-framed shades sit at the tip of his nose. Low on his forehead, flame red curls bob as if they were a theatrical wig.

To Liza, the day began as a new venture — her first day as the coordinator for the High Park sculpt-in. She can still hear the whirl of the helicopter above the crowd gathered at Nathan Philips Square where the sculpt-in, part of the city-wide Art Symposium, is being announced. All eyes are on the swishing blades descending near the three concrete arches that span the reflecting pool. The aircraft hovers for a few moments, then rises up in a wide circle over the Square to take in the panorama.

"They're marvelling at the view from above! Admiring the new City Hall!" Anna exclaims over the modulating drone.

"We should take a ride sometime," Liza calls out.

Although a helicopter tour is available any day, taking it with Anna would be more interesting. Anna could point to a building and rhyme off a whole wealth of information — its age, type of architecture, historical significance. She has been with the City's Department of Culture for almost a decade. It was her first job after high school and she is already office manager. Radiating confidence, she is an energetic go-getter, with dark hair she wears straight down her back, and never a dab of makeup.

Looking up at the helicopter, Anna says: "A bird's eye view of the eye? I'm all for it!"

The new City Hall has been nicknamed "The Eye of the Government" because, from above, it resembles a large eye. As a university student, Liza had written a research paper on the project. A couple of years later, the complex of structures representing two eyelids and a pupil is still the buzz of the town as well as a source of controversy. She had hoped to meet the architect at the opening ceremonies, but Viljo Revell died only months before the completion. His architectural marvel, however, has become the symbol of Toronto and has propelled the city into modernism. Likewise, the Symposium is seen as a forum for innovation in art and design. Liza's research on the new City Hall tipped the scale in her favour for the position of the coordinator.

A woman in a brown tweed suit turns to Anna. "We sure are starved for something edgy in this city. Love the concept — sculptors selected worldwide."

Anna nods with satisfaction. "Goodbye Muddy York! Farewell Hogtown! This is a historic moment!"

"It's more of an invasion," a gravelly voice interjects.

"Twelve sculptors from different parts of the world *occupying* High Park."

The women turn toward the voice. The man takes a bite of a burger in a paper wrapping. With lips closed and cheeks puffed out like a chipmunk, he grins and nods in acknowledgement.

Anna winces as if stung by a wasp and zaps him a look of annoyance.

He swallows his food and says: "Why not our own artists? Don't we have some home-grown talent here to take on the task?"

"Good to have some international flair," Liza says, smiling. "This will shake up Toronto's arts community in a big way!"

The man winks. "Wouldn't that be grand? Shaking up this sleepy old town." He wraps the unfinished burger, drops it in the waste bin, and moves a step closer. "Too bad old Revell didn't live long enough to see it."

"Who the heck does he think he is?" Anna says to Liza loud enough for the man to hear. "Viljo Revell died in his early fifties. Didn't get the chance to get old." She shoots an incensed look at the man, links her arm under Liza's, and leads her several steps away.

The white helicopter hovers for a few minutes longer then slowly descends to touch down on the cordoned off concrete slabs. Irving Burman, a middle-aged Toronto architect who spearheaded the project, steps out and, stooped over, runs to the side, beaming at the crowd.

Mark di Suvero, an American sculptor Liza met a few days back when he arrived to Toronto, follows. His posture is erect and his stride long and sure-footed, and she imagines him as a walking totem-pole.

Anna leans close to Liza and, looking at di Suvero, whispers: "Rumour has it, he supports the anti-Vietnam war movement."

Another man steps out. From the photos, Liza guesses it has to be Armand Vaillancourt. His long, disciple-like hair and beard make him appear a decade younger than his thirty-five, closer to her age, and she gets the sense that he will be easy going and pleasant to work with.

As Vaillancourt walks toward the group gathered by the edge of the reflecting pool, Anna tracks him with her eyes. "This job does have its perks. Meeting artists whose work you admire doesn't happen every day. Especially when they look like that. Too bad I have to run."

"Aren't you staying for the ceremonies?" Liza says, checking the program. "They'll be starting any minute."

Anna pulls out a pack of Luckies and taps out a cigarette. "Got to get back to the office. Late staff meeting."

"I've been asked to help out with the tour of the city. After the presentations. Won't you come along? Vaillancourt will be there." Liza raises her eyebrows and gives Anna a meaningful stare.

Anna strikes a match and lights the menthol tip. She inhales deeply and blows rings of smoke slowly through her pursed lips. "Now you're talking. I wish I could, honest." She places her hand on Liza's arm and, eyeing Vaillancourt, whispers: "There's talk in the office. That handsome Montrealer could be a separatist. Part of the movement René Levesque started, not long ago." She glances at her watch, then skims the crowd as if searching for someone. "But I've got to run. You'll be great! Call me this evening and tell me how it went. Maybe we'll grab a beer later on if you're up for it." Rushing off she turns and waves, cigarette grasped between her fingers. "And stay away from strange men!"

Liza feels a twinge of panic. She had hoped that Anna would join the city tour to answer some of the questions. Anna's parents had been members of the local historical board, and she knows some of the most obscure details about Toronto, as if she were an old-timer.

Burman is the first to speak. He emphasizes the significance of the Symposium and its role in Canada-wide Centennial celebrations. What he and the three levels of government on the planning committee had envisioned was an innovation in the design and the variety of material used in the sculptures — stone, metal, and wood. The committee had examined the sketches submitted by three hundred and seventy-five artists and had chosen the final twelve sculptors. The Symposium is autonomous — the artists would have full control of the design and the material. And although the ownership and the copyright of the work produced would remain with the City of Toronto, the City would have no control over any other aspect of the artworks created.

Burman expresses great interest in working in his own city. He talks about the proposal for his sculpture. It is to be comprised of three large stone carvings, two granite, and a Carrara marble as the centrepiece. The moment he saw this block of white marble it spoke to him, and he envisioned it as the crown jewel of his sculpture. His carvings would transform High Park and its visitors.

Di Suvero steps up to the lectern and announces that his sculpture will "embody the culture as we experience it." He plans to combine wooden timbers with structural steel. His installation will contain sections that will rotate and swing and enable the visitors to take a ride on the sculpture, and in this way interact with the piece.

Vaillancourt takes the mike and presents his plan for building a modern temple. As soon as he saw Sculpture Hill in High Park, he envisioned a Druid-like structure in its magnitude, made of large cast iron cubes. A foundry would have to be built, preferably in the park. He declares that, when his piece is finished, it will be unlike anything Torontonians have seen.

After two more speakers, Burman returns to the lectern for the closing remarks. He invites Torontonians to visit the sculpture sites, to talk to the artists and watch them work, and to experience a true "gallery without walls." The sculpt-in, which will take place in July and August, is the first of its kind in Toronto, and when the pieces are completed, Sculpture Hill will become Toronto's first permanent sculpture park. It will bring international attention to Canada's artistic heritage and lead Toronto into a new era of contemporary art.

"This is better than I ever imagined!" Liza exclaims.

"You always talk to yourself, young lady?" a gravelly voice calls out.

She spots the hamburger man smiling at her. A warm breeze sweeps through the Square, and she feels her zeal inflating. She unbuttons her cherry-red canvas coat and glances at her watch—just enough time to freshen up before meeting Burman and the sculptors for the tour of the city. Clutching a black folder under her arm, she walks toward City Hall at a fast clip, her patent leather pumps that match her coat clicking along the cement pads.

Burman catches up with her. "The tour has been called off."

"Great!" Liza exclaims. It takes her a moment to realize what he had just said. Her second "great" is that of disappointment.

CHAPTER 2

THE AIR IS perfectly still and, behind Osgoode Hall, the western sky is blushing pink. Liza and David chat by the reflecting pool now streaked with purple hues.

"Can't believe we're still here," Liza says.

David grins. "Glad those sculptors aren't into city tours. Gave us a chance to talk. You know a good restaurant?"

They perch on bar stools in the cocktail lounge of the Savarin Tavern on Bay Street, about a block south of City Hall, and wait to be seated in the dining room.

Elbows on the bar counter, David rests his chin on his fist. "How 'bout something little different? You like gin?"

She shrugs. He puts on an exaggerated British accent and continues: "How 'bout the Queen Mother special? Rumour has it she was known to have said before a trip, 'I think I will take two small bottles of Dubonnet and gin with me today in case it is needed'." He orders two Queen Mothers with an extra twist of lemon.

The waiter places cocktail napkins next to the tumblers and looks at Liza. "Just the way the Queen Mother likes it."

David raises his glass. "To you, Liza. And to this great day I met you."

Her face turns red as they clink glasses. He takes her hand gently in his. His hand is warm and dry and a bit calloused, and comfort settles between them.

Looking intensely into her eyes, David nods. "If the eyes in fact *are* the portals to the soul, you my girl are an angel. It's not often one meets an angel."

She pulls her hand out of his. "You using *lines* on me?"

He clears his throat. "I really mean that."

"How about we agree—no more lines, David." She takes a sip. "Nice blend."

He raises the tumbler toward the pendant light. "And the rose hue is eye-candy."

She props her chin on her hand and gives him a look of despair. "You always speak in … riddles?"

He shrugs and taps out a cigarette. "You win. No more *lines*. Where's your family from, Liza? Originally."

"My mother was from Belgrade. My father from Nuenen—that's in Holland. An odd combination."

"I went to Belgrade some years back. As a student. Great old city. So much history. But Nuenen? Oddly enough, that sounds familiar." He strokes his beard. "Of course, that's where Van Gogh painted the Potato Eaters."

She finds it hard to tell his age—late twenties, early thirties? *His bushy beard could use a trim.*

The maître d' announces that the table is ready. He points to David's jean jacket and tells him he cannot be seated without proper attire. David takes his jacket off, but discovers that he must have a dressy one. The maître d' signals to the waiter who promptly darts into the back room and brings out a restaurant-issue navy blazer.

"What an anachronism," David grumbles as he carries the blazer on his arm and folds it over chair back next to him. A few minutes later the waiter returns and asks David to put it on. David takes him aside and, as they exchange a few guffaws, he slips a bill into the waiter's hand, and the jacket remains on the spare chair. Every once in a while David glances at the jacket with disdain, as if it were road-kill.

A blond waitress whose nametag reads "Helena" approaches the table and passes out the menus.

David raises his eyebrows at her. "Hallelujah! Did they have to restrain you to put on that black garb? Didn't know you had a new job."

Helena waves her hand in dismissal. Her broad smile showcases her perfect teeth. She slips her hand in her pocket, pulls it out in a fist, and asks David to put his hand out. She places a small object in his palm and closes his fingers over it.

She smiles at Liza. "He can look when I'm gone."

Liza wonders what David meant by "black garb." Helena's black outfit is rather attractive. Her snug mini skirt and Lycra top outline her perfect curves. Her textured nylons and pumps with a front bow accentuate her shapely legs.

Liza studies the smirk on David's lips. "Well, you heard the instructions."

He opens his hand and reveals a white plastic lighter

in the shape of a woman in a pink bikini. He turns the wheel of the lighter, holds down the red tab, and the bikini top lights up at the same time as the bluish flame flares up.

"Ah, that's Helena, alright," he says. "She'd rather be dressed like this herself, believe me."

Helena returns with fresh rolls and butter. David flicks the lighter on and off and Helena gives him an incredulous look and they laugh. He introduces Liza as his new friend, and Helena as his old one.

Helena leaves the table and David says: "Surprised to see her here. Not her type of place."

Liza is tempted to ask about Helena. Then she decides it's too personal. She'll ask about his work. Has she seen him at the U of T's St. George campus? But instead she asks about his family. His mother is Irish and his father—in his words, somewhere there as well, Irish and Scottish.

Throughout dinner, Helena takes care of every detail as if they were her house guests. An unruly curl of thick blond hair has wiggled out of the tightly rolled bun and hangs over her right temple and down her cheek. She adjusts her tight skirt as if she is uncomfortable in it, and Liza has a desire to get to know that other Helena, the one David hints at, the fun Helena. But instead she says: "Your turn to tell me something about yourself. Your last name, perhaps."

"Gould. David Gould."

"Any relation to Glenn Gould?"

He laughs. And she thinks how his laughter makes her feel cozy, like a silk scarf she wants to wrap herself in.

He continues. "That eccentric pianist? The genius? No. You have an interest in music?"

"I saw him perform a few years back."

"Here, in Toronto? The man's a recluse."

"No, in Los Angeles. I was visiting relatives. With my mother. We were given the tickets—somebody couldn't make it. We sat in the third row. My mother was ecstatic. She passed away a year later. I found the ticket stubs still in her purse—April 10, 1964. So I never forgot it."

"I'm sorry, Liza. About losing your mother."

He takes her hand and gazes into her palm as if about to tell her fortune. He examines her fingers, rubbing his thumb over each one.

Liza takes a large gulp of water. She swishes the ice and listens to it jingle. "That was the only time I saw him. Glenn Gould. I don't think he's had any concerts since."

"Must've been quite an experience."

She lowers her eyes. A pang of longing at the memory of her mother lodges in her chest as if she'd choked on an ice cube that wouldn't melt. "What struck me was the way he sat in this low chair. Literally reaching up for the keyboard. He swayed his shoulders. I couldn't take my eyes off him."

"Did he hum to the pieces?"

"You know about that? My mother was fascinated by the humming. She told me to listen for it. Apparently some people were bothered by it."

"Funny," he says. "I recall that concert. Something he said about draft dodgers. Almost got kicked out of the United States. For a man who kept to himself, his words caused quite a stir."

"In support of the antiwar movement?"

David chuckles. "Sure thing, Babe. Except it got twist-ed. Turned into a question. Is Glenn Gould a pacifist?" An ironic smirk flickers across his lips. "Is Glenn Gould a pacifist," David mutters and shakes his head.

Liza examines his features — how that bitter look ac-centuates the sharp creases around his eyes. His murmur-ing reminds her of Glenn Gould's humming. Her moth-er's words resonate in her head. *Glenn Gould needed to compensate for the piano's inability to realize the music as he intended. So he hummed the notes.*

She'd felt that way about the violin lessons she began in grade nine in hopes of someday becoming a profes-sional violinist. But the violin could not produce the sounds she heard in her head. She tried humming the sounds, but her music teacher forbade it. She was told that she'd started too late to make a career of it. But she soon concluded it was the talent she lacked. She would not have made it as a professional regardless of when she'd started.

From then on, everything she did seemed off-key. The courses she took at university were not what she'd expected. The friendships she valued faded. And then she lost her mother — and fell into some sense of apathy as if nothing good would ever happen to her.

Until she landed her job with the Department of Cul-ture and met Anna. Anna has guided her on the corporate ethos at work, as well as coached her on ordering cock-tails at a bar. She encouraged her to apply for the position on the Symposium Committee. Liza's new assignment of reporting on the sculptors' work will be truly hands-on.

This is what she'd envisioned when she accepted the job with the ministry. And it's all thanks to Anna. Will she live up to her director's and her colleagues' expectations? Or will she fail, as she failed at becoming a virtuoso?

And now, as if the dam holding back her fears had burst, she is compelled to air out her misgivings about her off-key self—the misfit. But she met David only that afternoon. It wouldn't be right. Besides, she usually doesn't go out to dinner with strangers. Why did she accept his invitation? Is he also unable to air out the thoughts that preoccupy him? Yet, this feeling that the person across the table *would* understand is a shared moment, a subconscious connection—an odd conundrum. So she returns to the safe subject, to a conversation about Glenn Gould.

"Did you know Glenn Gould claimed his humming was subconscious? That he heard music in his head?"

David looks up as if he'd been caught off guard. "Glenn's groans and croons ... Sure thing."

"The way you said something reminded me of just that."

He narrows his eyes. "I groan for the war to end. The bombing to end. Napalming of Vietnam villages to end. The killing of children to stop. I croon for peace, Baby. Peace."

Something about David reminds her of Glenn Gould. The way David leans into that chair is suggestive of the way the pianist had been scrunched up in the chair his father had made for him. The one the pianist took to all his concerts. The one he refused to play without. The picture surfaces in her mind—of Glenn Gould on stage—as if the chair held the key to his talent. Was the repository of his genius somehow sheltered in that chair and he needed to draw on it—without which there would be only sound but not music?

And now she realizes what links the two men: the look of determination, some type of purposeful obsession she sensed in Glenn Gould—and she sees in David's face.

David leans his chin on his folded hands. "And you had to be all the way in California to see a Toronto pianist. You visit your relatives often?"

"Not any more."

He taps out another cigarette, and before she has the chance to remind him that he has an unlit one resting on the ashtray, he pushes it in his mouth. "And your father?"

"I never knew my father. He never knew he'd have a daughter. He was killed at the end of the war, 1945. He and my mother weren't married. She was a nurse and he a doctor. The clinic where they were stationed was bombed, accidentally ..." She catches herself. Why is she telling her life story, her parents' life story to someone she had just met? And why is he asking so many questions?

The maître d' appears by their table, silently, as if he's glided through air, and points toward the navy jacket folded on the back of the chair. Slowly, his irritation evident, David takes the unlit cigarette from his mouth and leans it next to the other unlit one on the ashtray rim. He slips his hand in his pocket, pulls out a few bills, and hands them to the maître d'. The maître d' nods as if he'd just remembered something and walks away just as silently, and Liza is glad. She could not imagine David in that borrowed jacket who-knows-who had worn. And she does not want anyone to disrupt the ease she feels sitting across the table from him. As if she'd known him all her life.

He is the most knowledgeable person she'd ever met when it comes to dining. They order glazed Cornish hen stuffed with wild rice for her and a steak with mushrooms for him, followed by chocolate soufflé for two, and the dinner is superb. They finish a bottle of French Merlot and now Helena places two snifters of Drambuie in front of them. The pianist is playing Moonlight Sonata, the lights are dim, and all is mellow and cozy.

Liza swishes the Drambuie and inhales the fragrance. David takes her hand gently in his, and fits the stem of the glass between her fingers, so that her palm cups the bowl warming the liquid within. "You hold the glass in the palm of your hand, like this," he says, "then you swish it a few times." Holding her cupped hand in his, he guides the glass to her lips. She takes a sip of liqueur, and then another, and a rush of heat descends to her chest, then radiates to her face, and she is not sure whether it's from the Drambuie or from David's hand on hers.

She stands up and makes her way to the ladies' room. She runs the water cold, slips her hands under, and presses chilled fingers against her cheeks; then takes a few deep breaths to collect herself.

When she returns, he pulls the chair out for her and meets her with a welcoming smile.

"I still know nothing about you, David Gould," she says.

He picks up the Drambuie and swirls the auburn liquid slowly. "I'm from Boston."

"You visit often?"

He looks at the unlit cigarettes on the ashtray as if deciding whether they are spaced evenly, and Liza wonders if he'd heard what she'd said, and as he continues gazing at the ashtray she realizes there is much more to this man than meets the eye. Finally, he says: "No, I don't. I don't visit. Unfortunately." He says it in a distant manner as if he's just remembered their conversation. The sadness in those words takes away her desire to ask more questions.

He picks up the lighter and flicks it on and off, absent-mindedly. Helena brings the bill to their table.

David looks up at Helena. "New job, ha? How are those classes going? Anything happening there?"

Helena stares at him icily. "Don't we have a deal?" She turns to Liza and says, softly: "Real pleasure to meet you."

She drops the black leather billfold in front of David, then turns and walks away briskly.

Liza reaches for the cheque. "Why don't I get this and leave the two of you to figure things out?"

He gently takes the billfold out of her hand. "Forgive me, Liza. I spoiled a perfect dinner."

"You didn't spoil anything. This *was* a perfect dinner. And Helena's a lovely girl."

David takes her hand into his. His touch is gentle, and she feels young and pampered, and all the tension dissipates.

The black billfold looks rather intimidating. It would've been more appropriate on a bank manager's desk than at a restaurant. The thick wad he takes out to peel off a couple of bills is even more intimidating.

Helena returns to the table. David hands her the billfold with, "no need for change," and she nods, sternly. She smiles at Liza and says how pleased she is to have met her, and without so much as a glance at David, turns and bristles away.

Liza wonders who Helena might be. He'd asked about her classes. Could he be her professor? But would a professor question his student about a decision to take on a new job? Clearly she did not appreciate his questions.

Later that evening, Liza sits in front of the mirror combing her dark hair. What did he see when he looked at her? She wishes her lips were fuller and her complexion finer. All during her dinner with David she'd wished for a different look. Less uptight, more relaxed and fun.

She recalls how David looked at her. Curiously, is the only way she could describe it. Even when he held her hand, she did not sense affection. Yet, the memory of him is comforting — as she no longer has to restrain herself from staring at him. He'd observed her features closely, watched her walking to the ladies' room. She knew he'd been watching her, she'd felt his eyes on her. When she returned, he asked for her telephone number.

"Okay if I call?"

She pulled out a writing pad from her purse and was about to tear out a page when he rolled up his sleeve. "Here. That way I won't lose it."

Her heart is racing as she recalls the scene. His arm is wrapped in a tattoo above his elbow and around his muscular bicep. Has she seen those symbols somewhere? The graphics are too dense, indecipherable. She clears her throat. "Where do you want me to write it?" He points to a bare spot of skin about the size of a ping pong ball. She leans her hand on his bare arm, brushes away a long tress that has fallen over her face, and as the ink forms the numbers, she inhales his scent mixed with a faint whiff of soap and cigarette smoke. The two top buttons of his white cotton shirt are undone, the fabric fraying around the collar. His breath is warm, and her face is inches away from his chest. She wonders if the rest of him is sun-tanned, and how did he manage that in April, and what it would feel like to press her lips on his bare skin. Her face is flushed and her palms are clammy and she is a bit shaky by the time the task is done. As he rolls down the sleeve he grins, seemingly amused. Then his eyes turn serious, focused on her lips. Slowly, she raises her face. He presses his cheek against hers, and draws her into an embrace.

And that's all. No kiss. Liza's heart is thumping and her face burning, just thinking about him. It's been a long time since she last jotted notes on herself or anyone else. Must've been in high school.

Would he call? Would she go out with him again if he did?

If her mother were alive, she would not approve of him. She'd call him a hippie. Anna seemed to dislike him at first sight earlier in the day at Nathan Phillips Square. Liza picks up the phone and dials Anna.

CHAPTER 3

"GOODNESS GRACIOUS!" ANNA exclaims, as two pints of draft are plopped on the table by the bare breasted waitress in gold leatherette shorts and white go-go boots, the mirrored sunglasses extending halfway down her cheeks.

"Thanks, sweetie," David murmurs and folds a bill into the waitress' hand. She blows him a kiss and he winks.

The waitress announces the daily special — chocolate covered ants, buy one get the second at half price — crunchy and peppery and yummy!

Anna rolls her eyes. "I thought it was chocolate covered worms."

"That was last week. We'll have them again tomorrow," the waitress enthuses without missing a beat.

"Can't wait," Anna says.

"We're adding chocolate covered crickets to the menu. Next week. Super crunchy!"

Anna shakes her head. "What's the world coming to?

That'll be the day, when I bite into a worm or an ant. Bring us some fries, will you, dear?"

"Love that about you," David says.

"Love me or hate me, I'm who I am. Why the heck would anyone eat insects?"

It's close to midnight and the crowds at Yorkville are warming up. Through the grimy window of the Mynah Bird Café, Anna notices several bikers sitting on their Harleys parked on the sidewalk. The colours are of the Vagabonds, and that familiar queasiness sets in at the sight of a motorcycle gang. But she keeps it to herself— there is no point in stirring up memories both she and David would rather leave behind.

Somewhere in the dark bowels of the cafe, the record player is stuck, and it keeps on scraping, "keeel, keeel," until somebody bumps it and sets it back to "... a Catholic, a Hindu," and it's jarred again as the scraping sound resumes, followed by "... Baptist, and a Jew," and it screeches again then continues with "... fighting for Democracy ... the Reds" and then it skips to "... peace of all," and is stuck again, and then picks up at "... all this killing can't go on." Then one long screech and the music stops.

Through the grey clouds of smoke, the bartender moseys to the back of the room and picks up the record player. He carries it to the bar, pushes aside an assortment of bottles and glasses on the counter, and sets it down. He slips a book of matches under one corner to level it, and the album is back on, the lyrics of Buffy Sainte-Marie's "Universal Soldier" softened by the grassy wallpaper and absorbed in the straw wrapping of the Chianti candles, in the dripping wax, and in the shrouds of blue fog exhaled in curls and billows. The crowd, a mélange of long hair, colourful beads, miniskirts, go-go boots, and sunglasses competing for size, cheers, and soon the whole room is singing along, out-of-sync lyrics trailing behind or suddenly taking the lead.

The bar is much better lit than the rest of the room. Colin Kerr, the owner, stands out from the crowd, with his shock of dark hair and his mynah bird Rajah on his shoulder, as usual. He moves about swiftly, one moment mixing drinks, and the next serving customers and clearing tables.

Anna flips her hair off her face. "There's Colin. He has a few volunteers for us." She picks up the glass and heads toward the bar. She plunks her beer on the counter and, chin on elbow, chats with Colin. She pulls a writing pad out of her purse and jots down the names of people willing to help organize the next antiwar demonstration.

David follows and sits on a stool at the far end of the bar. After a while, Anna picks up her mug and joins him. She shoots David a burning glare. "What were you doing there, anyway? Other than hitting on my colleague," she says in a low voice, and they both know that this is only the beginning of the grilling.

"You mean City Hall? The Symposium Ceremonies?"

Her stare intensifies. "No, David, the never-never land. Of course, City Hall. You were hitting on a woman I work with!"

The deafening noise at the bar magnifies the tension between them. He tucks his hands in his pockets. "I play by your rules, Anna. Appreciate your help. Guard your privacy. You said nothing, I said nothing."

He pulls out a cigarette pack and Anna wonders how many frayed white cotton shirts and fashionably worn jeans he owns in order to look as if he is always wearing the same clothes that have just been laundered.

She steps closer without taking eyes off him. The silky fabric of her purple mini dress moulds to her body, she knows, and her faux snakeskin slingbacks, although sensible, have these new heels, at once architectural and minimalistic and sexy in the way they make her feel chic. Her confident stance is enough to attract the attention of several young men strung along the bar like cheerful Christmas lights.

David taps out a cigarette. By the look on Anna's face he is certain that she is fully aware of the men's hungry looks and of the power she holds over her audience, including him, that very moment.

He slips the cigarette between his lips. "You look rather sleek today, wouldn't you say?"

She narrows her eyes. "Answer my question, David. This isn't about me, and you know that."

"If it's about hitting on your colleague, I wasn't exactly."

Anna flips her hair back over her shoulders. She picks up her mug as if it were a trophy, and squeezing between the patrons returns to their table.

David takes a long puff, puts out the cigarette in the overflowing ashtray on the counter, and follows. They're back at their small round table in the dark corner.

"How dare you stand behind me at City Hall, next to

me, or whatever, and pretend it's by chance? What's your game, David?"

"No game, Anna. Hoped to talk to you. Didn't know you'd be with Liza."

"We have an agreement. You don't come near my work. Or work-related functions. Where my colleagues could make the connection. No discussions whatsoever. About the demonstrations or anything else. Get it?"

"I didn't do any of that."

"I'd really prefer you didn't come near me when I'm around my coworkers. What you did was rotten. Butting in on my talk with Liza. Every time I turned you were there, somewhere behind me or next to me, clowning around. And you thought you were so charming. You made me really uneasy, David. Did that cross your mind?"

David nods. "I know I should've been more careful. It's the Commie thing, isn't it? But you're not in the States. It's not so bad here."

"Haven't you heard a word I said? Some of us need our jobs. Like me, for instance. The benefits, the pension, the whole shebang. I need it."

David shrugs. "I *did* want to be there for the opening."

"Sure. And happen to stand next to me. Oh, yes, and you certainly didn't want me to see you wallowing in self-pity. No, not you. Being a sculptor doesn't mean you get every contract, David. You have my sympathy. You really do."

He flicks the plastic bathing-suit-lighter and nothing happens. He shakes it and thumbs the flint wheel again, and is rewarded with a bluish flame that flares up as the fluorescent pink bikini top lights up and flashes on and off.

Anna shakes her head in disbelief. "I see you got yourself a new toy."

He shrugs. "It's a gift."

"You know, that's really degrading. Tells me how much you think of women."

"Quite the contrary. Toy, yes. But with no reflection on my view on women. C'mon, Anna. You know me better than that. It's a gag gift. From a woman, for that matter."

Anna rolls her eyes. "Besides, you haven't been sculpting for a while now. You have to practice your craft, David, or you lose the edge. Or the contract for that matter."

"The contract? Most of the winners are newbies. Irving Burman, for example. But why tell you what you already know?"

"The competition was fierce, David. So you didn't get it. Besides, you've been busy teaching."

David knows Anna has a point. The twelve sculptors who were chosen do have impressive backgrounds. And so does Burman. What burns him is that he believes his rejection had something to do with his being a draft dodger. It's not the money he is upset over — there is no money to speak of — a couple of thousand dollars for a whole summer's work. It's the recognition and the chance to challenge his creative self. The promise of a new beginning. Once he saw the two granite blocks and the slab of marble delivered at Burman's site, he became inflamed with a desire to be part of the venture.

He could work wonders with those pieces. And that

hunk of Carrara that sat atop the granite blocks? It spoke to him the moment he saw it. He envisions the sculpture trapped in it — stirring, shrugging off the excess stone that weighs it down, unburdening itself of the rubble, heaving sighs of freedom to become all it could be — an elegant woman with the physique of an athlete, struggling to rise from the rock in her full form and beauty. He is the only one who can free her! Without him, she will remain encased in that marble tomb forever.

He blows a loose smoke ring and, in the dissipating ether of the dark bowels of the bar, the stone woman emerges — and all at once he is elated by the possibilities and devastated by the reality that he would *not be* the one to unshackle her.

"You sure seem absentminded today," Anna says.

David stares into the distance, then rests his forehead in his palms. "No, not really." Hand over eyes, he invites the vision of the stone woman to settle in the quiet darkness of his mind. After a moment, he opens his eyes.

Anna scrapes off a dab of wax from the Chianti candle and moulds it between her fingers. The flickering wick casts yellowish shadows across her face. Her eyes remain downcast, focused on the metallic-purple glass. She pictures the fibres of a loosely twisted cord inside the bottle, imbedded in the wax — the soft-spun threads that by capillary action draw up to be burned a steady supply of the melted wax. How similar this apparently simple process is to human relations. Especially to certain people, certain men. What is it about David that draws women to him the way the wick draws oil to a flame?

David taps out another cigarette, pushes it between his lips, and observes Anna carefully, the crow's feet around his eyes deepening. "Is there a problem?"

She unwraps a new piece of gum. "I'm uneasy about the demonstrations. Even about being seen with you."

"Just being seen with a Commie. Not a good thing, as Allen says. Right?"

Anna winces. Allen Ginsberg has been a pebble in her shoe. Not that she has anything against the man or what he stands for — she is glad for his courage — but the office politics at work are rather complex. To David, he is a friend and an inspiration, a poet who uses his talent to stand up to convention and bureaucracy, unafraid to express his beliefs. To her, Allen is a rather curious writer who uses foul language to shock society into hearing what he has to say. When some of her coworkers refer to Ginsberg as "a screaming kite caught in the storm of criticism," she finds it difficult to totally disagree with a clear conscience. So she tactfully avoids the subject.

Anna is chewing gum as if her life depends on it. "Things seem so simple to you, don't they, David?"

"No, I realize. In your office, I'm sure ..."

"Just the mention of Ginsberg raises hackles in some circles. Especially with my boss! You've had your picture plastered all over the newspapers. You and Allen. I could imagine what my boss would say if he thought I had anything to do with either of you."

The gold leatherette shorts and perky breasts are back with cold beer. She sets two mugs of draft and a shiny clamshell filled with chocolate-y morsels. "Surprise! Our chocolate covered grasshoppers got here early! We're all so excited! The boss said to give out free samples!"

Anna shakes her head in despair, picks up one of the mugs, and takes a gulp. "Liza and I work in the same office. You must've figured out that much. Any idiot would've. And it's just a matter of time before she figures *you* out."

"Come on, Anna, things aren't that bad. You make it sound as if I'm ..."

She places the mug back on the table. "No? A lot of people know your involvement. You lead the demonstrations. You're friends with Joe Young. With Allen Ginsberg. Your teaching contract at U of T wasn't renewed. Anyone seen with you gets labelled."

"Is that what you're worried about? My teaching contract? It had nothing to do with politics."

"Sure, David. If you say so. But we both know the truth. As I said, I need my job."

He searches her face for meaning, the creases on his forehead deepening. "You're great Anna. You get things done. People look up to you. Just need to loosen up a bit."

Anna's blood rushes to her cheeks. She grabs the mug with both hands and takes a long swallow. "Did I hear you say, loosen up?"

He runs his fingers through his hair. "Everything's under control."

Anna pulls a paper fan out of her purse and snaps it open, revealing a large coral-coloured peony and a tall-legged bird, and begins to fan her face. "You know, David, you can do whatever you want." She places the fan on the table. "You have no attachments. You come and go as you wish. And you think it's nothing. If you got caught you'd be jailed for good. You do know that, don't you?"

"Relax, Anna. I haven't been caught yet, have I? Why would I get caught now?"

"Don't play with me, David. We know each other too well for that. Where do you cross, anyway? Buffalo, Lake Erie?"

"Yeah, yeah. A short boat ride. No biggie. My fellow Americans don't really care. What would they do to me? Jail me? Anything's better than fighting a war. Killing innocent people. I am not a soldier, Anna. But change can happen without a gun. You believe that, don't you?"

"You think I'd be here, talking to you, if I didn't?"

David leans forward, props his elbows onto the table, cups his face, and closes his eyes. After a long moment he opens his eyes, pushes his chair back, and gets up.

Anna stiffens. "For God's sake David. Go ahead. Walk away." Her voice softens. "You know I respect the work you do. Fighting for peace. Otherwise I wouldn't be putting my job on the line. And being a draft dodger? I sure don't blame you for that."

She grabs a few chocolate-y tidbits from the clamshell and stuffs them in her mouth. The next moment, with a revolted look on her face, she snatches the paper napkin off the table and spits into it. Holding the napkin over her mouth, she runs to the ladies' room.

David sits down and leans his chin in his hand. He wishes he could remind Anna that she and Ginsberg are on the same side, helping with the antiwar movement. Except that she is undercover, sort of. Her job with the Department of Culture means the world to her, and the politics *could* get heated if her coworkers found out about her involvement in organizing the demonstrations. She would be ostracized and that could be tough on her. He knows her heart is in the right place and her work with the movement is invaluable. She's an efficient organizer and a people-person. He sits down and guzzles most of the beer and places the mug back on the table.

In his mind, he goes over the speech he'd like to convey to Anna. He could remind her that Ginsberg is the one who had suggested that protesters should be *armed* with flowers to hand out to spectators, even to police and press and politicians. The use of flowers and toys and music was intended to reduce the fear and anger inherent in protests. The method proved very successful, and "flower power" became an integral symbol in the counterculture movement. Ginsberg is a beacon of the movement and what it stands for. David is ready to jog Anna's memory about all this. Then he reconsiders — she is too upset.

Anna returns. "For heaven sake, I just stuffed insects in my mouth! I've got to take a break from everything. All of this is really getting to me." She picks up the clamshell and sets it on another table.

"Things aren't that bad, Anna. Nothing comes easy."

"I just need some calmness here, in my world. No one depends on you. It's different for you."

"What's this about, Anna? Who depends on you? Who are you talking about?"

She sits down with a deep sigh. Deflated. "Forget it, David. It has nothing to do with you. Forget I said anything."

He taps out another cigarette. "I'm here for you. You know that."

She reaches into her purse, pulls out a package of bubble gum, and slaps it on the table. "Why do you keep lighting up one after another? Don't you see I'm trying to quit?"

She waves away the billows of smoke drifting from the table next to them and stares at the two large men in shirts with cut-off sleeves and mirrored sunglasses, puffing away. Bikers. A young woman squeezes out of the chair wedged between them. Her ample breasts are spilling over the yellow push-up bra and her thighs are bulging below the skin-tight purple shorts. With her waspish waist, she appears ready to take flight. Her blond hair is tied with white lace into pigtails. As she passes behind David, she leans over the back of his chair, grasps a handful of hair at the top of his head, and stares mischievously at his face. Then she plants a smacking kiss on his cheek.

Anna makes a gagging gesture with her index finger. "Hey, you!" she calls out. "Those two not enough for you?"

"It's Helena," the woman answers calmly. "Like Helena of Troy, you know," she says in a musical voice as she tousles his hair. She picks up David's unlit cigarette from the ashtray, flicks her lighter that matches David's, and after lighting up and drawing a few puffs, sets it back in the ashtray. She continues toward the ladies' room.

"You mean, Helen of Troy, don't you?" Anna hollers after her.

"Yeah, sure, whatever," Helena mutters and waves her hand without turning.

Anna wonders where she'd seen Helena before — must've been one of the bars. She pulls a pack of Luckies out of her purse, then shoves it back in. This is her last pack. After this, she'll quit. And she's given herself per-mission to make it last as long as she wants — weeks, months ... And by then, she would've quit, surely. Besides, one more cigarette and there would be no breathable air left in the room.

David rocks on the back legs of his chair and blows perfect smoke rings. He taps the ash off into an empty beer bottle on the table instead of the large purple ashtray overflowing with butts, and Anna wonders how he man-ages not to miss the narrow bottleneck, and in that brief moment, this mundane task somehow alludes to how he handles a lot of other things such as organizing the dem-onstrations, getting across the border without being caught, or when funds are short, paying out of his own pocket for the buses that bring in the demonstrators. Or how he manages to handle his ex-buddies, the Hells An-gels. But her top-of-mind concern at this point is that he convinced Liza to have dinner with him. What are the chances that he would start dating her colleague? He is going too far. Meddling with her job *and* her friend.

Anna locks eyes with him. "Did you have a good time? You and Liza."

"Liza?"

Anna casts him an incredulous look. "Yes, you do re-member Liza, don't you?"

David says gently. "She's a great gal." He takes a swig and sets the empty mug on the table.

Could Anna be reading more into their relationship than she should? David wonders. Is there something more than friendship between him and Anna? Their one occasion of intimacy flashes in his mind and he quickly dismisses it. They had agreed to never mention it. And they had not. It was not the way either would have wanted it to happen.

Anna looks into his eyes with steely determination. "How much does Liza know about you?"

"What's to know? The whole McCarthyism thing is really American bullshit."

"I'll say it once more, David. How much does she know about you?"

CHAPTER 4

June

A FTER A WEEK of intermittent rain, the afternoon sun seeps through the vapour veiling the tree crowns. Black binder under her arm, Liza stands at Sculpture Hill looking over the cluster of sculpture sites. She slips her shoes off, delighting in the coolness of moist grass beneath her bare feet.

She is preparing a progress report on the setup of the artists' work areas. Some sculptors have not revealed their plans yet. They are taking some time to get inspired by the setting, designing their pieces to suit the location. Others, like Mark di Suvero, are ahead of schedule. Di Suvero has already begun the construction of his *Flower Power*. He has asked the City for a set of tools: a crane, a cherry picker, a welding power supply, as well as accessory hammers and an assortment of hand tools. The local construction companies have been generous with lending the machinery and tools to the sculptors, free of charge, and the trades people are more than happy to donate their time and help out. The community has provided the artists and their families with accommodations. Encouraged by Toronto's enthusiastic support, di Suvero is planning to build two installations.

Using a crane to create a sculpture is not what Liza imagined. This is the first time she has seen an artist using this method. With the crane, di Suvero lifts the red I-beams she estimates to be seven or eight yards long, and moves them around until he finds the right position — the look he envisions. Then he climbs into the cherry picker, torch in hand, and is lifted to weld the beams into position. Some beams he fastens with steel plates. Three I-beams in the shape of a "V" about ten yards high have already been erected, and she imagines how this colossal installation will look when completed.

A five minute walk to the valley just south of Spring Road leads her to Bernard Schottlander's foundation for his weighty piece. Schottlander is manoeuvring a wheelbarrow with concrete which he empties into the wood frame of about three square yards. He pushes the empty wheelbarrow to the side of the foundation and greets her. He unrolls the plan for his *November Pyramid*, which will be made of large brown cubes, and tells her it will be a gathering place for children.

On her way to Wessel Couzijn's site, she is thrilled by the flurry of activity in the park. The birds are darting from one tree top to the next, as if on a mission. The squirrels are scurrying up and down tree trunks. The dog walkers pause to observe the work in progress, and the joggers weave among the sculpture sites. The visitors, some in groups of three or four, are updating each other on the development of certain pieces. The artists visit each other's settings and deliberate amongst themselves. Some of the discussions are quite boisterous, a lot of laughter and pats on the shoulders.

Couzijn, a middle-aged Dutch sculptor, is stretched out on the grass under a clump of birches. He turns on his back and gazes into the green canopy above him — Liza knows this is in an effort to get the feel of the place, to get inspired. The art has to suit the setting. She tiptoes through the grass and joins him.

He sits up and smiles. "That's a very Dutch thing to do, walk bare foot."

"I *am* part Dutch," she says.

"Yees, you told me. Your father was from Nuenen." His eyes appear small through his thick round glasses. He has that same half-smile on his moon-shaped face that always puts her at ease.

She sits next to him and clasps her knees. "Have you decided what to sculpt, Mr. Couzijn?" She says, smiling.

He winks. "A few times. But this time I got it right. It'll be about the park. This park and every other, but mostly this spot, right here."

"Here where we're sitting? So you've chosen your site?"

He gets up and paces among the birches, his slight figure moving as if he were weightless. The word, "yes" said in his drawn out way, encompasses a whole spectrum of plans and visions.

"It would have to withstand time and the elements," he says. "It is a park after all. The piece will belong here."

"And what will it be?"

"It will be a moment in life. As it evolves here, in this park."

His mischievous smile tells her that he isn't about to reveal any more than that. She waves goodbye. Later, his words would seep back into Liza's thoughts, the inspiration for the sculpture revealed to her in a way she had not anticipated.

Liza heads to Jason Seley's site — a pile of chrome plated car bumpers and other car parts. The sun dances off the shiny metal surfaces and the setting resembles a mini junk-yard. How would she describe this site in her report? The prospect of artwork made of old car parts *is* intriguing. The first in Toronto. Yet, visitors shrug doubtfully as they pause at Seley's collection.

She makes her way toward the Forest School. The clapboard building from the early nineteen hundreds, once a summer school for underprivileged children, is now used as an art studio for the sculptors and art students who assist them. In the shade of the veranda, two men are having a loud discussion. The sun is in her eyes, but she recognizes the voice of the school superintendent who looks after the inventory and schedules. The second man is Frank Gallo.

The superintendent waves her over. "Just the young woman I need! Frank here could use your help." The superintendent continues: "Frank's supply of epoxy resin is held up at the border. Customs won't release it. Questioning the chemical composition of the material."

Liza had already heard from Gallo, had contacted a friend at the customs office who knows the officer in charge of Gallo's shipment, and she is hoping to hear back any time now.

The first time she met Gallo about a month ago she could not believe how much he reminded her of David. David — who never did call. David — whom she has not been able to put out of her mind after only one date, almost two months ago.

The superintendent waves his arms in despair. "The customs people simply won't let it through. What do they think it is? Dynamite? I've done all I can, Frank."

Gallo steps hurriedly toward Liza, takes her hand and shakes it vigorously as if they were old friends.

The sun is suddenly searing hot and the humid air feels too warm to inhale. Liza leads Gallo toward the shade of the school veranda. They sit side by side on the wooden steps. A gentle breeze weaves its way among the wooden trellises and she is instantly refreshed.

Gallo gives her that same questioning glance as the day they met. It reminds her of the way David looked at her at the restaurant when he said: "Liza, you look lovely." It was just an observation. He could have been gazing at the Fettuccini Alfredo and saying: "That pasta looks lovely." A detached assessment.

Gallo rhymes off the dates and times he contacted the customs office looking for his supplies.

"I'll phone you as soon as I get some info," she says.

At last, he gets up, shakes her hand heartily, and hurries off.

Liza wishes she could put David out of her thoughts. Since the sculptors arrived in Toronto, the whole city has been altered by their presence — David somehow part of the whole scene. *Even if he did phone, I would not wish to see him, not after so much time has passed.*

The sculptors have left their sites for the day. Gallo's hosts have invited the artists and their families to a garden party. The locals take turns holding pot-luck dinners — the chance for the neighbours to chat with the sculptors and to get to know their families. Liza has excused herself. She could use a quiet evening. She checks her watch. There is enough time to draft the report while the information is fresh.

She heads to Couzijn's site, sits on the grass in the cradle-like hollow between the birches, and works on her notes. The fog has lifted. The late afternoon sun lights up the tips of the tree crowns and lengthens the shadows below. How should she report on Gallo's site?

By the Forest School where she and Gallo had been, a man is sitting on the veranda steps. Her heart beat quickens. It *is* David. He stands up and walks toward Keele Street, his back to her. His navy and white tie-dyed T-shirt hangs loosely over his jeans. He turns and she watches his profile. His shoulder length hair and bushy beard glow red in the sunshine.

He strides down the hill and pauses at the site for *No Shoes*, di Suvero's second piece. It's just a cordoned off grassy patch with a few I-beams stacked in a pile. Seeing David here feels personal. Close to home. She is glad that he is not aware of her presence. *Another chance meeting?*

A few weeks back, Liza saw David at the Love-in at Queens Park. He did not recognize her. She had sprayed gold sparkles in her hair and tied a multicoloured bandana across her forehead; an artist at the Love-in had drawn a pink tulip on her cheek; hot pink lipstick and oversized sunglasses completed the look.

She had gone to see Leonard Cohen and Buffy Sainte-Marie's performance, and the excitement of the event took hold of her. She can see it now. Cohen is singing her favourites — "Suzanne," and "So Long Marianne," while wearing flowers behind his ears, bare feet planted in the grass. He tells people he loves everybody and spring had called him to come to Toronto.

A woman hands Liza an armload of tulips and daffodils and asks her to hand them out to others. As Liza distributes the flowers, Buffy Sainte-Marie is singing "The Universal Soldier," and the crowd joins in. In another section of the park, Earle Birney, poet in residence at University of Toronto, is reading poetry. The place is throbbing with music and sing-along. Some people are dancing barefoot. The venues are free of charge and the performers have volunteered their time. A long-haired teenager dunks a plastic ring into a soapy dish and offers it to Liza, and as she blows into the ring, gigantic rainbow bubbles drift over the crowd. Several people are sitting on the grass, cross legged, and meditating, their palms upturned to the sunshine, eyes closed, faces serene. A group of teenagers are smoking banana peel and singing Donovan's "Mellow Yellow." *High on the song, if not on the banana peel*, Liza ponders.

And then she spots David, sitting on the grass in a group of people, she estimates about ten, and passing joints. They have a few going, and seem relaxed, engaged in conversation. A few pizza boxes are passed around as well. Cans of pop are propped up between them, here and there. She recognizes a few faces from the newspaper articles — organizers of the antiwar demonstrations, seen as socialists. She gets closer, debating whether she should say "hello" and catches a few words — about deserters and FBI agents, and the difficulties of finding jobs. She walks away. *What would I say to David?* At the end of the day, David and a few others organize the clean-up of the park and everyone helps. While picking up paper cups and discarded food cartons, Liza remains a safe distance from David. *If he wants to talk to me he would call me.* The next day's newspaper articles praised the organizers for bringing the community together and keeping the event peaceful.

Now, seeing David at Sculpture Hill checking out the sites, she wonders if she should walk over and tell him that she had seen him at the Love-in. She could use it as an excuse to talk to him. He continues toward the Forest School, and she loses sight of him. He reappears not far from Colborne Lodge Drive where Irving Burman's two boulders of granite and a block of marble have been sitting in the crates since they were delivered, a few days before the opening ceremonies.

He stands by the stones, arms crossed, rocking back and forth on his heels. She is dizzy just watching him. What does that say about him? Insecurity? Discontent? Or simply contemplation? Then he turns in her direction. She lowers her head and brings the sunglasses from her hair down over her eyes. She buries her face in the open pages of the report and hopes he does not notice her.

When she looks up, he is passing not far from her, and she is glad the shrubs and trees obscure her hideaway. He continues up the hill toward Mark di Suvero's *Flower Power*. He stops by the red I-beams that have been erected in the shape of a large "V" and remind her of a gigantic peace sign.

She is not surprised by David's interest in di Suvero's work. The name *Flower Power* di Suvero chose for his second piece confirms his empathy with the hippie subculture and the antiwar movement.

Liza has kept clear of the rallies and maintained the "clean" and "disciplined" look of the corporate culture. While at university, she stayed away from the "cool" kids and wild parties and stuck to a tight study schedule and a part time job at the school library that, in Anna's words, had kept her out of trouble. Now she wishes that she had broken out and experienced the "wild side." She has missed out on the freedom the hippie subculture offers. Yet it's everywhere, all around her. She could smell it but not taste it, she could see it but not touch it — as if she were wrapped in gauze to prevent being infected by it. And all she has to do is reach out. But how? Going to the Love-in was her way of trying to, in a small way, get the taste of the subculture. But it was only a one-day adventure.

She's always been a bit of a loner. She does not fully belong to the corporate culture either. This feeling of not belonging is amplified by her conflicted existence. In principle, she fully supports the antiwar movement — that she does nothing about it gnaws dully at her like hunger pains after a skipped meal.

Liza now has a clear view of David. He steps over the

plank barrier to examine the partially erected V-shape of *Flower Power*. He passes his hand over the red I-beams. Then he steps out of the cordoned-off area. He pats his jean pockets, pulls out a pack, taps out a cigarette, and pushes it in his mouth. With the unlit cigarette hanging from his lips, he sits on the grass and stares into the distance.

I etched my number in his skin, for heaven sake. She turns her attention to the report. In the corner of her vision, his red hair glows in the late-day sun.

The draft report finished, she snaps the folder shut. The shadows have enveloped the hill and filled the valley, and the last rays of sunlight illuminate the I-beam apex of di Suvero's *Flower Power*. The man with the red hair has vanished.

CHAPTER 5

"**T**HIS LITTLE BUG never lets me down."

Liza pats the hood of her Volkswagen Beetle she's squeezed into the last available parking spot on Colborne Lodge Drive near the Forest School. Returning from a gruelling Friday afternoon meeting in Etobicoke, she drove straight to the park to visit the sites and update the report.

She clutches the door handle. Should she search for another parking space down the road? The forest green Ford Galaxy parked next to her is rather close. She has been careful not to have the car dented or the paint scratched. Although she'd bought the robin-egg-blue Beetle second hand, it had been well cared for, and is immaculate for its age. On the other side, a cherry red Camaro convertible with the top down and white leather seats is parked a safe distance away.

Instinctively, she scans the sculpture sites. Irving Burman's two large granite blocks and a slab of marble are still strapped in the wooden crate in which they were delivered. She had been puzzled by the combination — Carrara marble and granite — and as much as she tried to pry details about the design, outside of his announcement at the opening ceremonies, Burman remained as silent as those stones. But his enthusiasm was high. The day of the delivery, he remained near the blocks well into the night. When a man appears from behind the blocks, she expects it to be Burman. But his red hair and beard quickly give him away. David runs his palm along the face of the marble as one would run a hand along the back of a horse, caressing and connecting. *He is as captivated by those stones as Burman is,* Liza thinks.

He looks up and their eyes meet. He waves to her as if they'd agreed to get together right there.

"Liza, that's some bug you've got," he says approaching, a broad smile on his face.

"This Beetle's my baby," she says.

He taps the car's headlight. "Mine was a yellow one." He rubs his palm over the hood. "Original. These bugs are some works of art. A piece of art should never be re-painted." His hand glides over the fender affectionately.

His tie-dyed shirt is almost the same colour as the car. He is squinting hard with his right eye to keep the sun out, the left one remaining large and unblinking as if it were a translucent blue marble. Fine lines gather around the corners of his eyes. Creases have set in his face as if he has spent too much time in the sun. She is reminded of the Clint Eastwood rugged good looks. Except that the man facing her has a heavier build — at least in comparison to the movie-screen Eastwood. She has to admit that

David's tall frame enables him to carry a bit of extra weight very well. She usually towers over her female friends, including Anna, and it's a nice change not to feel taller than the man she is with. Up to now, it did not seem to matter, but somehow, with David, it does. It gives her a sense of comfort. He looks older than the first time she met him — perhaps late-thirties?

Searching for a writing pad, Liza fumbles through her briefcase, then sets it on the pavement. She takes off her sandals and dangles them on her finger by the heel straps, opens the car door and shoves them under the passenger seat. From the back, she picks up a pair of slip-ons. When she straightens, David is back by the stone blocks. She heaves the briefcase onto the back seat and locks the door.

She walks to the granite pieces and stands by him. "I'm off on my usual rounds. Would you like to join me? Check out the sites? We'd just be following in each other's footsteps anyway."

He smirks. "We would, wouldn't we?"

She fixes her eyes on him. "I've seen you here a few times. You have an interest in the Symposium?"

"This is huge. First of its kind."

"Sure is. And I do love this job," she says.

"I figured that. You're here a lot."

"And?"

"Hard to explain. I wasn't sure... how..."

"What is it, David?"

He shrugs. "I'm a draft dodger."

"Oh?"

"You OK with that?"

"What is it you do? I mean, what kind of work?"

"I teach sculpting. When I can get work." He adds: "Toronto Arts College. Used to teach at U of T."

She tightens her lips and gives him a long stare. "This all makes sense."

"It does?" He bows subtly, slowly reaches for her hand, and brings her fingertips to his lips. Gently, he pecks each fingertip, then plants a soft kiss on the back of her hand.

Heat clambers her cheeks, then her ears, and the hilly ground beneath her feet shifts ever so subtly.

Liza looks up—everything around her is vibrant and brilliant, the sculpture sites alive with possibilities.

He takes off his red wooden bead necklace and hooks it around her neck.

"Friends?"

CHAPTER 6

July

"TAKE A SWIG, Baby." David pulls the paper bag out of his knapsack and hands it over to Liza.

"You can't be serious," she says. "And don't call me Baby." She takes the bag from him, pulls the thermos out, and laughs. "It's just a thermos. A nice canary yellow. Why keep it in a paper bag?"

"Guilty mind, I guess," he says and takes her hand.

This should count as our fifth date, Liza ponders, and an inner glow overtakes the guarded persona within her. Her doubts about seeing him and her fear of falling for him wane in his presence. But Anna's subtle warnings gnaw at her. *What do you know about him, Liza?* She tries to push them away, but they linger, persistent enough to make her feel that she is doing something wrong. Up to now, she had no secrets from Anna, and David is the first man Liza is uneasy mentioning. Is Anna protecting her from him? Even more puzzling, she seems to know each time Liza and David see each other—eerie to feel spied on by a close friend.

They get up from the bench by Colborne Lodge Drive and walk to *Flower Power*. From this vantage point at the top of the hill, the sculpture sites below them unfold, each a theatre stage in itself, with park visitors as audience to the work-in-progress. On a sunny Sunday afternoon, the sites are a magnet not only to the Torontonians but also many tourists.

David spreads his jean jacket out on the grass, sits on a corner, and playfully pulls her on his knee. "This better?" He draws her into an embrace. Liza unscrews the thermos, fills the cup, and takes a sip. She smacks her lips at the taste of fresh lemon and honey.

He laughs. "Got you! Didn't I?"

"Surprised me, yes," she says. "I know you'd rather have a Queen Mother."

"I see you've got your report on you. Is this a working date? Or just your way of luring me here to your lair?"

"I could stay like this forever, but I better get working on that report."

"It's Sunday afternoon. No one works on a Sunday afternoon."

"Need it for tomorrow morning. Monday staff meeting, as usual."

They walk down the hill to Pauta Saila's site. David wraps his arm around her shoulders. "See Pauta down there? Making the two-month sculpt-in an event to remember. The man's committed."

"Everybody's talking about his 'Dancing Bear'," Liza says.

David rubs his beard. "Sure thing. A polar bear balancing on one foot! That's challenging."

"Growing up on Baffin Island has its benefits—Pauta's been seeing polar bears all his life."

A group of visitors are gathered outside the rope cordoning off Saila's site. Some are taking photos and others are chatting with "artists' children" patrolling the sites. The children of the artists, joined by a number of local kids, have organized a patrol group to help answer visitor queries and in this way free up the sculptors to work on their pieces. They have taken on the job as the self-appointed tour-guides and have become part of the scene at Sculpture Hill.

After chatting with one of the young tour-guides, a woman with a beehive hairdo and a hot pink mini dress turns to Liza. She points to Saila who is working on his piece. "Is that the Eskimo they're talking about? In the paper."

Liza smiles. "That's Pauta Saila. Highly respected in his field."

A man in a baseball cap, camera in hand, joins them. Looking at Liza, he says: "You keeping tabs on these guys here?"

Liza winces. "Not sure what you mean."

The baseball cap points to Pauta and continues: "His wife and three children. Having time of their life. Getting used to drinking coke and watching television."

Another man steps closer. "Sure thing, man. On government expense."

Liza shoots them an incensed look. "Miserly two thousand dollars for the whole summer's work. If he was flipping burgers he'd make more than that."

David turns to the man. "It's not easy to uproot a family and go to a strange place. Saila has talent. I'd give anything to be in his place."

The baseball cap takes a few more shots. "I wouldn't mind playing with that stone if somebody paid me."

Liza takes David's hand and they make their way to the other side of the site. Pauta looks up through his large goggles, nods to them, and then continues with his work.

As they walk to another site, David murmurs: "Chipping away at his stone bear like there's no tomorrow. The man's a workaholic."

She wraps her arm around his waist. "You and Pauta have much more in common than you're letting on."

He stops to light the cigarette and takes a long drag. Slowly, he blows out the smoke. "I can't say I wouldn't like to be in his place. Pauta's. No, I couldn't say that. I just wouldn't trade *this* place." He tightens his embrace. "I wouldn't trade being with you for anything."

"Oh, David, don't say that."

"Why not, Babe? There's more to life than getting the contract. It gets to me every once in a while. But I'm over it. Was over it months ago, soon as I found out. If you can't do it, you teach it, I always say."

"You don't sound like you're over it. And nobody said you couldn't do it. You simply didn't get the contract. And neither did the other few hundred artists."

"Twelve did. Let's just see if the judges made the right choice. The work will speak for itself."

"You've done incredible things, David. Standing up for what you believe in. Leaving your own country. Adjusting to a new life here. Getting a teaching job at the

TAC. That's more than some people accomplish in a life-time. You shouldn't feel bad."

"Feeling good, now, Baby, feeling good. Toronto Arts College is a good place to teach. I'm done with U of T and their politics."

"I'd really like to see some of your work."

"And that you will, soon. I promise."

He closes his eyes, and traces her features with his fingertips — the bridge of her nose, her lips, the curve of her chin, the outline of her neck, her collar bone.

Seeing David transported into another world, she wonders what he envisions in that realm of his imagination.

She is taken back to the previous weekend and their trip to Wasaga, about a two-hour drive north of Toronto. She is behind David on his Harley, riding along the newly-built Highway 400, and then along the winding side roads meandering through the perfume of pine forests and scent of farmland — through the waves of swaying wheat, and the spans of green corn stalks, and the sweeps of purple clover. They arrive at the golden shore of Wasaga — the longest fresh water beach in the world — and Liza feels as if she has entered another realm. This is her first time in the Georgian Bay cottage country, her first time at this sun-drenched expanse of water and sand and sky.

She soon realizes that the *Globe and Mail* write-ups about the Yorkville Hippies moving to Wasaga were not totally exaggerated. Hundreds of young people the articles referred to as "long-haired hipsters from Yorkville" had made themselves at home all along the beach. They set up temporary camps—blankets, knapsacks, bags of chips and pop bottles, and some tents perched here and there among the sand dunes—along the shore. The store-keepers smile at Liza, but give David, with his long hair and unruly beard and cutoff jean shorts with fraying fabric hanging down his thighs, unwelcome looks. *Good thing he took off his biking leathers*, Liza thinks.

While having lunch at a restaurant overlooking the lake, Liza catches the snippets of conversation—about all night parties with loud music and young vagrants sleeping on the beach and among the sand dunes, and how the influx of uninvited "hipsters" makes the townspeople edgy. Reports of shoplifting and petty crimes hype up the panic. Apparently, a woman reported her laundry being stolen from the clothes line in her yard, towels and shirts and bathing suits. A man called the police because his grocery bags were taken from his shopping cart. He had left the groceries in the cart in front of the store for only a few minutes to pick up his car from the parking lot, and when he drove to the front of the store to load the groceries, his cart was empty. He caught sight of a group of teenagers running away with what he claimed must have been *his* bags of food and laughing. He yelled after them, but they took off. Others complain about the "long hair bearded drifters" smoking dope, making love on the beach and drinking beer, and corrupting the local youth.

Strolling along the main drag, Liza and David pass a vendor cart. "No," Liza chuckles looking at David. "We just had lunch."

David shrugs. A minute later he runs back and buys

two hot dogs smothered in mustard and relish. He brings them under her nose, and she gives in.

"They're best from vendor carts," David sums up after they finish eating them.

They walk along the beach to the secluded section, away from the strip lined with stores and restaurants and ice cream huts, far from the crowds and the blasting music.

They swim in the warm, crystal clear lake, and sunbathe by the edge of the gently splashing waves. David scoops the sand with his cupped palms and piles it up in the shape of a mermaid. He closes his eyes, and with fingertips gently traces Liza's features. He shapes the mermaid's face, his fingertips moulding the curves. He opens his eyes, looks intently into Liza's face, and makes a few adjustments on the mermaid's. Liza is astonished at her likeness — high cheek bones, deep set eyes, full lips.

David raises his eyebrows. "What say you?"

"Amazing."

The look on the face made of sand is too realistic. Almost eerie. Almost. She feels a knot in her stomach. And the image remains etched in her vision.

Now, scanning Sculpture Hill, she suddenly realizes how difficult it must be for the sculptor in David.

"You okay, Babe?" he says.

She punches him playfully on the shoulder and begins to run. He catches up with her.

"The only way to keep you, wild thing, is to hold you tight, like this." He gathers her into his arms and sprints toward the forested area. She wraps her arms around his neck, her face splashed by the patches of sun spilling through the green canopies of oaks.

CHAPTER 7

THE FULL MOON illuminates the park and blanches the stars in the sky. Liza sees a glimmer in the grass next to David's shoulder, as they lie in an embrace, their nakedness swathed by the shade of a large maple. He is sprawled on his back, she pressed against him, head on his chest. She reaches for the glimmer and picks up the lens that has fallen out of his sunglasses. Lens over an eye, she gazes into the sky — several stars are brightened in the ellipse of the lens. If it wasn't for the red I-beams of di Suvero's *Flower Power* the moon has painted purple, she could imagine being anywhere. She has always feared what it would be like the first time. At times she wondered: Would she ever fall in love, or would she stay a virgin forever? And now she knows. Gently sweeping hair from her forehead, David kisses her lips, and she dreads having to part with him and go home. But it's Thursday night, and she has to be in the office early in the morning.

Eyes closed, Liza stands in the shower as the water streams over her head, her shoulders. It's five in the morning, and although she has not slept, she is elated. Eager to get to the office and catch up on the work she has pushed aside over the past week, she slips on a long skirt printed in white daisies, a white Indian cotton shirt, and gathers her hair in a girl-ponytail for a semi-casual Friday. After work, she will have dinner at David's place in Parkdale. From the back of the dresser drawer where impulsive purchases shy away, she retrieves the pale yellow halter-top. It would go well over the skirt. He has never seen her wearing anything sensuous. If not in business attire, she is usually in a casual dress. She splurged on this silk top on a whim at The Colonnade on Bloor Street where she sometimes drops in after work. She finds a pair of lacy panties in a corner of the dresser, beneath a pile of practical cotton lingerie — and stuffs it in the bag. This will be her first time at his place.

Only last week she refused his offer to cook dinner for her. She saw it as a trap — a visit to his bachelor pad, his love nest. How many women has he seduced there before her, showing off his culinary arts? She will not be a notch on his bed post. But last night in the park, things just happened. Unplanned. This time, she was not strong enough to resist. Or was it he who was not strong enough to refuse? She practically tore his clothes off under that maple shadow that hid them from the moonlight as if they were delinquent teenagers. What had come over her? Was it the full moon?

And now, her face is flushed just thinking about him. Until David came along with his casual arrogance and his clichéd nickname, Baby, for her, she usually lost interest in a man before the third date.

A sense of wrongdoing floods her, as if she has committed a mortal sin — sin against her own guarded self. As if she has somehow betrayed an oath to herself, unspoken yet understood. Her apprehension mushrooms by the need to be with him. Her fear of lovemaking has now been broken, and in its place her want of him has set in like obsession. It would be twelve hours before she sees him, twelve long hours she needs to fill with urgent tasks, complex enough to put him out of her thoughts. The scent of his skin, the caress of his hands, his body against hers — the taste of tobacco on his lips … She never imagined the taste of cigarettes on someone's lips could be so deliciously addictive.

She steps out of the shower and scrutinizes the image in the fogged mirror. Her virginity had been intrinsically linked to her notion of self-worth — part of her old-world mentality on sex entrenched by her mother. She does feel different — something in her has changed. But worthless? No, by no means.

She has never fallen in love with anyone before David. And this need to be with him, all consuming, suddenly offers relief. She has no regrets. On the contrary — she has completed a monumental task that has loomed over her and prevented her from living life the way it should be lived. She no longer has to worry about her virginity. It is no longer there.

Her momentary alarm dissipates. She reaches in her

purse for the makeup pouch, and a small plastic object falls to the wood floor. It's David's lens she stashed into her purse the previous night. Lens over her eye, she examines her reflection in the mirror—and is reminded of the previous night's sky, where all is surreal.

In the subway, she stands grasping the rod above her hoping the rattling of wheels on the metal rails might shake the previous night out of her thoughts. Reading the ads, she comes across a poster featuring a likeness of Michelangelo's David. Another is promoting Davy's Cafe where singles mingle. Yet another offers end-of-season discounts at David's Designer Shoes. Clearly, the subway world is conspiring against her resolve to stop thinking about David.

Liza gets off at the Yonge-Bloor station. Instead of continuing on the southbound train to College Street, she decides to walk to the office and clear her head.

CHAPTER 8

AT TORONTO ARTS College, David breezes through his lecture as if in a dream. The usual close interaction with his students is absent. He feels disengaged. Focussed on the back row where faces blur one into another, he delivers a sermon—instructions that do not elicit questions or debate—a presentation of facts. The echo of his own voice is disruptive, as if it belongs to someone else. He wishes he could skip the sterile facts and move on to his own approaches and works.

But doubts linger. *Have I proven myself as a sculptor? Have I created anything worthy of recognition? Anything that will live on after me? Or am I one of those, if-you-can't-do-it-you-teach-it impostors who give themselves the right to lecture others without being able to put in practice what they profess?*

In his mind, he goes over the pieces he has sculpted. He had his own one-man exhibit in Boston. The exhibit sold out. But that was a long time ago.

He had featured a number of experimental pieces—a few marble ones and some bronze figures he saw as reflective of a more rough-hewn period of his sculpting. One of the bronze pieces stood out from the rest. It began as an experiment of combining different mediums for creating the form before it was cast in bronze. When the sculpture was finished, it became his favourite piece. He had named it "Child Soldier." It was of a young woman planting a daisy in the barrel of a gun held by a teenage soldier. It was only about a foot tall. At first he had planned to keep it as an example of his new approach until he further studied and developed the method. But his desire to share the success of the new process compelled him to include it in the exhibit. He had priced it high, secretly hoping no one would buy it. He never considered the possibility of it being stolen.

Finding out it had disappeared during the exhibit made him furious. As if his essence had been pilfered.

But soon he wondered who the thief could have been. Perhaps a student who could not afford to purchase it? An eccentric collector? Another sculptor? Was his art so inspiring, so irresistible? The notion was romantic, enticing. He imagines it hidden and admired secretly.

The exhibit did well, and the gallery owner offered to hold another one when David was ready. But he had left, escaped to Canada. In Toronto, he took a few months to find a place to live and to get a job. After that, his work with organizing antiwar demonstrations and helping new draft-dodgers and deserters adjust to their new home— helping them to obtain legal status in Canada, especially difficult for deserters—has taken up most of his free time. The competition for the Centennial project renewed his enthusiasm for sculpting. It offered the chance to prove himself to his new county, to get back to the craft. The chance to dive in with all his zeal in the hope of easing the pain of losing the one who had inspired "Child Soldier" —the one who meant everything to him—the chance to soothe the ache he carries that cuts into him like shards of broken glass.

Not winning the contract hit him hard. He sees it as a personal failure. Similar to losing a student he thought had an extraordinary talent, a rare capacity for sculpting —expressive use of line and shape, originality in composition, sensitivity to line and colour. It happened only a few weeks back. The student was in her second year when she quit the program. She reasoned that most instructors are not artists. If they can't do it, how could they teach it? David's efforts to keep her in the program had failed. She decided to move on and practice her craft rather than be taught by those who had no artwork to call their own —which, technically, includes him. And now he has fallen in love with a woman who coordinates the sculpt-in. And works in Anna's office. Could things get any more complicated?

Anna's warning about his relationship with Liza plays out in his thoughts. In Anna's words, why is he leading Liza on? He is not the settle-down type. Her reasons— his involvement with the antiwar movement, with the Socialist Party of Canada, and his lack of job security, not to mention his contentious relationship with Hells Angels. How could he convince Anna that her fears are unfounded?

The first time he saw Liza, something in him broke—
it broke the way one breaks a crystal glass, the way one
throws the glass against a stone and it shatters into a million pieces. He had felt it that day at Nathan Phillips
Square—that fracture that gives off a thin, musical note
and lingers. He could hear it in his lonely nights the way
one hears the lyrics of a song. He had to say something to
her, make himself visible. So he'd turned into a wise-
cracking, donut-eating buffoon he never thought he'd
pull off. But it worked. Someday, when they are old and
grey, sitting on their favourite park bench and holding
hands, he will tell her—you had me at "hello." It won't
sound like a cliché because they will have lived a life
together. It will be true. Someday, it will feel just right.

This vortex of self-doubt trundles through his head
on those late nights when he lies on his bed staring at the
flashing red Parkdale Pizza sign across the street and
plans the next demonstration, or the following day's lecture, or a way to keep a fellow draft dodger or a deserter
from being deported. His thoughts rattle like the wobbling wheels of a stolen shopping cart he would roll down
the hill when he was a young boy. He imagined the cart
to be his motorcycle, rumbling along the highway. Now,
when he rides with the Hells Angels, disguised behind
red shades, he is once more that boy.

He never thought he would fall in love again. Since
he lost the woman who gave meaning to his life, he had
buried himself in a vault—a sarcophagus that kept him
safe in its confinement. And now, Liza's caresses have
settled in the forefront of his thoughts, a screen through

which his day is sifted — his morning coffee, the lecture he gave today at the college, his motorcycle ride home.

Back at his apartment, the first task of the day going smoothly is the dinner preparation. He placed the Cornish hens in the oven and is about to take a shower when the phone rings. He lets the answering machine pick up. It's Anna, asking if he would mind her dropping in on him later that evening to work out some details about the upcoming demonstration.

He has already made the wild rice stuffing, one of his favourite dishes. He kept the recipe simple — sautéed onions and garlic with finely chopped celery and carrots mixed with partially boiled wild rice. He has stuffed the birds with the rice mixture, rubbed some olive oil with chopped rosemary and thyme over them, and placed them in the oven on a timer. The main course is pretty much ready. Even the salad is done — fresh spinach with olives and goat feta drizzled with roasted pine nut dressing. The fragrance of savoury herbs and garlic is mouthwatering. He and Liza could have a leisurely aperitif on the rooftop terrace without the worry of a burnt dinner.

Should he have invited Anna to join them? She *is* Liza's closest friend. Why hide his relationship with Liza? Here's the opportunity to bring things out into the open.

Then he reconsiders. Anna has been very clear on his relationship with Liza. He is to back off and not ruin Liza's life. Or at least that's what she told him. Is there more to this than Anna's fear that her work with the anti-war movement will be revealed to her coworkers? Liza is not the type who would tell on people. And she is also strongly opposed to the war. From the first time he met Liza, he felt that he could trust her. There was an ease between them, not to mention the attraction. He is planning to let Liza in on all of his involvements. Perhaps she'll join the movement. The sentiments against the war are growing in Canada and Anna's fear of losing her job is unfounded. Should he tell Anna all this? No. It would turn into an argument and would lead to even more tension between them.

But that is only a small part of the problem. Explaining to Liza why he has been hiding his friendship with Anna is a bigger one. At City Hall, why did he pretend not to know Anna? Would Liza understand that he did not mean to deceive her? Things evolved, somehow, without intention.

He had hoped that Anna would tell Liza about her friendship with him. Anna and Liza are not only colleagues, but also friends. Anna could find the way to explain it—women are better at it. But Anna decided to, in her words, let him stew in his own mess. Let him solve his own problems.

How did he get himself into all this? Having to hide his seeing Liza is juvenile. He will tell Liza everything. He rewinds the tape of the answering machine to make room for the recordings and heads to the shower, leaving the bathroom door open in case Liza rings the doorbell.

CHAPTER 9

SHADED BY A tall maple, Liza stands at the front door of a rooming house on Sorauren Avenue just north of Queen, where David lives. The acrid odour of asphalt from the newly patched up potholes along the street stings her nostrils. In the late afternoon sun, the neighbourhood cicadas are in full orchestra.

Before buzzing David's flat, Liza checks her reflection in the door glass pane, hoping the halter top with a plunging neckline she slipped on when she changed in the ladies' room after work is not too revealing. She rushed out without checking herself in the mirror for fear of being seen by coworkers. And this whole braless feel, combined with free buffing — she accidentally dropped her lace underwear into the toilet bowl while trying to change into them, and the cotton ones she removed she'd already discarded into the sanitary napkin disposal unit — is suddenly making her feel as if she were a star in a porn film. Queen Street is only minutes away. She could find a lingerie shop and buy a pair of underwear, and with luck, a liquor store as well—for a bottle of wine she forgot to bring—unless this is a dry-area where store sales of alcohol are forbidden.

She turns and walks back down the three steps and along the short pathway toward the street. In spite of the missing undergarments, the daisy-printed skirt, white patent leather sandals, and wide, matching belt that accentuates her slim waist and shapes the silk top make her feel elegant. Her steps quicken. Behind her, the front door opens and David calls out: "Liza, my wild thing, where're you off to?"

She stops, face burning. And the next moment he is kissing her and leading her back to the entrance. The oak-panel slab groans as he opens it.

… The worn wood stairway leading to the third floor … an open door freshly stripped of paint … a large bouquet of pink peonies on the marble coffee table in front of a brown leather sofa … a humongous bed with white linen crinkled from drying in the sun … red hummingbirds among the green leaves and orange blossoms of the Dutchman's pipe vine painted on the ceiling of an airy room with white walls … a black wrought-iron headboard that begins to squeak—an incorrigible violin being tuned, each resonance a different string.

After they make love, they sip the Queen Mothers—the QMs—on the rooftop deck.

With bare feet and cut-off jean shorts, David looks carefree. His indigo tie-die shirt makes his eyes appear bluer. He disappears through the patio door saying: "Chef David is needed in the kitchen."

Curled up in the rattan basket hanging by a chain from the rafter above the deck, Liza tugs at the bottom of David's oversized shirt she'd slipped on after they'd made love. The magentas of the tie-dye pattern over her breasts morph into a heart-shaped swirl. A sunray streaming across her hair falls over her shoulders. Swaying gently, she is warm and dreamy and illuminated from within, as if the sun had penetrated her body and made her fluorescent.

She does not mind David's insistence on making dinner on his own; does not mind him leading her to this swaying basket each time she gets up to help; she certainly does not mind his kisses. If she could only keep those kisses planted all over her, keep them thriving like orchids on wood. She gazes at the refilled glass in her hand and swishes the ice, round and round. Those helpless ice cubes, melting in the burnt orange liqueur the way she melts in David's arms. She closes her eyes and descends into the warmth of the sun and the taste of David's lips that lingers on hers, and the scent of his nakedness.

The fragrance of rosemary and thyme mingles with the roaster and wafts through the open kitchen door and Liza realizes that her last real meal had been the evening before—before she and David had first made love, before this gripping want of him—when she was her old self. *Kind of my last supper … before … before …* David is back on the patio, balancing the flow blue china platter with hors d'oeuvres. He sets the plate on the bench and pulls the table across the patio toward her. The rattan legs dragged along the wooden deck cause the round glass table top to quiver in its frame and the blue ceramic jug with pink peonies to rumble, and she fears the jug could topple and shatter. She jumps out of the basket and grabs the other side of the table.

After they set the table back in its place, she inhales the fragrance of the peonies. "Gorgeous. I thought they'd be finished by now."

He leads her to the porch railing and points to a secluded nook in the backyard. "They're a bit later in the shade."

"And that pile of signs next to the peony-patch?" She reads the signs face up: "End the Vietnam War, Now! Until Americans Stop Killing and Being Killed in Vietnam ..."

David shrugs. "Oh, that. From the last demonstration. Getting them ready for the next one. Some got smashed when a fight broke out."

"You not worried? About being ostracized. In my office, demonstrators and socialists—all the same."

David rubs his beard. "People need to stand up against this war. Against babies getting napalmed in Vietnam. Women, men, children. Dying as we speak! And for what?" He begins to pace the deck. "The fear of socialists. That burns me. If I can do something to stop the killing of innocent people, you bet I will."

Liza takes his hand. "I said in my office. Not me."

She reads another sign leaning against the fence: "Is it Better to Burn a Draft Card or a Child?"

She places her palm against his cheek. "I'm glad you're not in Vietnam. I wish the war would stop. I feel bad for the

American soldiers. They're just following orders. Ordered to kill and be killed. What irony!"

He wraps his arm around her shoulder. "Glad you think so, Babe. Let's keep the war out for the evening."

He leads her to the table and lays a small flow blue plate, a different pattern than the large one, and a slightly tarnished, mismatched silver spoon and fork in front of her. He arranges the same for himself, his plate in yet another flow blue pattern.

"The most charming table setting I could imagine," Liza says.

David grins. "My thrift-shop finds. It's amazing what you can get in Parkdale for a few bucks. Love it here." He flips a white linen napkin and spreads it on her lap. "For you, Mademoiselle."

They sample from an assortment of cheese and crackers; a glazed pâté log with a tiny ceramic duck next to it; a cluster of white grapes; and two barbecued shrimp skewers.

Her right leg is crossed over the left one, and the right foot is hooked under the left calf, when her elbow knocks down the glass and spills the liquor on her shirt — David's shirt — and her bare legs. Her face scalds in embarrassment. David laughs. "Can't waste the liqueur," he says and kisses her where the liquid had tinted her skin. "And you'll need a clean shirt."

They are back on his bed still rumpled up from their lovemaking. David pulls out a peony from the vase on the night table, plucks the petals, and scatters them over the bed, over Liza. "I love you, Liza," he says. His eyes are the blue of winter clouds and he looks sombre. She saw this frosty look not long ago, when he talked of death and the Vietnam War.

"Don't say it," she whispers.

"It's been many years since I'd said it."

A dreadful sense of foreboding lurks somewhere deep in her. David's words are at once exhilarating and frightening. The ideology of the period rushes through her mind—people living in times of emotional conflict. Coexisting, a drive for justice and peace and the pursuit of immediate pleasure. As if the accomplishment of the former could somehow diminish the latter—sap the joy of everyday life. Or does the war give context to the drive to live in the moment? For no one knows what the future could bring?

He loves her? Why does it seem so surreal? Is it because she thought that she'd never fall in love, and if she did, it would not last or it would not be with the right person, or simply *it would not be*, whatever that meant, whatever that little insecure voice contrived it to mean? Or is it because death seems to be everywhere—every news station reporting the gory scenes from Vietnam, burned and mutilated bodies of women and children and old farmers?

And now he is kissing her and he is part of her, and if she could only wave that magic wand and dispel the fear.

She pats him on the shoulder. "I can't, David. I can't get the war out of my head."

They are back on the patio when the stove timer buzzes and David announces that dinner is ready. They arrange the plates—Cornish hen, a dollop of wild rice, and a few sprigs of asparagus. The aroma is appetizing, yet she hardly murmurs a few words of praise. Her taste

buds, though, are heightened, every bite superb. She lifts
her wine glass and suddenly realizes she has drunk too
much. Even lifting the fork takes effort. She asks David
for a glass of water. When he returns she says: "No more
wine for me, please David." Are the words rolling out
slurred? As he brings a jug of water with slices of lemon,
her first impulse is to gulp it down as if she has just been
rescued from a desert. But she sips slowly, and is instantly
refreshed.

It occurs to her, suddenly, that all those years of
guarding her virginity — all through university — now
seem futile. If she had died two days ago, she would not
have known what it means to be truly alive. All that propa-
ganda about love — love buttons, love slogans about making love, not war — would have remained just jingles to
her. She would not have known how it feels to love — completely. She lifts her heavy eyelids and sees him as if
through haze. "You okay, Babe?" He asks. She gets up and
floats over to his chair. She takes the wine glass from his
hand and sets it on the table, then slips her hands under
his shirt. The bed is too far away, and they find themselves making love on the wooden boards of the deck, as
dusk descends on the tree crowns.

Later, unable to face the prospect of waking up at
David's place, with no clean clothes and a likely hangover,
Liza insists on returning to her own house to sleep. He
wheels his Harley onto the sidewalk and, as they drive
off, Liza hears someone call his name. She turns. A few
street lights back, she glimpses a tall man and next to
him, waving, a much shorter woman. Should she tap
David on the shoulder? The loud rumbling of the motor

is throbbing in her head, and her shakiness on the bike convinces her to keep her grip on David and to focus on retaining her balance. The silhouette of the woman reminds her of Anna. *No, it couldn't be.* It would be best to tell him of it once they get off the bike, and she is safely on the ground.

CHAPTER 10

Suspended from the high ceiling of the second floor landing at Mynah Bird, a glass cage begins to glow, and a silhouette of a nude dancer twirls around a metal pole.

Helena, balancing a tray of beer mugs, approaches. She is dressed in yellow shorts and a shiny red bra, midriff painted in red hearts. She empties the tray at the table next to Anna and David and turns to them.

"Get you anything?"

David's face lights up. Helena tousles his hair and plants a kiss on his cheek. He takes her hand in both of his and holds it for a moment.

"Ah, if it isn't Helena of Troy! Love your artwork!" Anna shouts over the din of the crowd.

Helena smiles. "Paint-in. At Grab Bag. It'd look delish on you."

Anna knows that coffee shops and convenience stores in Yorkville host local artists who paint designs on women's and men's naked bodies. She has been tempted, but thought better of it considering the office politics.

"I see you two know each other well," Anna says, staring at David.

Helena shrugs. "Maybe I know ya," she says playfully to David and heads toward the bar.

Several bikers stroll in and take up a corner of the bar. Anna decides that the place is far too noisy to carry a conversation. They need to finalize the details for the next demonstration.

She turns to David. "Let's get out of here. Can't hear a word."

"Good move," he says. "Need a quick chat with Ricky. Be back in a flash."

Anna's eyes widen. "Ricky James? Is he playing tonight?"

David waves to someone. "Tomorrow. And there he is."

Making his way among the tables, David wonders whether he should let Anna in on Ricky's situation. She knows a lot of people and might be able to help, and yet, the more entangled she becomes, the more chance that too much involvement could backfire. She could lose her job, or be ostracized—things could become difficult for her at work. She is much more valuable to the antiwar movement than she gives herself credit. He shouldn't ask for more. And then there is this attachment—hard to explain.

The one-time intimacy is not exactly the reason. Although he cannot fully put that out of his mind. It sits there, unspoken of, like shame. If only he could talk to her about it and explain. But explain what? There was no other way out of a situation that could've turned ugly. Yet, if they could only talk it out. Perhaps Anna had put it out of her thoughts long ago. Why bring up an old ghost? She knows that he stopped riding with the Angels after that—unless he really needs to when crossing the border. Although he still tries to keep peace between the gang and the demonstrators—a precarious position to be in. Strangely, they let him out without incident. And they have not been too difficult during the demonstrations. There had been clashes. Some Angels had stormed the protests and a few demonstrators ended up with body casts and bandaged heads, but that could not have been prevented.

David needs to warn Ricky that an FBI agent has been seen in the Yorkville area. Although Ricky has changed his name to escape being deported as a deserter, he is still a target. The earlier Americans who crossed the border as draft dodgers were mostly university students and academics opposed to the war they did not believe in, like David. But in the last year or so, the number of de-serters has been growing, and they have a much tougher time—harder to find jobs, and even harder to obtain an immigrant status. A number of FBI agents have been sent to Canada to seek out the deserters and bring them back to the United States to face justice.

Ricky arrived to Yorkville a few months back, still wearing his U.S. navy uniform. He walked into Mynah Bird to have lunch, met the house band, and was hired the same afternoon as the band's lead singer. David was there, and they quickly became friends. The band manager even provided Ricky with a place to stay. But the tensions in the band have led to accusations that could get Ricky deported, and David hopes to convince Ricky to hide out for a while until things cool off.

Through the smoky haze of the bar, Anna can make out Ricky's handsome figure, his shoulder length Jheri curls a sure giveaway. She has seen him play at the Mynah Bird. His music is electrifying. His soulful voice and sharp looks draw the Yorkville crowds, not to mention the hordes of girls whose greatest dream is to date a musician. Anna could never understand this affliction of so many young women. Band members have the reputation of treating girls as if they were disposable napkins.

She is not part of the hip Yorkville scene — boys looking for girls, girls looking for boys, people looking for dope. She enjoys a night-out-on-the-town, listening to music or just people-watching. And Yorkville is perfect for that, with its many cafes and bands. It's also a great place for meeting David and other organizers. Her boss and her coworkers are not likely to wander off into this bohemian hippie-haven where "love-children" drop their inhibitions. No, not likely.

Anna catches David's eye and motions that she'll be waiting outside. On the sidewalk, she lights up a cigarette and inhales deeply. *Ah, the fresh air, the summer breeze,* and then she scoffs at the irony and grinds the cigarette into the sand of the floor ashtray in front of the Mynah Bird. She has been quitting for as long as she has been smoking, since her teenage years.

David comes out and says: "The man won't hide out. Says he needs to work. Says, what's life without music? The guys in the band love him. But he's got trouble with the band manager."

Anna looks at David. "You do mean Ricky James?"

David nods. "Needs another place to live. But that's hard. He's a night owl. Likes to practice at any ungodly hour. Very talented, though."

Someone taps David on the shoulder. It's Ricky. "Glad I caught you before you left, man," Ricky says. "I'm okay for a week or two. Not that urgent. And thanks, man." He looks at Anna. "You're the gorgeous lady David won't introduce me to."

Anna steps closer to Ricky, barely reaching his shoulder. "I can do that all by myself." She extends her hand to him. "Anna."

Ricky takes her hand in both of his. "Annie. I'll call you Annie."

David inhales a long drag of his cigarette and eyeing Ricky lets it out slowly. "Now that you no longer need a place ..."

Ricky shrugs. "No rush, but I do need a place." He turns to Anna. "Take me home, lovely lady."

She laughs. "Now, that's an offer I can't refuse."

Ricky winks. "Not kidding, Annie. I *do* pay rent."

David squints an eye and stares at Ricky. "I'll see what I can do for you, man."

"The rent money *would* come in handy," Anna says and pulls out a small writing pad from her purse. She rips off a slip of paper, writes on it, and hands it to Ricky. "Here, call me and come and see the place. See if you like it."

Ricky kisses Anna on the forehead. "I *like* it. I'll call you." She props on her tiptoes and pecks him on the cheek and he lifts her into a hug.

David whistles through his teeth. He steps away a few paces, and arms crossed on his chest stares at them, shaking his head.

Ricky lowers Anna and she says: "You're not a Commie, are you?"

Ricky laughs. "Me, a Commie? Not a chance. Just a musician who doesn't believe in war."

"We better get going," David says to Anna, "or you'll blame me tomorrow for being tired in the office."

Ricky waves good-buy and David says: "Good going, Anna. What's all this about?"

She squints at the neon lights that seem to be radiating outward from behind him. "Aren't we going to the Riverboat?"

Although it's close to midnight, hundreds of people crowd the streets. The line-up in front of the Riverboat is still long, curving around the block—Gordon Lightfoot is playing. They're tempted to join the line, but Anna does need to be in the office early in the morning.

A long haired man in an orange tie-dye shirt punches David's arm jokily, and after enthusiastic greetings, they're invited in as friends of the band. No need to line up. "Go, go, round ..." Anna hums Lightfoot's lyrics.

While waiting to be seated, David clears his throat. "What was that whole thing about? With you and Ricky?"

"It's about my coach house. And the apartment next to it I'd like to rent."

"I thought you said the raccoons were occupying your coach house, free of rent."

"Got rid of them. You should've seen the mess. It stank so bad you couldn't get near. Our guys ripped everything off, rebuilt the roof. Using the space for making signs and storing supplies. And that two bedroom apartment attached to the garage that's been sitting empty is now good to use."

David shakes his head. "Ricky James is a nice guy. But a deserter. You not worried?"

Anna gives him a defiant look. "Hundreds of Torontonians are renting to draft dodgers and deserters. Haven't heard of any problems. And he's got a job. This is business, David. Besides, this could be good for me if something did come up — you know, about my involvement and all. And I need the rent money. Everywhere I look my house needs work."

"Anna, if you need money, I can ..."

She cuts him off. "You can come and help me clean up the place."

He agrees.

Anna smiles. *Ricky James, ha? The rent money won't hurt, either.*

It is long past midnight, and Anna and David realize that public transit stopped running some time ago. Anna is so wound up by Lightfoot's music, she feels as if she could fly. She coordinates her steps to the rhythm as she hums the tune of his "Canadian Railroad Trilogy," and sings about surreal forests from the past. David offers to hail a cab, but Anna would prefer to first clear up a few things. She leads the way to a bench — to unwind and get some details worked out for the new group of draft dodgers.

She had found a place they could share and has some job leads for them as well.

A group of Vagabonds rumble by, circle the block, and dismount only steps from Anna and David's bench. They stumble toward the bar.

Anna stiffens. "What are the bikers doing, swarming all over Yorkville?"

David shrugs. "How would I know? Checking out the chicks! Looking for a one-night stand!"

It takes him a few moments to realize what he said. And to remember how sensitive she can be. He should have been more careful. He would be lost without her. The Riverboat was too noisy and she has been edgy all evening. Now he realizes it must have to do with the bikers.

Anna gets up to leave and David wonders how to reel back in what he just unravelled. How could a few clichés hold so much baggage? He should not feel guilty for what happened that night long ago. Why does it keep popping up when he least expects it? It had been no one's fault. Yet, every once in a while that twinge of remorse gnaws at him. Perhaps he could have stopped it before things got too far. David feels himself shrinking to the size of a toy action figure. He takes Anna's hands into his. Their eyes lock. And in that fractured moment between silence and speech, both fear the unspeakable that has expanded its bloated form over the past few years, yet both know that it would lie limp between them like a rotting rodent, and neither would dare poke at it.

❧

Walking along Yorkville, Anna makes a mental list of the Canadian volunteers and their tasks in organizing the upcoming protest in Washington. She is helping David arrange for the Canadian supporters to be bussed to the march on the Pentagon.

"Have you arranged for the buses?" Anna says to David. "We need those lined up."

"October's a long time from now. But you're right. Better to start earlier."

"I've got people signing up every day. Could be the biggest demonstration ever."

"Our first national rally," David murmurs, "and our biggest. It'll be unlike anything we've seen." He raises his hand to hail an approaching cab.

CHAPTER 11

LIZA UNLOCKS HER bike from the rack by the forest school. The sun is setting, just enough time to cycle the trails before dusk. She spots Wessel Couzijn at his site, under the birches where she stood only a few minutes earlier. Most artists have begun working on their pieces, while his site remains empty.

She turns back, drops the bike on the grassy slope, and walks toward him. With feet spread well apart and arms folded on his chest, his small frame appears taller than usual. There is a curious self-assurance about him. His eyes twinkle behind the silver-rimmed lenses as if he'd just won a lottery and can now afford to build all those sculptures he has envisioned.

His greeting—"Liza, my girl, just the young lady I want to see!"—is uncommonly enthusiastic.

She smiles. "Have you decided what to sculpt, Mr. Couzijn?"

"Yees," he replies. "This time it's the right decision." He studies her face carefully. "What is the most important thing in the world, Liza? I need to hear it from you."

"I don't know, really. I've no idea."

"You do," he says. "What makes life worth living? One word, my girl. One word tells all."

He leans against the white birch trunk. "Art is an imitation of life, as old Ari said. But we already agreed on that, didn't we?"

She recalls their talks on the meaning of sculpture as an art from, and how it affects people. His hand sweeps the air with a flourish as if he were conducting an orchestra. "You and I are of the same cloth, Liza. The garb of Aristotle. When you see my sculpture, you'll know."

"And what will it be?"

"Oh, no, young lady. First, your answer to my question. What makes the world go round?"

"But Mr. Couzijn, why such a question?"

He winks. "Your answer, Liza, is what my sculpture is about."

A whole week has gone by since Liza visited Sculpture Hill. She approaches Couzijn's site at a fast clip, glad that he has finally begun the work on his piece. She is intrigued by a whale shaped contraption of boards and plywood wedged between the birch trees. The sun has set. She thought that Couzijn had left for the day, but he rises behind the wooden frame.

He waves her over. "Come, come."

He is covered in sawdust. Two sawhorses crudely put together hold an assortment of boards. A hand saw hangs from a nail on the side of one of the sawhorses, and a few more tools are scattered on the grass. A couple of red metal tool boxes hold a jumble of devices the purpose of which she could only guess.

He brushes his hands along trouser legs. "You have something to tell me, Liza, my girl?" He resumes cutting the boards and building the frame.

Liza sits on the grass. Mark di Suvero's ubiquitous truck with the logo "Make Love, Not War," printed on its side in red letters the size of a person is parked by the Forest School. Love buttons, and every type of love-insignia, are everywhere, as if love were a new candy that everyone should taste.

She takes David's lens out of her pocket and places it over her eye. Through the dark tint, the twilight streaks shades of mauve over the park. She looks up into the sky and spots the moon, pale yet already risen. It appears unusually close, and she now understands why it has been immortalized in myth and legends across many cultures. Why people sing about it, write poems, have their cows jump over it, why lovers try to catch its beams for their sweethearts, or wish to be flown to it. A patch of translucent fog sits atop its sphere — *it must be Chang, the mythical woman of the moon who guides lovers on their uncharted journeys, or if need be conceals them below her veil. She is the lovers' muse and guardian, who appears to those in need of her magic.*

And now, Liza is ready to answer Couzijn's question.

She gets up and walks over to his structure of boards and plywood. "*Love* makes the world go round."

"You've got it, Liza. Now you know what my sculpture is about. Take a good look. What does it remind you of?"

She examines the wood crate carefully, but all she sees is about a two-yard wide, by about seven yards long contraption of boards that mean nothing to her. It has an irregular shape that resembles a large whale.

He is amused. "Give it a week or two. You'll know when it's finished."

CHAPTER 12

FOR THE LAST few nights, since Wessel Couzijn poured concrete into the plywood mould and his sculpture took shape, Liza has not been able to put the image of the two entwined whale-like shapes out of her thoughts. He has named the figure *Midsummer Night's Dream*. Had he seen her and David making love in the park? The two entwined figures in an embrace evoke that image.

"Not surprised you inspired old man Couzijn," David had said. "You're *my* muse, Liza. And soon, I'll have a surprise for you."

Watching him asleep next to her, naked under the sheets, red curls strewn over his forehead, drool at the corner of his mouth, Liza smiles at the boyishness of his calm face, at the vulnerability that vanishes in his waking hours, only to peep out like a timid fairy, when he is unaware—when they make love. Careful not wake him, she gently pulls out the corner of her silk nightgown caught under his leg, slips out of bed, and tiptoes to the kitchen. His teasing about her love of silk makes her smile. The long, backless negligee he'd given her with the plunging neckline held by spaghetti straps could easily pass as a gown at a black tie gala.

"You're my enchantress swaddled in silk," he tells her each time he presents her with yet another garment. Her assortment has grown—baby-dolls and nightgowns and a kimono she adores, with birds of paradise and gigantic peonies.

She plugs in the kettle and drops a chamomile pouch into the tea pot. David's crumpled sport jacket lies on the sofa, a large Love button pinned on the lapel. She places the jacket on a hanger and hooks it on the mahogany stand. The web of creases remind her of David's life—full of secret tucks and crevices. She wets her hands and passes her palms over the furrows to smooth them, but they remain firm in the fabric.

Liza opens the small drawer of the coat stand and pulls out a Love button matching the one on David's jacket. He picked them up as they walked along Yonge Street toward the subway station, after a bike ride on Centre Island. She presses the button against her chest and the word, "Love," reflected in the tarnished mirror of the stand becomes distorted—as if some bizarre malice were lurking just below the thin crust of reality. She stuffs the button back in the drawer and shuts it.

She plucks a white daisy from the bouquet on the stand and slips the stem into the lapel buttonhole just above the Love button. Cary Grant would be pleased.

And so will David. Boutonnieres are symbols of love un-
defined, yet captured in a single bloom.

After the tea, she treads softly up the steps and nestles
beside David. Through the window, the moon shines
upon a round peace button on the night table — a white
dove, in its beak an olive branch. David must have placed
it there.

Her gaze moves to David's tattoo — under the metallic moonlight, the graphics on his bicep appear three
dimensional. She sees it now — the same symbol — a white
dove with an olive branch stands out from the rest of the
drawings. She fathoms another symbol below the dove
— a skull. Hells Angels' logo, Death Head. Is that what he
is trying to hide? Her vision magnified, she discerns yet
another emblem superimposed over the others. Another
peace sign — the ubiquitous circle with an inverted V
known as the crow's foot design. *It hides semaphoric shapes
for letters N and D (nuclear disarmament) and was inspired by
Goya's peasant before the firing squad, with arms stretched out-
wards and downwards.*

She sits up in bed. *So this is the enigmatic tattoo I've been
trying to decipher since the day I met him. Symbols, logos. One
layer of his life upon another.*

She recalls him riding his bicycle on Centre Island,
the same boyishness of the David sleeping in her bed
evident in the way he shows off his flip tricks to her. He
pedals his Raleigh Sports Roadster ahead, pulls on the
handlebar, lifts the front wheel off the road, and as he
continues riding on the back wheel, he spins the bike
three hundred and sixty degrees. She catches his glance

— he knows she is watching — and she adores the vulnerable boy in need of attention, more than she ever thought possible. Her need to protect this man with paper-cut lines around his eyes and keen involvement in the antiwar movement, this communist-in-disguise, overpowers the fear she has come to know as premonition. She hardens her resolve against the fear. *You don't believe in superstition, Liza, do you?* She hears David's voice.

She settles under the sheets again — the lure of his nakedness. He stirs and enfolds her in an embrace.

Hells Angels. Hells Angels. Hells Angels. Throbs in her head.

She jumps up and turns on the lamp.

"You okay, Babe?" David murmurs.

She shakes his shoulder. "Wake up, David."

He sits up and rubs his eyes.

"Tell me about Hells Angels," she says.

"Now? What time is it?"

"Yes, now."

He rubs his forehead and mutters: "I rode with them. For a bit."

"Rode? So you don't any more? Why would you ride with them?"

He gets out of bed and begins to pace the floor. "A childhood friend, an Angel, helped me escape to Canada."

She sits on the edge of the bed, props her chin with her hand, and stares at him.

"He risked his reputation in the gang. And his safety. All for me."

She shrugs. "How?"

"That's complicated, Babe. Angels are in support of the War. To them, draft dodgers are traitors."

"So you joined the gang?"

"I rode with them here and there. Paid for beer. Posted bail for a few. Angels are always short of money. This was my way to get on their good side."

"Because a friend helped you?"

"Angels often attack the antiwar rallies. They beat the protesters so badly, they're feared more than the police. I thought if I pay some of their bills, they'll leave the protesters alone." He rubs his beard. "And, yes. Because a friend helped me. As I said, it's complicated."

"They still attack the rallies, don't they?"

David shrugs. "Not as badly. And not as often."

"You're still *friends* with them?"

"Got to keep them off the protesters' backs. Got to try, at least. Every once in a while, I bail out a guy. But that's all."

Liza gets out of bed and paces the floor with him. "This is more that I can handle."

David embraces her. "Nothing to worry about, Babe. Tomorrow in the daylight, all of this will look different."

CHAPTER 13

IZA LEANS ON the large cement planter on Yorkville
Avenue and waits for David to park the Harley in the back
lane. He was able to reserve a table at the Riverboat — a
difficult task considering Leonard Cohen is performing
this evening. Cohen is extending his stay in Toronto after
taking part in the Victoria Day's Love-in at Queen's Park,
which drew thousands.

She has left her flats in the storage pack of David's
bike. On her finger, she dangles new stilettos by the straps,
about to slip her bare feet into them. Looking down Yorkville, she is surprised by the changes that have taken
place in the couple of years since she began working for
the City.

As a student, she had frequented the Bohemian Embassy — a coffee shop on the second floor of a run-down
warehouse on Saint Nicholas Street, constantly threatened
with closure by the fire department — where Margaret

Atwood and Milton Acorn read poetry to a packed room, and Joni Mitchell often sang. Since then, Yorkville has taken on a different flavour. Where the sound of jazz and folk once wafted through the coffee houses, now rock bands blare, and hordes of young people, many from the suburbs and surrounding towns, hang out on the streets of the so-called "Toorotten's hippie cultural centre," the new Yorkville.

Narrow one-way streets are packed with cars. The three-block drive along Yorkville Avenue took her and David nearly half an hour, with drivers honking and gawking and passengers yelling to the crowds jamming the sidewalks and spilling onto the streets. The media had not exaggerated reports about Yorkville becoming the teenage hangout. Toronto's draconian liquor licensing laws prohibit most coffee shops and clubs from serving alcohol, which means the teenagers are welcome. Yorkville has become a hangout for high school students simply killing time, standing about to see and be seen. After about ten at night, when the crowds begin pouring into the bars, the teenagers usually mange to get in and drink themselves into a stupor and rowdiness.

"Move along! Move along!" Two police officers instruct as they shuffle among young people crowding the sidewalks. "No loitering allowed."

Liza has managed to fit one foot into her new sandal when an officer approaches. "It's past your bedtime, young lady, wouldn't you say?"

Standing off balance with one bare foot on the sidewalk and the other in a high heel sandal, Liza is caught off guard. "I beg your pardon, officer?"

"How old are you?" the officer asks.

"Officer, what's this about?"

"Got your birth certificate, young lady?"

She pulls out her driver's license and hands it to him. He looks at it for a moment, turns it over, examines it again, and hands it back to her.

"This better be real," he says.

Liza slips the driver's license back in her wallet. It had been a number of years since she'd been carded, and she would have found the experience humorous if it was not for the paddy wagon parked at Hazelton and Yorkville she and David had passed by, with police eager to arrest anyone under eighteen, or anyone without ID suspected to be an adolescent, hanging out in Yorkville past the ten o'clock curfew.

She breathes a sigh of relief. She'd almost left her wallet at home — David had suggested it — as the weekend crowds were becoming known for purse snatching by underage youth looking for excitement and easy cash. The officer meshes into the crowd, his head towering over the swarm of teenagers. He can't be much older than her. Has she imagined that spark in his eyes, that flash of a smile that told her he had other interest in her than making an arrest? And the stern voice is a put-on, she is sure. He turns, and their eyes meet. Her face turns hot as if she'd just had a shot of Drambuie. The sandal she had placed on a planter drops to the sidewalk. Her skirt is too short, so she squats down, picks up the sandal and slips it on, and when she stands up, now with both shoes on, the police officer is still there, eyes glued on her, beaming. She waves goodbye, and turns away.

And now she remembers where she had seen this cop. At the Love-in, at Queens Park. She can see him now — leaning on the seat of his parked motorcycle a group of hippies had decorated with tulips and daffodils. Gathered around, they're serenading him with, "For he's a jolly good fellow," at which he blushes profusely. As soon as the singing stops, he rides off.

He did not see her. She stood aside and observed. Even if he saw her, he would not recognize her, now. She was practically "masked." She teeters on her pink stilettos and instinctively pulls on the hem of her mini skirt trying to cover her thighs. David approaches. "You alright, Babe?" He takes her hand and they head for the River-boat.

From her purse, Liza pulls out a pair of heart-shaped sunglasses, hoping they'll conceal some of her unease. But she cannot contain her excitement about Leonard Cohen's concert. If his performance is anything close to the Love-in, this will be the best night ever.

The lyrics from Cohen's "Famous Blue Raincoat," which Liza heard for the first time this evening, replay in her mind. The song has not been released yet, and Cohen was testing it on his audience. She finds the rhyme hypnotic, addictive, and she makes a mental note to buy the album as soon as it becomes available. But the words are so sad, they are lodged in her chest, and she cannot free herself from them. The song is written as a letter about a love triangle. About loss. It makes her think of love and death

— and her and David. About his involvement with the antiwar movement. And the Hells Angels. Especially the Hells Angels. He greeted a few gang members at the Riverboat. He offered to introduce her, but she used a washroom excuse. When she came back, they had left — they were not interested in Cohen's music — and she was grateful. Now that she knows what David's tattoo means, she cannot put it out of her thoughts.

Liza went to a tattoo parlour on Yonge Street and found out that a tattoo *could* be removed. The only risk is some possible scarring. She did not, however, like the atmosphere at the place — it seems to be run by bikers, and she wonders how hygienic it is. The hepatitis scare in Yorkville has saturated the Toronto media. Although the sharing of hypodermic needles by drug users, primarily the Yorkville crowd, is seen as the main means of spreading the virus, she fears that the needles used at a tattoo parlour could also be contaminated. *I must talk to David,* she resolves, and drifts off to sleep.

CHAPTER 14

ANNA GETS OFF at the Keele Street subway station, crosses Bloor Street and walks to the corner store out of habit. She pulls the *Daily Star* out of her bag and dumps it in the garbage container. But she cannot get the article about the young woman, found in the back alley just outside of Yorkville, out of her thoughts. The woman was dumped into the large garbage container and left for dead, the article said. A passer-by spotted her and called the police. She was taken to the Women's Centenary Hospital and, miraculously, she is expected to make a full recovery. But the doctor reports that she had been gang raped so brutally, her internal organs have been permanently damaged and she will never be able to bear children. She has regained consciousness, but the only thing she recalls is being at a party in Yorkville.

Standing in the entrance of the crammed shop, Anna summons up a mental picture of her fridge contents and well-stocked kitchen cupboards. What does she need to pick up on the way home? She takes a few minutes to collect her thoughts. Her mind drifts back to the article. *Who could this unfortunate sixteen-year-old be?* She recalls an advertisement by the new private eye agency that just opened up in Yorkville: "Looking for your son or daughter? Have you checked Yorkville? If you can't find them, we can." She has seen parents carrying a photo of their daughter or son and asking passers-by and store owners if they have seen them.

David has joined the Diggers, and has been helping the teenagers find jobs and a place to live. But Anna is not sure that is the answer. Too many kids have been pouring in, and too many bikers have been taking them under their wings and turning them to drugs and prostitution. The gang rapes of young girls have become a horrific scare — they used to be unheard of in Toronto before the teenage "exodus" into Yorkville, and before the bikers moved into the area. Rumour has it, the bikers have made a deal with some of the hippies to supply them with "fresh virgins" from Yorkville — the young women who flock to the city and have no means of supporting themselves. Some of the "old timer" hippies are horrified. They feel that the newcomers are not the "real hippies" and do not respect the qualities the hippies stand for — love and peace and freedom to express themselves, be it through the clothing they wear, or art, or lifestyle. And the fervent opposition to war and violence of any kind.

Anna feels nauseous just thinking about the unfortunate young woman in the article. She needs to keep her mind occupied. There must be something needing replenishment in her fridge. A carton of milk for her cat. Although most people advise against feeding milk to cats, she sides with the cat. She compares it to smoking and her perpetual attempt to quit. Milk to her cat is what a cigarette is to her—helps to calm her. She mustn't forget a can of tuna for her other cat. After paying for her items, she is back out crossing Keele Street on the south side of Bloor. Walking up the hill along the sidewalk bounded by the park on one side and Bloor Street on the other, Anna heads towards the bench at the edge of the park. On the way home she often pauses here and takes the time to unwind. To leave the work behind. To regain her balance.

Sitting on the green wood slats, watching the steady flow of cars along the street below, and sheltered by the tall oaks bordering the park behind her, she looks up into the sky. *Where were you, God, when that girl got raped? Yes, I'm talking to you.*

Anna turns and scans the wooded hillock behind her. She never could venture out into the deep entrails of the park she lives near. Not even in the daytime. The paved paths and the well-tended gardens in the centre near the restaurant is where she takes her walks. But not in the unpaved forested sections. No, never. As if she would lose herself, lose the grip on everyday routine and all the familiar aspects that define her place in the world. That, she could not risk—this sense of security that is linked to her workplace, that office on Bay and College she lives in five days a week, and even on weekends when work needs to be done.

How the two are linked, her office and the deep forest of this park, this urban sanctuary, and why they are exclusive of each other, irreconcilable, she cannot explain. They just are. A photo from the 1920s with an inscription, *Lovers' Walk*, flashes in her thoughts. It's a sepia snapshot of a dirt path in the forest, somewhere in High Park, donated to the Toronto Reference Library. Did it have special meaning to the anonymous donor? Was it known as lovers' hideout? She cannot allow herself to go there, mentally or physically. Going there would mean losing herself, losing a grip on the intricate threads that bind all the vital segments of her existence, hold them together as one perfectly oiled machine. Stepping into the forest would be akin to leaving this machine out in the rain to rust, would cause her life to come apart.

The forest and its wilderness belong to Liza. And David. She'd seen them at the sculpture sites during some of her walks. One time she was heading to her favourite bench under a gingko tree near the maintenance building. They were by the *Flower Power* and did not see her. She did not greet them—they seemed to be in their own world, and she needed time to herself as well. Have they ventured into the recesses of the dark woods forbidden to her? Perhaps they have. Most likely.

But what does it matter? She and David never did see each other as more than friends. What happened between them that night had nothing to do with how they feel about each other. She had pushed that memory out of her thoughts. Now, she and David are on a mission—the antiwar movement. She worries when he sneaks across the border. If he gets caught, he'll be jailed. As long as he remains in Canada, he is safe.

Every once in a while, though, her memory takes her

back—back to the scene with the drunk and drugged gang that night. She had tucked this event away in a compartment of her private life she keeps separate from her public one. In her mind, she carefully scrutinizes every decision, gesture, and word, against these two lives she lives—each exclusive of the other, yet both continuing in parallel universes—as if uniting them would trigger an inner atomic bomb.

These two lives are kept in balance by one common element—David. He is aware of her public life only, and a molecule of her private one—the very molecule which, literally, conceived her private one. She could cut him out of her life. Could stop helping with the antiwar movement. Could stop the clandestine work that fuels the fears for her job and a communist label. But that is her link to David—her life-link—as vital to sustaining her secret private life as oxygen is to breathing.

Lately, she finds herself going back to that night at the Hells Angels' clubhouse just outside of Boston and realizes that only David could have pulled it off. He had been riding with them for a while—a fugitive in his own country. After he escaped to Canada, riding with the Angels was a way to get back to the United States and help with the antiwar demonstrations without being arrested —a way to hide. He had been dividing his time between a chapter in the US and another one in Canada, a precarious position for any Angel—and especially perilous for a draft dodger who is not a member but just a friend. David has been a master at mediating between the Angels and the bar owners, paying for damages, and bribing police officers to drop charges for unruly and drunken gang members. Rumour has it David has been squandering his inheritance and the Angels don't mind being the benefactors. Besides, when riding with them, he transforms into a picture-perfect biker with his red hair and beard and mirrored spectacles that never leave his face. They call him Flaming Davy Do-good. In their eyes, Davy's downfall is his cleanliness and his measure of propriety and justice — not to the Angels' code of conduct.

Yet that night they listened.

One of the women had accused Anna of going after her *ol' man*. After that, everything happened quickly. Several women had encircled her. One had ripped open Anna's shirt, and they had begun tearing off her clothes. The scene flashes in her mind.

"Wanna fuck ma ol' man, don' you, bitch," a woman hisses.

She steps toward Anna, her blood gorged face only inches away. Watery blue eyes like thawing ice, launching menace. She grins. Her canines and molars are missing. Her front teeth are stuck in her gums like an unfinished picket fence. She flicks a switchblade and presses it against Anna's nostril.

"I'll make a flower out of that pig-snout," she spits, and scratches a semi-circle across Anna's cheek. She traces the blade to the corner of Anna's mouth.

A few intoxicated Angels crowd around them. One yanks the belt from his oily jeans and drops it on the floor, and the heavy buckle thuds like a hammer on the worn boards. Another unzips his fly and thrusts his hips, ready for action. Beer in hand, more Angels stagger from the bar and throng into a loose line-up. The women are clapping and whistling and yelping: "Fuck the bitch, fuck her brains out ..." Foot-stomping and grunting, the gang-rape about to commence.

David pushes through the crowd, grabs Anna by the arm, and drags her out of the mob, his Engineer boots reverberating like cannons, his voice barking and snarling and hissing profanities—unlike anything she'd imagined. She was his *momma*, and he would be the one to inflict the punishment. No one dare come near him and his *ol' lady*! She never could believe they actually bought his act. After she and David had made love—to the vulgar growls and shouts of exhortation from the frenzied gang—he'd held her close all night, keeping at bay the Angels eager to "share with" and "help" their buddy. David's barks were coarse that night. She never forgot that snarl in his voice, although she'd never heard it again. He was as much the wounded animal as she was. And she felt safe in his embrace.

CHAPTER 15

ANNA CRINGES. THE bar is full of bikers. From the second floor, she hears a crash of falling furniture, as if someone has thrown a chair across the room. A loud thud as if a table has collapsed. Gruff mumbling. A number of guests raise their drinks and cheer the Mynah Bird's resident ghost.

Someone yells: "Hey, ghost, have a beer, man. You'll feel better."

Another says: "Take it easy, dude."

And another: "We ain't here for no reason but fun, good time man."

And "Peace, man," and that prompts many peace signs in the smoky haze and many shouts: "Peace an' love man, peace an' free love."

"Our ghost don't like the porns, dude. He's religious. No porn for 'im, dude," someone says.

"He ain't religious, man. Or he'd be in heaven. With God," another says, and others join in a jumbled chorus.

"Maybe this is heaven, dude. Whiskey an' burgers, an' all the beer you want. An' girls. Maybe he ain't a ghost. Maybe we're in heaven."

"That ghost up there's mad, man. Throwin' furniture. We ain't in heaven."

"Well, you know, that's like your opinion, dude. Very free spirited."

"He don' like nudie girlies, that's what he don' like. The ghost."

Someone yells: "Whatsa matter, ghost? Why you don' like nudie girlies? I like nudie girlies. An' free love. An' peace. An' did I say free love?"

"Yeah, man. That's what that ghost needs. Some real good lovin', man. Then he wouldn't be so angry. Wouldn't be throwin' those chairs 'round."

"That's free spirited of you, dude. That nudie girlie up there can give our ghost some good ol' fashion lovin' …"

The smell of marijuana is thick, and combined with the whiff of perfume some patrons claim is dispensed by the ghost believed to reside on the second floor, it conjures up a taste of sweetness. It reminds Anna of burning incense at Saint Joan of Arc church at Bloor and Keele, except that this is anything but a church—not a house of God in any way, no. Or is it?

It is at strange places and in peculiar circumstances that Anna finds herself contemplating God. When she is at a place of worship, she reflects on the art and the architecture and the rituals—the icons, the stained glass, and the pagan rites that have morphed into religious ceremonies. But not on God. God she searches for in bars and coffee houses, at street corners where old men and women with gaunt faces and faded eyes beg for spare change. In "needle parks" where teenagers overdose and thirteen-year-old girls sell themselves to depraved old men.

She took her niece Jane, now a toddler, to the neighbourhood playground and found a used syringe in the sandbox. The notion that the teenagers who inject themselves might have played in that same sandbox only a decade earlier, eats away at her like rust on iron. How could she protect this child from such a fate?

Does God venture out to Vietnam where children are burned by napalm? She wonders.

She does not buy into the theory of God's acolyte, the devil, being responsible for all the horror in the world — a cowardly method of explaining away and shifting responsibility. Just as she knows that her own contemplation of God's existence does not lead to any resolution.

She is not an atheist. She cannot deny the existence of a Supreme Being. She considers herself an agnostic. *How could anyone prove or disprove the existence of God?* The concept of an agnostic, always controversial and always evolving, she had inherited from her parents who were followers of Thomas Huxley. But she had not been indoctrinated by them — she was to make her own choice when old enough. Now, she finds solace in this noncommittal position about God and sees no reason to change. Yet, every once in a while, she senses a presence. *Presence within my own thoughts. Is it the spiritual side of me, the divine? My conscience?* She wonders. *Is that my God?* To her, places of worship offer a glimpse into a philosophy on life and existence — an expansion of her horizons. But when she inhales the fragrance of a rose, or glimpses a smile on a child's face — she thanks her God.

More people pour in and the bikers blend with hippies, students, artists, business people, and tourists. Soon they tune in to the debate with the resident ghost — offering to appease it with beer or advice. Some patrons claim that a prankster upstairs is set up by the owner to amuse and draw the crowd. Others declare there must be some form of energy. A restless spirit? Anna is uneasy. And it has nothing to do with the ghost. She is uneasy about the living unquiet type — there are too many bikers. They seem to be everywhere.

She checks her watch. David should be here by now. She is having second thoughts about renting her apartment to Ricky — taking in a deserter. She'll give David a few more minutes and, if he doesn't show up, she's leaving.

David rushes in and catches sight of her, and she wonders if he has some ancient mariner compass implanted in him to be able to spot her so quickly in this hazy cauldron of people and smoke and glimmer of Chianti candles. He signals to give him a moment and makes his way to the band. After a brief chat with a lead guitarist, the music stops.

David takes the microphone and announces that he has some very sad news to share. "A great man, a singer-songwriter, a folk-musician and an inspiration to many — is dead. If I tell you his guitar carried a slogan, 'This machine kills fascists,' you'll know who he is."

A murmur passes through the crowd. Glasses clink

along with words of regret. Of praise. "Here's to you, Woody, wherever you are. You're the man, Woody. You rock, man."

David says into the mike. "Woody Guthrie died last night. After a long and cruel illness." He invites everyone to join him in a moment of silence in honour of this American icon.

Afterwards, David says: "I'm sure many of you know that Woody's most famous song is 'This Land is Your Land.' He wrote the American version, and it's been adapted by our new homeland here."

He waits for the applause to subside, then continues. "On the typescript submitted for copyright of 'This Land Is Your Land,' Woody wrote: 'This song is Copyrighted in U.S., under Seal of Copyright # 154085, for a period of 28 years, and anybody caught singin it without our permission, will be mighty good friends of ourn, cause we don't give a dern. Publish it. Write it. Sing it. Swing to it. Yodel it. We wrote it, that's all we wanted to do.'"

Again cheers and shouts of affirmation swell through the bar.

David says into the mike: "Just for the record, as we speak, a number of organizations claim copyright for many of Guthrie's songs."

The crowd boos and hisses.

The band begins to play "This land is your land ..." and everyone stands up to join in the lyrics.

When the song is over, another version of Guthrie's hymn, "The Travelers," popular with Canadian folksingers, gushes out.

When Anna stops singing along, she raises her arms

toward the smoke-filled ceiling, and cries out: "Bet you enjoyed this? Ha?" She turns. David is now next to her. He lifts his eyebrows and says nothing and she is glad. She couldn't exactly explain her conversation with her God, could she?

Suddenly the answer she has been looking for comes to her. Woody lived life his way — for his music and the causes he believed in. Not unlike Ricky. And in a way, not unlike her own. Except she feels crippled by fear — fear of openly supporting the antiwar movement, of being ostracized by her coworkers, of losing her job, of being labelled … *No, I will not be ruled by fear, no.*

CHAPTER 16

August

LIZA STEPS OUT of the elevator at her fifteenth floor office at College and Bay. Balancing a coffee cup in one hand and a briefcase along with a small bouquet of pink roses from her garden in another, she passes a police officer standing by the Department of Culture's double panel doors, flipping through his notebook. She enters the office, nods good-morning to the receptionist, checks her message box, and proceeds to her desk, anxious to finalize the Symposium progress report before the department's weekly Monday morning staff meeting.

She rushes to the ladies' room and fills a vase with water for her flowers. A few minutes later, notes spread out on her desk, she is typing the report and is startled by the receptionist's rapid double knock on the door.

"Sorry to interrupt, Liza, but there's a police officer asking for you."

Liza shrugs, puzzled, picks up the vase with roses and inhales their fragrance, needing a few seconds for the words to sink in. Walking toward the reception area, they exchange questioning glances.

The policeman standing by the front desk looks up. "Miss Liza Grant?"

It's the same officer she had passed in the hallway — six foot four, trousers too short, as well as his jacket sleeves. If it were not for his dark bushy eyebrows, he would look more like a high school student in a poorly fitting band uniform. He shifts his weight from one foot to the other nervously as if it's his first day on the job.

Suddenly, Liza recognizes that look. *Of course, he's the officer who carded me at Yorkville. The same officer whose bike got decorated with tulips at the Love-in. He wore a better fitting uniform, then. And his buzz-cut has grown out.*

Liza extends her hand. "What can I do for you, officer?"

He tilts his head and squints an eye, and she realizes that he might recognize her as well. But their Yorkville encounter was at night, and she was dressed very differently. At the Love-in, she was practically "masked" and part of the crowd — he did not notice her.

The phone rings and the receptionist picks up. "She is not available right now. Can I take a message?"

Palm over the receiver, she turns to Liza. "There is a reporter calling from the lobby. Wants to talk to you. From *The Telegram*."

"A reporter? What about?"

"Didn't say. Sounds rather pushy. I'll tell him you're in a meeting."

The receptionist continues into the receiver: "You need an appointment, Sir. Miss Grant is in a meeting."

She looks at Liza, exasperated. "He's not there any more. Sure hope he's not on his way up."

Liza turns to the policeman. "Officer?"

"You need to come with me to the station, Miss Grant," the policeman says. "We need you to make a statement."

"Me? A statement? About what?"

"I'll explain on the way."

Liza glances at her watch. "Officer, can't this wait? I have a meeting at ten."

There is a loud knock at the door and the next moment the door swings open and a flash lights up the monochrome interior. Two men stumble in as if someone is chasing them. One is holding a camera and the other a microphone.

"I'm looking for Miss Liza Grant! I'd like a few words with her!" The reporter thrusts the microphone to the receptionist's mouth. "She works for the Department of Culture. Correct? She is on the Symposium Committee. The High Park one. Correct?"

The receptionist stands up. "Please leave these premises or I'll call security."

"Just a short interview. Five minutes. Which way is her office?"

The receptionist sits down and dials. "Security? Fifteenth floor, please, fifteen o'two. Department of Culture. A newspaper reporter's trying to muscle his way in."

"Miss! She is on the Symposium Committee? You could confirm this, couldn't you?" The reporter jabs the microphone at her.

The receptionist places her hand on the mike. With a disgusted look on her face as if the microphone and the reporter's hand that seems glued to it were contaminated, she pushes it away.

Liza and the policeman stand in silence, taking in the confrontation.

The receptionist calls out to the policeman: "Officer, can you please do something? These reporters have no permission ..."

Seeing the policeman, the reporter and the photographer excuse themselves and quickly back out of the door and into the hallway, still apologizing as the door closes behind them.

A smirk of satisfaction flashes on the officer's face. He takes on a confident stance as if he'd just won a boxing match.

"Officer, what's this about?" Liza asks.

"We need to talk to you. About the last time you were at the Symposium site. In High Park. If everything was in order. That nothing was missing."

"I visit every Friday for the report update. And I live just a few blocks north of the park. I'm there every spare minute I get."

"You know the sites very well, then."

"Yes, of course."

"Last night, a block of stone was stolen. A large block. Belonged to one of the artists."

"What did you say? That's preposterous!"

"That's what some others said. Who'd steal a block of stone? But it's gone."

"That stuff weighs tons. It's not like somebody just walked in and took a rock from the park. It can't be!"

"We think it's a professional job." The officer's voice drops an octave. He straightens up and takes on an authoritative tone. "It had to be. They'd need a truck and a mini crane."

"That's impossible. What kind of stone?"

"We believe it was a large block of marble. White Carrara."

"Have you been to the site, officer?"

"No, that's what the report says. Haven't seen it for myself. But then, how would I? It's not there anymore." The policeman laughs. He squints an eye and studies her curiously, "Have we met? We have, haven't we? Yorkville, right?"

She shrugs. "There's only one block of marble there. I've got to go to the park. I need to see this. How about I meet you at your station in an hour or so?"

"The Sergeant wants to talk to you. We need your help, Miss Grant. You can refuse, if you want. It's your right."

"What if I was at the park today? On business. You would've come looking for me there. Right?"

"This is urgent, Miss. Mr. Burman, the sculptor who owns that stone, came to the station this morning. He was furious. The Sergeant hopes to get to the bottom of this. Quickly. This Symposium's the biggest thing Toronto's ever seen."

Should she call the police station and ask to speak to the sergeant? Why should she be asked to go to the police station? And could she not go to the station after the meeting? The officer locks eyes with her and smiles. *He did save me from that reporter.*

"Give me a minute," Liza says. "I'll get my purse."

In her office, Liza pauses. *I have to see the sites first.* She picks up her purse and walks to the reception. "Officer, please call your Sergeant. I'd be glad to come to the station with you, after I see the sites in High Park. I need to check that *it is* missing. And not just moved somewhere else. And if anything else is missing. Otherwise, I am not coming with you, unless you arrest me."

He shifts his weight from one foot to the next and shrugs. "Wait here," he says, and steps out into the hallway.

A moment later the officer returns. "You win, Ma'am. Any problem going in my car? I'll drive you back."

The officer opens the back door of the police car. "Sorry Miss Grant. Procedures."

They drive south along University Avenue. He searches for her in the rear view mirror — that spark of recognition still in his eyes. He couldn't be much older that her, she thinks.

"What did you say your name was, officer?"

"I didn't."

Liza smiles. "Come to think of it, weren't you supposed to give me your name?"

"No, I wasn't. Just the badge I showed you when I came in. No name there. Only a number."

She fumbles for words. "Any rules against using names?"

He nods. "Personal safety." A coy little smile plays across his lips. "But you can call me James."

She brushes an unruly strand of hair away from her face and catches his eye in the rear-view mirror. "Ok, James. I feel a bit better. Now, with a wave of my magic wand, I will turn this police car into a black limo."

He laughs, and his brown eyes sparkle as if a match was thrown into a pile of kindling.

James parks the car on Colborne Lodge Drive near the Forest School. As soon as they step out of the vehicle, Liza's heart drops. The marble *is* missing. Not that she doubted James' words. But seeing it makes it real, somehow. The CFTO Television crew is filming the sites and interviewing curious onlookers who are gathered next to Burman's blocks of granite.

"They don't waste any time," Liza says, looking at the film crew. "We better wait until they leave. Or they'll badger me to death with questions."

They get back into the car, and Liza suggests they have coffee at the Grenadier Restaurant.

James glances at his watch. "Almost lunch time," he says. "My treat. How about it?"

After lunch, they walk toward Burman's granite blocks. The film crew has left, and curious visitors pace the sites and chit-chat. James takes a few shots of the tire tracks.

Liza produces a paper napkin out of her purse and uses it to collect some cigarette butts she wraps in a few more napkins and gives to James.

He laughs. "You're a real detective, aren't you?"

"Aren't you going to take some close up photos of this place?"

"Another officer was here early this morning."

Liza gives James a tour of the sculpture sites, then they drive to the station.

The Sergeant questions Liza about her work and her involvement with the Symposium. At first, he is direct and somewhat impatient, as if he knows the answer even before she gives it. He asks about Greenwin Construction and the companies which donated the use of its equipment, and she wonders why he needed to talk to her. He could have gotten the same information from the Human Resources. Then he turns edgy—how often she visits the park, when she was there last, who are her friends, whether she suspects anyone, and why, in her opinion, would someone steel a block of marble. He pauses at her answers and glares at her. *Is he doubting me? Or the sincerity of my replies?* Instinctively, she keeps David out of it. *Why should I divulge personal details? Am I a suspect?* It is late afternoon by the time she finally returns to her office.

CHAPTER 17

ANNA STRIDES ALONG Yorkville Avenue fuming.

She's left two messages on David's answering machine asking to meet him. Marching to their secret place where pressing matters are usually aired, she almost misses the Riverboat. Next to the coffeehouse, she turns onto the side street that leads to the back alley. He is leaning against the wall, hands in pockets.

"I want the truth, David. And I want it now."

He winces. "What's up, Anna?"

"You a great actor or a great liar?" she snaps, as they walk back to Yorkville Avenue. In front of the Riverboat, three teenagers are sitting on the newspaper boxes lined up along the sidewalk.

She props her hands on her hips. "What do you know about that missing marble, David? The papers are plastered with speculation. And things are heating up in my office."

The city noise has subsided and her voice carries in the stillness of dusk. She glances at the youngsters on the boxes and they smile.

"Don't know anything about that, Anna. Just as I didn't know you'd have your own audience here today. Should I pass the hat or let those three stooges get a free show?" David waves dismissively and turns his back to the trio.

The teens rest their chins on their hands and glare, intent on not missing a word. One has long dark hair spilling over his forehead and covering most of his eyes. He waves a folded newspaper page with a picture of Burman's two granite blocks with a heading: "High Park stone thief," and says: "It's cool, man. Stone thief in Toronto."

His buddies repeat after him: "Yeah. Cool."

Anna marches over to them. "Let me see that. I didn't see this one."

The youth flips his mane, and looks at her. Then he hands the article to her. "It's all yours, lady. Knock yourself out."

Anna takes the paper over to David. "Have you seen this?"

David strokes his beard. "How 'bout a drink?"

Anna walks over to the newspaper boxes and hands the paper back. Then drifts down the steps that lead below the street level to the Riverboat. David follows. He takes a long puff, butts out the cigarette in the can of sand on the window sill, and they enter the smoky darkness of the club. They sit in a red booth across from each other, surrounded by pine walls and brass portholes.

From her purse, Anna pulls out a piece of newspaper, unfolds it, and plunks it on the table. It's the front page of the *Toronto Daily Star*, featuring a photograph of the same blocks of granite, taken from a slightly different angle, with a heading: "Who would steal a block of marble from High Park?"

She pulls out another page and unfolds it. This one is from *The Telegram* with a heading: "Toronto thief." She irons the pages out with her hand.

"Have you seen these? Since that marble disappeared, that's all anyone talks about."

"I've seen some. You collecting them?"

"The police are there a lot. Took pictures of the tire tracks. Witnesses have come forward. Said they saw a flatbed, late Sunday night."

"What do you want *me* to do about it?"

"They've questioned Liza."

"What could she know? She doesn't sleep there."

Anna shakes her head. "The 'artists' children' are playing amateur sleuths. Scouring the area for clues. Collecting cigarette butts. Turning into little detectives. And having a ball."

"Ah, my buddies. Doing a good job. Keeping those relentless visitors at bay so the men can work on their pieces."

Anna winces. "It's not just the children any more. The locals have joined in as well. They've organized shifts to patrol the sites. The park has many eyes. There's always somebody out there who sees what happens."

David nods. "Hope they get him. Or her. Whoever stole that piece. I hear Burman's taking it hard. The quarry offered to replace it free of charge. But he refuses."

"Or her? You think a woman did it? You making fun of me, David?"

"Well, well. You seem to have your finger pointed at me. And how do we know it's not a woman?"

"Because it never is."

"Oh? And what if it happens to be a sculptress who fell in love with that stone? What do you say to that?"

Anna's face turns red. "Now we're on to something. And that's what worries me, David. I saw you coveting that piece. There was something about that block of marble. And that wistful look on you every time it's mentioned. The way you caressed it that day in the park ..."

"I thought you didn't like the park. You prefer your garden. Or your porch."

"I go for a walk there, like everyone else. Was surprised to see you there. But then, I figure, with the Symposium and all."

She gives him a long, hesitant look. "The way you were leaning your greedy paw on that boulder, David." She waits for him to speak, and when he doesn't, she continues. "After that piece disappeared, the sight of you and that stone kept flashing in my mind. My gut feeling tells me you have something to do with it."

"Your gut feeling's wrong, Anna."

Her eyes narrow. A mischievous smile scans across her lips. "You're the stone thief, aren't you, David?" She says it slowly, without taking eyes off him.

"Almost wish you were right. That *was* a nice piece."

"So where were you last Sunday?"

"You know where I was. Same place as you. The Sit-in."

She takes the gum out of her mouth, unwraps a new piece, and begins to chew noisily. "Oh, didn't know you saw me."

"Yep. Said nothing. Like we agreed."

"I left when the arrests began."

"Glad you did. I'm still trying to clean up that mess. Still trying to get some of the protesters out of jail. You've seen the paper."

The Star reported that the Yorkville Sit-in, which was staged as response to the failed Talk-in between the Foragers, a community activist group, and City Council, had become a Jail-in. The protesters had been dragged off to Don Jail.

The article said that the Sit-in, organized by the Foragers, drew hundreds of residents who sat on the road blocking traffic to protest the grid-lock of vehicles that had plagued the street ever since it became a gawkers' mecca. The Yorkville old-timers were joined by the hippies and the youth. They demanded that Yorkville Avenue be closed to traffic and turned into a pedestrian mall. The protest grew to a few thousand. They formed a human chain to show the bridging of the gap between the youth, the hippies, and the old-timers of Yorkville — and to send the message that the influx of vehicles was the problem and not the influx of youth. Anna was not surprised when the police showed up, but she was stunned by the show of force she thought completely unnecessary. The police ordered the protesters to leave, and those who refused were beaten and dragged away to jail. The youth were a particular target. Anna found a telephone booth and called a friend at City Council. Although she knew he would not be in the office, she felt the need to report it, and calling the police would not have helped. She left an urgent message, and followed up with two more messages since. But

three days have gone by and he still has not returned her
calls. She realizes the issues are a lot more political then
they appear, and she just might have to go in person to
see him. But now, her suspicion of David's involvement
with the missing marble pushes her worries to the edge.

Anna shrugs. "Stealing that marble was a late night
job. Where did you go later on?"

"To bed. Where else? I was in bed, Anna."

"Why don't I believe you?"

"After a day like that, where do you think I'd be?"

David had spent the afternoon getting the protesters
out of jail. He had managed to get some released, but
many are still held for questioning.

He runs his fingers through his hair. "Getting dis-
couraged with the Foragers lately."

Anna nods. "I see your point. I sometimes wonder as
well. When that girl got raped ... I thought, if there is no
help here, maybe the teenagers would stop coming." She
heaves a sigh. "But then, things could get worse. The
youth really depend on you guys. Especially the homeless. For everything, food, shelter."

"Too much dependence, if you ask me. Too many
teenagers pouring in daily. The help's supposed to be temporary. But it's turned into a way of life for some. A free-
ride. And the number's growing."

Anna knows David has a point. Many teenagers, in
their zeal to stand up to convention that includes just about
everyone, from parents to educators to employers, leave
their homes and flock to Yorkville. In return for food and
shelter, they're expected to look for employment and help
other newcomers. But the teenagers' focus on having a

good time. David has been patient with them. To him, this is all part of the big picture, and change could not happen without this wave of free thought that has swept the world and turned Yorkville into "the eye of the storm."

She shakes her head. "After all that mess at the Sit-in, you went straight to bed? And that's it?"

"That's all, Anna." He squints his right eye and his left one—the one that sometimes turns into a lazy eye—is frozen and ice-blue, staring right through her, and she wonders how does he manage this? Is the eye-squinting some type of subconscious self-preservation technique? And what does it mean? After all these years she still cannot decipher his lazy eye and what message it holds. One thing she realizes, though, is that there is no point in continuing the discussion. This is his stubborn mode.

"If I could only believe you had nothing to do with that missing stone," she says.

"Believe it," he says, his lazy eye a clump of ice.

Anna wonders if she is being too hard on David.

Accusing him of stealing that block of marble may not be fair. Why did she reach her guilty verdict even before talking to him? She could've probed for answers gently. He takes on too much. Clearly, dealing with the failed Sit-in is stressful. And so is trying to broker some semblance of peace between the homeless youth, the hippies, and City Council. Would he actually risk his freedom and his reputation for a block of marble? Besides, he is becoming fond of Liza. And she is in charge of that project. Would he risk drawing her into such a perilous situation? No, that doesn't seem reasonable. Now, she is really remorseful. How could she make it up to him?

David leans back in his chair and rocks on the two back legs. He takes a long puff, then blows the smoke into the bluish haze hanging low.

"What the heck," Anna says and pulls out her pack of Eve — the last pack she'll ever smoke. She'll quit after this one's finished. She'd sworn. She's been pacing herself, taking a few puffs when she can't resist, then putting the cigarette out and stashing it back into the pack. She shakes out a half-cigarette, picks up David's flashing-nipples-lighter off the table, and lights up. She draws in deeply, then lets the smoke out slowly. *Courage, God, give me courage to quit.*

She heaves a sigh. "Okay, David. I'm relieved you had nothing to do with that stone."

After several heavenly puffs, the butt scorching her fingers, she grinds it into the ashtray. "Got a friend at City Council. Left a few messages, but haven't heard back. Owes me a favour, though. I'll go see him tomorrow. Twist his arm a bit. See what can be done about those jailbirds."

CHAPTER 18

"HERE'S THE KEY to the side door. Use the path from Glendenen Road through the backyard—a bit more secluded. There's a lot of rental housing around here. Nobody really cares who comes and goes. Careful with the fire escape. Hasn't been checked for a while—since my folks died a few years back. Don't think you'll need it, though—sure hope not. And this large key's for the garage door—need to jiggle it a bit so it'll catch. The garage's cluttered with stuff my folks collected. Mom was an antique buff and God knows what's in it. But if you need to store something, you'll find some room."

Anna presses the keys into Ricky James' hand, props up on tiptoes, and kisses him on the lips. She shoots him an alluring smile. "If you'd like to see me, you still need to ask me out. You know, on a date. Can't just sneak down to her boudoir and fuck your landlady any time you like."

Ricky smiles, lifts Anna in his arms, and the next

moment they're making love on the Qum Persian silk rug which Anna's mother bought on her trip to Iran. With one foot, Anna pushes off her panties caught on the ankle of the other, while she struggles to pull Ricky's shirt over his head. His trousers are in a pile under her and the belt buckle is pressing sharply into the fleshy part of her but-tock—*and we're off to cloud nine*, Anna imagines.

As Ricky dresses and hums the Mynah Birds' new song, "It's My Time," he inserts Anna's name into the lyrics about loving her every day. Anna sits on the red plastic sofa in the attic apartment and sways to the rhythm as she sips lemonade. It had been a few years since she'd closed off this unit from the rest of the house to save on heating bills. She'd used it as a teenager for pyjama parties and sleepovers, and as she glances about the small but airy space with peaked ceilings, she recalls it strewn with sleeping bags and knapsacks and bowls with chips and Cheezies and plastic Koolaid glasses and some favourite teddy bears girls cuddled imagining they were boy-friends. Now, it harbours a sentimental aura of times long ago, some gloomy and written off, and others pleasant and cheerful. Having Ricky use it is a meaningful way to bridge the past and the present. Besides, the plumbing in the apartment above the garage is too old and the knob-and-tube wiring too dangerous—all too costly to replace. Ricky's glass of lemonade, sweating from condensation, is perched precariously on the radiator.

"You like it spiked, Ricky?" she asks. "Some vodka in your lemonade?"

He nods and reminds her of their dinner date before his set starts that evening. "You'll be there, Annie?"

She pours the liquor straight from the bottle. "Sure thing, Ricky. Toby's Goodeats?"

"How 'bout The Pilot?"

"No problem. You meeting the guys there before the gig?"

"Not sure who'll be there. As long as you're there, my foxy lady." He downs the lemonade, gives her a smoldering gaze and a long kiss and says: "You're the sweetest thing, Annie."

That hungry look in his eyes makes her wish he did not have to leave so soon. The chemistry between them is ablaze. But there is also this emptiness as if they were actors in a movie and their affair would end when the filming wraps up. In her mind, she replays "You're the sweetest thing, Annie" in a Humphrey Bogart accent—he is Humphrey Bogart and she Ingrid Bergman in *Casablanca*, playing their roles. *Oh, what the hell. The sex is good. That's why they call him the chick-magnet.*

She picks up Ricky's glass and puts it on a tray. *Good things in life don't last.*

She opens her new package of birth control pills and is glad that the first pill is missing from its spot—she had not forgotten to take it that morning, after all. She's lived in mortal fear for the past couple of weeks, since Ricky entered her life and her bed, until her monthly cycle put her mind at ease and, in her words, Aunt Flo from Red River visited. She gives a sigh of relief. *I get pregnant before the guy pulls his pants on, for Pete's sake.*

She lifts the lid of the console, drops in a Bob Dylan album, and moves the stylus to the third song, "It Ain't Me, Babe." She pours some vodka into her lemonade and leans back into the sofa. She listens to the lyrics and begins to hum along—and the song reminds her that she and Ricky are all wrong for each other. She is melancholic as if the lyrics are intended for her. Did she choose to be with Ricky *because* he is not the settle-down type?

After finishing her drink, she walks down the staircase to her bedroom on the second floor, retrieves the photo album, and slowly peruses it. She picks up the phone and dials, and is thrilled when her sister in Ottawa answers on the second ring. They chat and Anna asks to speak with Jane. Anna's tone becomes girlish. "My little Janey! It's your Auntie Annie. How are you, my sweet? My darling little girl! You playing with your dolly? She's saying, mama? Mama! And how old are you today? No, no, that was yesterday, my sweet. Today you're two and one hundred and thirty two days. Yes you are! Here, you say it now." After they sing, "Teddy bear, teddy bear, turn around ..." and "Hey, diddle, diddle ..." and after many kisses sent over the phone, Anna sets the receiver back in its cradle. She wipes the tears off her cheeks. "How I love you, Janey," she sighs and begins tidying up. She always tidies up when harnessing in the nervous energy. She pauses by the assortment of Jane's photos on the wall, kisses the tip of her finger and places it gently on each photo.

She ties her hair in a ponytail and splashes her flushed cheeks with cold water. It's Saturday night and a more dramatic look than usual is in order. Ricky and Neil Young and the revived Mynah Birds, which had become the R&B house band at the Mynah Bird Café, are playing in their new outfits designed by Colin Kerr, the owner of the coffee house. Rumour has it that Ricky and Neil and the other musicians had reluctantly agreed to the costumes, and from the few swear words Ricky used when describing the outfits, Anna wonders how the evening would evolve. Looking her best would be the way to go. *Ricky likes me looking hot!* She picks out a mini dress with a plunging neckline and sandals covered in glitter. A long, cool, shower before dressing is the best way to refresh for an evening with Ricky and his band.

CHAPTER 19

COLIN KERR HAS been promoting his revived house band for a whole month. In addition to the band's new outfits, he has hired a new dancer and spruced up the façade of the coffee house.

As Liza and David approach the Mynah Bird, David whistles through his teeth.

Liza stares at the façade. The second-floor glass booth is aglow with lights that fade into purple, blue, and radiate back to red, with a voluptuous go-go dancer gyrating to rock music, her waist-long black hair swishing to the electric guitar's "waaang" and "chung" spilling onto the sidewalk.

She stops in front of the entrance: "Colin's gone all out! No expense spared!"

David passes his palm over his eyes. "It's a big night for the band. I asked Ricky to save us a table."

"Ricky James?"

David nods.

She pulls out a pair of cat-eye sunglasses from her purse. They are trimmed with rhinestones and hide almost a third of her face.

"That's some disguise!" David says with a chuckle. "Did I tell you I love your dress?"

Liza laughs. "Only five times." She runs her palms along the Campbell Soup labels printed on the cellulose fabric of her paper dress. A friend brought a few patterns from the Montreal Expo, where they are featured in the pulp and paper pavilion, complete with matching paper plates and napkins for a party theme. Liza chose the Campbell Soup pattern, inspired by Andy Warhol's design. She would have liked a Marilyn Monroe and an Elvis Presley print as well, but they were all sold out. She has been fascinated by Warhol's Graphic Art style works — paintings of iconic American objects — Coca-Cola bottles, electric chairs, and famous personalities.

David wraps his arm around Liza's waist, pulling her into him slightly. "Let's just hope it doesn't rain," he chortles and raises an eyebrow pretending to ogle her.

They enter the bar and the band is in full swing. Colourful strobe lights are flashing and the crowd cheers wildly as Neil Young goes into the band's feature song, *Big Time*. As the lyrics call upon the spirit of the past to guide the present, Young tosses the harmonica to Ricky James. To the crowd's delight, Ricky catches it and gets into the song. Bruce Palmer, the bassist, is playing with his back to the audience. His faceless gangly figure in black reminds Liza of a character from a horror movie. The rhythm is electrifying, and the club pulses with beat.

A waiter points Liza and David to a table not far from the stage.

Looking at the band, Liza calls out over the noise: "I just saw those weird outfits on the newsflash! For a few seconds. Didn't hit me it was them."

The bulletin on CFTO Television showed the Mynah Birds stepping out of a black limousine only to be chased by a group of screaming girls who ran after them through the Eaton's store on Queen Street, pleading for autographs.

"A promo stunt. Set up by Colin. The man loves the spectacle," David says, looking at the bar owner who is humming to the song and passing drinks over the counter, his mynah bird Rajah on his shoulder, and as he moves about, the bird's black feathers take on a translucent purplish hue.

On stage as in the broadcast, the musicians are decked out in black leather jackets over yellow turtlenecks. Their tight black pants are tucked into black leather boots with Cuban heels dyed yellow.

Liza props her sunglasses on her head for a clear view. "Their music's great! But the outfits?"

"They're supposed to look like mynah birds. Ricky and Neil were ready to walk. Give up the whole thing. But they're the house band here. Hard to get gigs like that. So they gave in." He takes a drag of the cigarette and adds: "Colin wanted them to shave their heads to look like his damn bird."

Liza rolls her eyes and props her chin in her hands. "I'm sure that didn't go over well!"

The section of the room where Liza and David sit is

lit mostly by candles in Chianti bottles. The flashes of strobe lights accentuate the clouds of smoke and obscure reality, and Liza feels as if she is in a cave of sorts, inhabited by otherworldly creatures.

Their drinks arrive. Liza takes a sip of the Pink Lady and smacks her lips. "Gin and grenadine — delicious!"

Another waitress empties a large tray of beer on the table next to them, occupied by a group of hippies shrouded in clouds of smoke that hang low and filter the dim light. Men in tie-dye shirts and scruffy bellbottom jeans with rips exposing bare knees. Women in paisley skirts and halter tops, accessorized by love buttons and peace symbols, and some with flowers in their hair. Slumped in their chairs, they look dazed, passing around the platters of edibles and half-finished joints in slow motion, as if bored by it all.

Pockets of excited teenagers, loud and attention hungry, an annoyance to many. *How did they get in?* Liza wonders.

A few Pink Ladies later, Liza is rather relaxed, her movements deliberate and leisurely as if she were imitating the hippies.

A group of bikers in sleeveless shirts showing off their Death Head tattoos and club logos occupy a corner, greasy ponytails part of the whole getup. Liza is reminded of David's defaced tattoo cowering under his sleeve. She needs to tell him that it *can* be removed. But doubts linger. Would he be offended? She needs to find the right moment — a good way to let him know how it makes her feel.

Here and there she spots couples and singles who she believes have nine-to-five jobs like her. And David across the table from her looks more like a hippie than a post-secondary instructor.

The band announces it's taking a break. The musicians put down their instruments and the record player is back on, screeching noisily.

Liza excuses herself and heads to the washroom. After stepping out of the cubicle and washing her hands, she discovers that the pull-down towel is a muted shade of every colour except white. She steps into the hallway, rummaging through her purse for a tissue. She is a bit tipsy from too many Pink Ladies. As she makes her way along the dim hallway fumbling through her bag, she collides with another woman. She looks up. It's Anna. They stare at each other in surprise. Anna looks gorgeous in her orange mini dress, and Liza is stunned. Anna usually does not wear fancy dresses. After a moment, Anna says: "Isn't it a fantastic evening! The Mynah Birds! They're fantastic!"

"Sure are. Fantastic. You look gorgeous!"

"Love your Souper dress. M'm! M'm! Good!" Anna rhymes off the Campbell Soup commercial. They hug as if it has been a while, although they see each other in the office every day. But that's not the same. They haven't been hanging out as they used to. After work. And on weekends.

Anna's eyes are wide, cheeks flushed. "Isn't Ricky hot?"

"Hmmm, sure," Liza murmurs, feebly. Then she adds with more enthusiasm: "The band is amazing."

There is a moment of awkwardness and Anna says: "What the heck. If you like the man. You only live once."

"David? You talking about David?"

"Ricky. I'm fucking Ricky."

Liza stares at Anna. It's not like her to use those words.

Anna runs her fingers through her hair and flips it off her face. "It's your business, girl. Who you date. I was worried, that's all."

Liza's eyes widen. "Worried about me seeing David? Why? Give it to me, straight. Isn't that what friends are for?"

Anna puts on a cheery smile. "Let's put it aside. Let's talk about fun stuff. You two fucking yet?"

Liza's mouth drops in disbelief. "You alright?"

Anna shrugs. "Yeah, yeah. Fucking. Making love. What's the difference?" She draws Liza into an embrace, and Liza wonders what's going on with Anna. Her cheerfulness is feigned. Does she sense a spark of sarcasm? What's bothering her? She takes a deep breath and resolves to say nothing. Things have been tense between them lately, so it's best to just go along.

Anna wraps her arm around Liza's waist, and leads her to her own table. David and Ricky are talking about acoustics, and they all move toward the bar where some of the musicians are leaning on the counter, drinks in hand.

Neil Young is holding a tall glass of water in one hand and a sandwich in the other. He bows slightly to Liza and she nods. There is a certain look about him. Eyes intense, he appears aloof, self-contained. In this whole noisy crowd, he seems alone. It would be some time later when he becomes a Canadian icon that she would recall this meeting with much fondness.

Palmer's eyes are concealed behind round yellow lenses and his long hair hides much of his face. But away from the flashing strobes, his energetic, friendly demeanour makes her feel as if he were an old friend.

The band is back on stage and the place is rocking. Liza and David join Anna at the cluster of tables reserved for friends-of-the-band, and Liza wonders whether meeting Anna here was not by chance. Did David and Ricky arrange this meeting to smooth things over between her and Anna? David is clearly more than casually acquainted with Ricky. But the evening is magical and she pushes aside the petty details.

Another waitress sets a large tray of beer and cocktails on their table and is welcomed with — snookums, sugar-lips, sexy-pants — and asked where she's been their whole life. She is wearing a pink diaphanous mini dress. A large gold bow holds her bleach-blond hair in a ponytail high at the top of her head, and her shiny white go-go boots reach half-way up her thighs. She has hearts and flowers painted on her bare arms and legs. Her midriff, veiled by the see-through fabric, allows a glimpse of similar artwork. She greets the customers by name, and answers the many questions in clipped sentences — Paint-in at Penny Farthing next door ... Be-in at City Hall ... last-minute Sit-in. Spotting Liza, she waves enthusiastically and shouts over the din of the crowd how great it is to see her, then pointing at Liza's dress, rhymes off, "M'm! M'm! Good!" Liza laughs and shouts back some pleasantries and wonders who this woman could possibly be.

Anna rolls her eyes. "Goodness gracious! If it isn't Helena of Troy." She turns to Liza. "You two know each other?"

Liza is perplexed—the waitress' voice sounds familiar but she cannot place her. Her smile—the way her lips curve upward in such a charming way to reveal those perfect teeth and the way those large blue eyes light up —makes her wonder where she had seen this woman before. There is something about her—this serenity—as if she belongs in another world and her presence here, in this crowded bar, is just a disguise. As if she were an angel sent from heaven on a mission.

Anna called this woman, Helena. The same Helena who waitressed at the Savarin Tavern? Suddenly David's comment about the black garb makes sense.

A few more drinks later, Liza makes her way toward the washroom again. The room is swaying as she shuffles between the tables and chairs and knees and elbows and instead ends up at the bar. Helena is leaning on the counter, downing tequila shots with a few friends: a woman whose body is painted with words "love" and "peace"; a few men bare waist up, chests and backs painted with wiggly stripes that resemble waves. They lick the salt sprinkled between the thumb and forefinger, take a gulp of tequila, and bite into a slice of lime. Liza joins them. After a few shots, she mumbles something about looking for the little girls' room.

Helena picks up the tray refilled with drinks and heads to a table nearby. Liza lets go of the counter and weaves toward the flashing neon light. Finally she is in the washroom. The cubicles have shrunk in size and she keeps bumping into doors and walls. Stepping out of the washroom, she wipes her wet hands on her skirt and shrieks. Peering closely at the damp patch of her dress,

she is relieved—the paper fabric is a bit rumpled, but still
in one piece. Although a bit dizzy, she recalls that the fabric consists of two layers of paper sandwiching a rayon
scrim for strength, and she breathes a sigh of relief. Now
her head is spinning, but there is nowhere to sit down, so
she heads to the alcove at the end of the hallway, leans her
back against the wall, then slides to the floor. Seated on
the parquet in a secluded nook, legs extended in front of
her, she closes her eyes and exhales in relief.

After a while Liza hears her name called. When she
looks up, Anna is settled next to her. She is saying something but it's difficult to hear because of the blasting noise
all around. Helena is slumped on her other side, eyelids
drooping, eyebrows raised as if tired of fighting gravity.
But the joint between her thumb and forefinger is held
firmly. Her pinkie is extended as if she is a little girl having a tea party using her mother's china cups. They pass
the joint and Liza recalls that she hadn't done this since
university. Now, Liza discerns that the conversation is
about the Paint-in at the Penny Farthing coffee house.
Hundreds of people had themselves painted as a way to
demonstrate the importance of freedom of expression.
Anna unzips her dress and pulls the top down to her waist
to reveal the red hearts and cupids armed with arrows
painted on her voluptuous breasts—a surprise for Ricky.

Helena gets up and weaves her way toward the bar.
She is back carrying a platter of cucumber sandwiches she
sets on the floor next to them. They begin eating hurriedly as if they'd been starved for days. Liza is amazed at
her voracious appetite and how quickly the plate is emp-
tied. They are talking all at once loudly, but Liza is not

sure what about, except that it's really, really important. And funny. They're laughing so hard her stomach hurts. All the while the music is pounding, and Liza keeps saying how good the band is and how she really gets it. Really gets it! She kicks off the stilettos and as the sandals bounce against the wall, they laugh because it's sooo funny. They're drinking some red coloured juice and gobbling corn chips out of a noisy bag. Helena produces a pair of tweezers to hold the end of the joint, and as they draw in the smoke and pass it around, she keeps saying: "This some real fuckin' ass shit."

Liza looks up to the stairway landing where the glass booth glows fluorescent as if it were Moses' burning bush. Inside the booth is a shapely female figure, making love to the stainless steel pole and Liza thinks it such a blasphemy, making love in front of the burning bush. What would Moses say? Her eyelids are heavy and she lets them rest for a moment, so she doesn't have to witness this sacrilege. But she can't stop wondering and she yells out loud: "What would Moses say?"

"Margaret Atwood. Po, e, try. Po, e, try," Helena repeats, and Liza shouts how fantastic it is. Fantastic! Anna keeps saying that Ricky's a real fucking machine if she'd ever seen one. That chick magnet.

Liza now feels hot tears burning her cheeks. All she wants to do is go to the moon with David in his gigantic bed and make love. She whispers in Anna's ear: "We go to the moon and make love."

Anna's eyes widen: "You and David? Make love?" She caresses Liza's wet cheeks in her palms. "Oh my dear girl. Congratulations! At long last! I thought you'd never let go of it. What a burden it must've been."

Anna announces that they have to celebrate — Liza's been cured of virginity. They get up holding on to each other and the wall, and walk along the hallway lit up on-and-off by the flashing neon sign.

Anna shouts: "My dress!" — and covers her bare breasts with her hands.

Liza places her palms under Anna's breasts and lifts them with a gentle bounce. "They're gorgeous! Gorgeous! The hell with the dress!"

Helena removes Liza's hands from Anna's breasts. She does so methodically as if it's part of her everyday routine. "Now, now," she murmurs, as she pulls the dress up over Anna's chest. She tugs at the zipper and finally the satiny garment is back on.

Liza is sad that they are leaving the burning bush behind, but they have to celebrate. She drops on her knees and picks up her sandals, then settles on the floor and struggles to slip one on. She tries to stand up on the stiletto, wobbles, kicks it off, and is relieved to be barefoot again.

"This way," Helena says. "So the boss doesn't see me" — and guides them to the back door below the "Exit" sign that leads to the street. And then, Liza is stunned. All is magic! The street is decorated with lanterns that cast streams of colourful light. Some of the trees are leaning as if they'd been uprooted, but the crowns straighten out as she passes under them. The sidewalk has wobbly potholes she tries to avoid with long strides.

"Don't step into the potholes," she shouts. There is a swishing noise in her ears and she wonders if Helena and Anna can hear her.

"Where are they?" Anna calls out.

"Everywhere," Liza says.

They try to coordinate their steps so they could avoid the potholes, but Liza yells that they are stepping right into them, and it's sooo funny, they have to crouch down and laugh and laugh. They pass their hands along Liza's dress and recite: "M'm! M'm! Good!" Liza feels a bit woozy and wants to sit down on the sidewalk and rest, but Anna reminds them that they have to continue. Because they have to celebrate.

Down the street at the Bohemian Embassy, they climb a narrow staircase, and Liza warns them to be careful because each step tilts as they put their weight on it, and as the staircase winds up and up, they laugh, and laugh. Finally, Margaret Atwood is reading poetry. The place is jammed. Beer mugs are placed in their hands and Liza gulps eagerly, the thick foam gathering into a moustache above her upper lip. Beer never tasted so good. They sit on the floor and Liza strains to hear the words. She repeats after Atwood, and the stanzas drift and sway, and paint the images in her thoughts—images of lakes and trees and love and death and immortality. Liza imagines what love looks like under the moonlit sky—she misses David. After the reading, someone waves a copy of Atwood's booklet of poetry, *Double Persephone*—a few copies are still available at fifty cents each. And then Atwood is signing it to Liza. To the nearly six foot tall Liza, Atwood appears diminutive like a china doll come to life—with sparkling blue eyes and a wave of black curly hair framing her flushed face — and Liza can't help but enfold the inspirational poetess into a hug. She feels sublime. Her misfit self is dissipating like the froth in her mug.

Back on the street inhaling the warm wind, they head to the Riverboat. Joni Mitchell is singing, and as the audience joins in the refrain, Liza envisions the scenes from the song, and recalls *the places I have been, and the wondrous things I have seen*. Joni's voice cuts through the chorus and reverberates through the bar. She takes a break. Helena makes her way through the crowd and introduces Liza and Anna, and Liza wants to pour her heart out and tell her how much she loves her music, but what comes out is something like, love you Joni my sister, and the moment is magical. They're all soulmates and love is all around.

Joni returns to the stage and sings of a girl who is alone at a carnival and goes for a ride on a Ferris wheel. Liza is now that girl, and all she wants to do is close her eyes and fly to the moon, *where Chang, the enchanting woman, guides lovers on their uncharted journeys*. And she does just that.

CHAPTER 20

AFTER GIVING HIS morning lecture, David strides along the hallway at Toronto Arts College, eager to get back to his desk in the part-time faculty office. He has a session with a group of students to discuss their project. In the afternoon, he will be meeting Liza at Sculpture Hill, where a large gathering is expected. Neighbours not only from the High Park area, but also from the Roncesvalles Village, Bloor West Village, Swansea, the Junction, and Parkdale, have decided to take the matter of the stolen marble into their own hands. The police have not made much progress, they said, so they invited a fortune teller. See what she has to say. In their words, this type of blatant disrespect for Torontonians doesn't happen in *Toronto-the-good*. Although talking to a soothsayer is not David's idea of solving the theft, he could not refuse Liza. Since that stone disappeared, her enthusiasm for the Symposium has dampened.

Burman blames the lack of security at the sites and is holding the City responsible. The police are questioning Liza. *And now the neighbours have invited a psychic.* David shrugs and picks up the pace.

By the open office door, a young police officer, the one David saw talking to Liza in the park—too young for the job, David deliberates—is scribbling in his note pad.

The officer looks up. "Mr. David Gould?"

David sits on a park bench by Colborne Lodge Drive with a clear view of Irving Burman's two granite blocks that still remain on the site where they had been delivered. Next to them, on a wooden post stuck in the ground, a hand-drawn sign reads: "Please bring back the marble block. This sculpture cannot be completed without it." Attached to the post is a see-through plastic pouch that holds a petition with pages of signatures. A few pens and sheets of paper are tucked inside for those who wish to add their name to the petition.

Two elderly women, arms linked, and a man walking with a cane, veer off the sidewalk and struggle up the hill toward the post. The man leans his cane against the post and removes the petition from the pouch. They take turns signing it, slip the sheets back in, and leaning on each other, slowly make their way back to the sidewalk. They walk past David, and the words of the kind of person who would do such a thing ... flap on the wind like a torn flag.

Does stealing a block of marble count as art-theft? David

wonders. It is, after all, raw material—a chunk of stone that has been gouged out of the earth in a similar way as a lump of clay.

It has been a few years since he has sculpted anything of note. He needs to get his hands on a project that will bring attention to his work—that will garner interest, excitement, recognition—a commissioned piece people in this city he's made his new home would look forward to. A piece he would be driven to work on. He had lost that chance when he lost the contract for the Symposium. Or when he did not win the contract, as Anna would say, although to him it's all alike. Losing or not winning—semantics—the result is the same. He prefers to think of it as losing. It gives him reasons to feel he's been wronged. And it's all over now. The sculptors have been chosen and the work is progressing, and there is nothing he can do about it.

The rumour about Burman not being able to move on with his sculpture without that piece of marble sits heavy with David. He can certainly relate to it. That's how he felt when his "Child Soldier" disappeared during the exhibit in Boston. He became disillusioned. He has not sculpted anything worthwhile since.

What is it about that block of marble? David wonders. The first time he laid eyes on it he sensed a figure trapped within. He stared at it for hours. He spent the night on the hillock next to it, imagining the figure entombed in that block of Carrara stone, shaping the vision of a woman he glimpsed in his mind's eye. That night, in the surreal dreams during his fitful intervals of slumber on the grassy lawn next to it, he saw her form.

Now, thinking back, he shrugs off the apparition. *An outlandish notion, a fixation.*

He seems prone to that lately — to his flights of imagination — as the first time he saw Liza at City Hall. He tried to avoid her after that, to block out his attraction to her — to his inspiration. But he kept seeing her here, at sculpture sites. She had been consumed by the project beyond her work duties and had been spending much of her free time here. At first, he tried to stay away from the park. But he found himself drawn to the sites, drawn to her. As if she were Burman's block of marble and he a chisel. He began visiting the park on Friday afternoons just to get a glimpse of her. Although they now spend much of their free time together, he still hurries to the park on Fridays after giving his lecture, to be with her.

He never thought it would happen to him. She has given new meaning to his life. A new purpose.

The gathering next to Burman's two blocks of granite has grown to about a hundred, he approximates. He gets up from the bench and stands at the periphery of the crowd. Liza has arrived — many people are trying to get a word with her, and he thinks it best to stay aside for a while.

Next to the granite slabs is the soothsayer, sitting on a plastic folding chair. She is sporting a flowery kerchief, garish gold hoop earrings dangling almost to her shoulders, and a wide skirt covering her knees and spilling onto the grass. Her face is wrinkled and sunburned, but her eyes are vivid green.

The psychic covers her eyes with her palms and sways to the left and to the right, then begins to hum and murmur in another language. *Probably not even a language*, David reasons. *Gibberish*. People in the gathering hush each other and suddenly all is silent, except for the traffic noise subdued by the gusts of wind in the towering tree crowns.

The soothsayer stops muttering. She gets up and lifts her hands toward the sky as if she were a saint in prayer. "Great talent," she declares in a breathy voice, looking up as if talking to the white feathery clouds. "Stolen." She shouts: "Stone thief! I call on you! Bring stone back!"

She repeats her call three times, her voice rising tremulously with each cry. She pauses and scans the crowd.

"You bring stone back, thief. All forgiven," she says, exhaling loudly, as if she just dropped an immense burden.

She takes a long pause, breathing deliberately, as if depleted of oxygen.

"You keep that stone, thief, and you cursed!" Her voice now threatening, cuts through the wind. "You hear me, thief? You cursed! Stone cursed! Forever!"

She gets up and stumbles, seemingly exhausted from the task. Then she straightens up, props her hands on her hips, and scans the gathering, now wild eyed.

"Stone cursed forever! Stone bring bad luck to them who have it!"

Liza is pale, as if her face is made of white marble. David has never seen her so pallid. Walking back to the bench to wait for her, he has a sudden urge to turn. He stops cold. The soothsayer's green eyes are staring straight at him, and although he is several yards away, her peridot pupils pierce right through him.

A construction truck with a company logo rumbles

by on its way to another site. The psychic points to the truck and shouts. "Like that. Stolen."

A man from the gathering grumbles: "Why would that construction company steal a block of marble? They've donated all kinds of equipment and material to the project."

"That stone didn't walk away. It had to be picked up by a truck," a woman from the crowd opines. She waves her hand in dismissal. "What are we doing here? Waste of time. The question is, who? Not, how."

Another man from the group shouts: "It'd be easy for these trucks. Rolling in any time day or night. You know what a slab of Carrara marble that size is worth? I think we'd all be surprised."

David shrugs off the uneasiness that has suddenly overcome him, and continues to the bench.

Soon, the gathering disperses, and Liza joins him. She slumps on the wooden slats as if her body is a burden she needs to drop.

"I'm jinxed," she says.

David wraps his arm around her shoulder. "Bad luck? Nonsensical superstition! Preposterous!"

"My first hands-on project," Liza murmurs. "Doomed."

"Now, that's a bit harsh, wouldn't you say?"

Liza jumps up and lifts her hands toward the sky, mimicking the soothsayer. "The curse is an ominous cloud looming over, ready to disgorge malice."

He stares, unsure what to think of her performance. *She couldn't be serious, could she?*

"I need to get back to the office. I'll see you later." She waves a hasty good-by, and heads toward the Keele Street subway entrance.

"What's the rush, Babe? It's Friday afternoon," David says, but she's gone.

He sags into the bench. *She has taken the theft personally.*

What could he do to dispel Liza's gloom? Should he tell her it was simply a chunk of stone that could be re-placed, and not a work of art? And contrary to the psych-ic's claim, no talent was stolen. Should he remind her that fortune telling is a charlatan's game? He'll explain to her that the psychic is wrong — that she simply cannot distin-guish between raw material and art.

He'll tell her about his sculpture that vanished during the Boston exhibit. Now, the way his "Child Soldier" dis-appeared from the exhibit is different. That's finished work! That's art-theft, alright!

CHAPTER 21

*l*N THE SUBWAY ride back to the office, Liza feels exhausted. It's not like her to be so lethargic. And queasy. *Is it something she ate? Maybe a touch of stomach flu.* Sucking on a straw, she downs a can of ginger ale and feels her nausea dissipate.

Just before she left her office for the soothsayer's session, James called and insisted on meeting with her. He offered to meet her at the sculpture sites, but she and David have plans for the evening, and she did not want the meeting with James to go on too long. The office is a better place—easier to keep the discussion brief.

Last time she and James drove to Sculpture Hill, the meeting took much of the afternoon. They checked Burman's site and looked for suspicious details. He photographed the tire tracks, and she gave him a tour of the sites. They had lunch at the Grenadier Restaurant in the park, which gave her the chance to fill him in about her favourite park and the neighbourhood she'd grown up in. And then, James asked if she would go out to a movie or a dinner with him, sometime. Or a walk in the park.

Now, thinking back, she has to admit—if it wasn't for David, she would have accepted.

Later that evening, David had asked if she had enjoyed her lunch with the cop. How did he know? This was too much of a coincidence. It *was* just business. But he had smiled and said: "Sure thing, Babe." Then he had asked the question that gave him away: *Do you love me, Liza?* The question she dreads. The question that brings on that tightness in her chest—the tension that prevents oxygen from reaching her lungs—the fear that she will lose him if she declares her love for him. Isn't what they have enough? Why does he need the reassurance she cannot give?

She did enjoy James' company. There was something charming about him—his awkwardness, his apologies about the questions he asked, the rubbing of his large hands that stuck out of the uniform sleeves that were too short for him. There was also this sense of *earnestness* about him—old fashioned honesty and trustworthiness she does not often come across among those of her generation. Reminds her a bit of Anna—except that Anna has been acting strange lately.

Over the next few visits to her office, James began asking questions about David. And now, his insistence on meeting with her on a late Friday afternoon annoys her a bit. She would have rather gone home after the park. She is not feeling well, and she puts a lot of extra time at the office—she would have appreciated a quiet afternoon at home.

Should she get off at the next subway stop and use the telephone booth to cancel her meeting? She could turn back and be home in no time. But then, she would spend the weekend wondering about the urgency of this discussion. Might as well get it over with.

On Monday morning, on her way to the office, Liza is still upbeat from the Sunday spent with David. She can't get him out of her thoughts. It is more than just having fun cycling at Centre Island, picnicking by the lake and sipping surprise health-booster he blends and brings in his yellow thermos. This time it was a carrot-mango-papaya-juice concoction. It was delish, as he put it. *The man is a walking oxymoron*, she ponders. He gobbles up hot dogs from vendor-carts and chips and donuts as zestfully as he savours gourmet dinners at trendy restaurants. He carries freshly squeezed juice in a thermos. One minute he is a junk-food buff and another a health-food fanatic, and yet another, a gourmet-food lover, as well versed in food etiquette and fine wines as he is in art and history and rock 'n' roll—this draft-dodger deeply immersed in the anti-war movement.

Yet, the more time she spends with him, the more she feels the need to keep her admiration of him in check. But that is becoming rather difficult. He had coaxed her into spending the day with him cycling the Toronto Islands instead of finishing her report for this morning's meeting. To be fair, there was not much coaxing. All he did was ask her. She loves visiting the Islands that appear far away from the city although only a twenty-minute ferry ride from downtown.

After biking, they had dinner at a Harbourfront restaurant—with a Queen Mother special, a bottle of merlot, and a cognac—sitting at a patio overlooking the lake. He had suggested a nightcap at his place. She had nodded in agreement. Her head was swimming and she'd wished the night would never end. There was also this want to be at his place, to sit at the sofa where he sat, to walk through his kitchen with the juicer always ready for a new health-booster, to run her palm along the table where he had the breakfast of granola he made from scratch, to smell the garlic bread he keeps in the freezer for heating up in the oven—the oven where he baked the bread he brought to the picnic. His bed.

At this, she sobered up. His bed—that place of magic where her body blends with his and her mind flies off to the moon and makes her think of the mythical Chang —has she also become addicted to his bed?

She had turned down his suggestion for a nightcap. She needed to go home and get ready for work. He said that was fine. If she wanted to be a good girl—a diligent civil servant—as he put it, in a tone she saw as patronizing, as if he had this power over her he could exercise at will. She was glad that she had gone home and was in her own bed before midnight.

She could not sleep. Could not get him out of her thoughts. The scent of his skin warmed by the sun, that look in his eyes each time they were about to kiss, the taste of tobacco on his lips. She, who has never smoked, is now addicted to the flavour of tobacco? But it's not the tobacco. *It's David I've become addicted to — David's kisses. I am now craving them like people crave tobacco.*

The realization makes her cringe. David the unpredictable? The man who vanishes for days, and then just pops up next to her at the park by *Flower Power* where she usually spends her Friday afternoons updating the reports? He turns on his charm and clowns around. His favourite put on is imitating Charlie Chaplin, begging forgiveness with flowerless stems until he makes her laugh. And that would be his tip-off that she'd forgiven him.

He said he would be gone for a few days, maybe five, maybe a week, to work on the upcoming demonstration. To meet with other organizers. She can hear him now.

"What about your classes?" she asks.

"Got a colleague to cover for me. Not a problem."

He did not say where he was going nor with whom he was meeting. She did not feel comfortable asking. At least this time he told her he'd be gone. She knows his commitment to the antiwar movement comes first. Everything else takes second place — everything, including her. Perhaps Anna has a point. She wishes she could have a chat with her — now that the silence about David has been broken. Find out why Anna dislikes him. Why she disapproves of her relationship with him.

But that's another problem. Anna and David seem to know each other much better than they are letting her believe. She can tell from their conversation — careful around her. *Afraid of hurting my feelings? Don't they realize this is much worse?* Liza is so wrapped up in her mental discussion with herself that the trip to her office is but a flash.

And now, her heart sinks. Her schedule for the day is

daunting. She has not finished the report over the weekend. Working on it the previous night proved futile. Her thoughts kept drifting off to David. Then to James. She had kept her last Friday's discussion with him short and agreed to a meeting this afternoon.

Would this be about David again?

David told her about the conversation he and James had—almost the same one *she* had with James.

A group of teenagers—an older group of "artists' children"—that hung out in the park on the night of the theft saw a flatbed truck with its headlights turned off. They did not see a company name, nor logo, nor the vehicle's license plate.

"It must've been covered. Clever move," James had said.

But they did see a man wearing a Maple Leaf baseball cap. They were fairly far away—about seven or eight carlengths. One of the teenagers pointed a flashlight and the beam caught the white maple leaf patch of the cap one of the men wore. And a silhouette of his bushy beard. Her discussion with David plays out in her thoughts.

"James thinks it could've been you, David. That you could've hidden your hair under the cap. He said you spend a lot of time at the sites."

"That's preposterous, Liza. This unruly shock of hair under a baseball cap?"

"I'll tell James you were with me that night, David. And end the questioning."

"Promise me you'll never do that, Liza. Lie for somebody. I already told James I was home that night. Alone."

"The teenagers told James they know you. They said

it wasn't you. The bearded man was shorter and skinnier. But James is not convinced."

"That cop is under pressure to find the culprit and appease the community."

"I'm still worried, though. What if somebody else witnessed the theft? Anyone with a beard could be a suspect. What if somebody picks you out in a line-up, David?"

"It's all speculation, Liza. I spend a lot of time at the sites, yes. I am a sculptor—what is so strange about my interest in the biggest art symposium in Toronto's history? Why should I have to provide an alibi? And how could I? I was sleeping in my bed like the rest of the world. They're targeting me because I'm a draft dodger. Let them find proof. Evidence. Let them lay charges. I have nothing to hide."

CHAPTER 22

AFTER A DAY of intermittent rain, the evening is dark and humid. The low churning clouds weigh heavily on the tree crowns that overhang the narrow sidewalk along Colborne Lodge Drive. A few late joggers scamper by and a lone cyclist whizzes along the pavement heading south toward the lake. David's arm is wrapped around Liza's waist as they turn toward sculpture sites and slog down the rain-sodden slope. Flashes of light illuminate the hill and the looming trees as if the whole landscape is a scene from a science fiction movie. Armand Vaillancourt's foundry, built in the north-east valley of the park, in which he casts iron cubes for his as yet unnamed sculpture, has become the focus for local residents. They flock to the site for an evening show of light and fire and the pouring of the molten metal. The whole city is brewing with anticipation of this colossal project.

They pause to take in the scene. The workers' silhouettes lumber about the site, coming into view against the glowing fury of the foundry furnace and then vanishing into the darkness.

David chuckles. "He's a night owl, isn't he? The man doesn't sleep. He's been here night after night." They move several steps to get a better view. "Any news on the sculpture? Any decisions?"

"Just what we already know."

Vaillancourt had revealed some of the details—it will consist of about a hundred cast iron cubes, weigh several hundred tons, and be, in his words, a reflection of his will power and all that is inside of him. *The Globe and Mail* referred to it as the sculptor's seven-hundred-ton torture.

Liza takes David's hand and presses it against her cheek. *How the aroma of tobacco takes on a pleasant scent on his skin.* He certainly has a keen interest in the project. He keeps an eye on the sites as if he was a self-appointed night watchman of Sculpture Hill.

David shakes his head in disbelief. "Quite a venture he's taken on. Convinced the City to pour in more money for the foundry. And he still doesn't know what the sculpture will look like. Now, that troubles me."

"Each cube will be lifted by a crane and moved around until he decides on the location. Then the pieces bolted together. And the whole installation could end up about thirty yards. Maybe more. He hasn't decided yet."

David whistles through his teeth. "Ah! The man might've bitten off more than he can chew."

It would be a few years later when the project is abandoned and the cubes of cast iron lay scattered at the site in High Park, many Torontonians would comment that hundreds of thousands had been wasted. Some would argue that the sculpture was not completed because of Vaillancourt's refusal to be confined by a blueprint. Others would claim it was his lack of vision. Yet others would point to the controversy over the potentially un-patriotic name he chose for the piece.

"He wants the installation to grow in a fluid man-ner," Liza says. "Without a blueprint to constrict its form."

But David is not convinced. "Those blocks weigh tons. He's looking at a colossal assembly. The sheer mass of those pieces ..."

"He's determined," Liza says. "The spirit of the Sym-posium! Loves the crowds. The inquisitive minds, as he calls them. Unlike a few others who keep to themselves. Like Bill Koochin. Glued to that granite slab. I can't get a word out of him. He ho-hums and nods. And that's the sum of his conversation."

"Bill's great. Keeps his nose to the grind. Has a family to support. Eager to get the job done and get back home."

"You know him?"

"Collaborated on a project. Have much respect for him."

"A project? When was that?"

"Some time ago. At Emily Carr College in Vancou-ver. Where Koochin lectures. We were featured at an art exhibit. I was living in Boston then."

"You've known him for a while? You never said any-thing."

"Not much to say. We met some years back. The first group travelling with Contiki Tours. It was organized by a New Zealander. He's now the owner of the company. Clever guy. Came up with the way to finance his own tour of Europe. Brought together a bunch of backpackers and offered himself as a guide. I happened to be there. So was Koochin. And Anna. That's how we all met."

"Wow, David. You're full of surprises. Didn't know you and Anna go way back."

"Not much to know, Babe."

"Not saying anything is a little strange, wouldn't you say?"

"Sure, Babe. But what's to say?"

Heat rushes to Liza's face. *No, she will not confront him, no. What would be the use?* But anger builds in her until she can hardly breathe. Why had Anna and David kept their friendship a secret? After the evening at the Mynah Bird, she had accepted their explanation — keeping their involvement in the antiwar movement covert. Although the reasoning does not sit well with her. Now he tells her they go way back. What else are they hiding? Even if they had been lovers, she could see no reason to keep it from her.

Liza takes a deep breath and tries to sound calm. "Well, perhaps you could talk to Koochin. Isn't the whole Symposium a type of an outdoor art gallery? An art-classroom of sorts. Which means the public is welcome to watch and ask questions. Isn't that what it's all about?"

David laughs. "I'm with you. But the artists have to eat and feed their families. If they answer every question, they'd never get done. Some people hang around here killing time, quizzing these men as if it's the Spanish Inquisition. And not only about their work. As if the miserly honorarium they get gives people the license to dissect their lives. I know I wouldn't like being asked piddly things like what I had for breakfast."

David had hit a sore spot—he certainly does not divulge much about himself. She would like to ask about the meetings he never elaborates on, about the people he mentions casually—Joe Young, Allen Ginsberg—clearly he knows them much better than what the newspapers write. He talks about them as if they're friends. She does not ask questions. Does not invade his privacy. If he wanted to say more he would. But his absences and his preoccupation with the antiwar movement that first evoked her curiosity, and she must admit, admiration, are now causing her to worry about his safety. And there is this uncertainty about him. On the one hand, his mention of the meetings with the antiwar organizers implies that he is not hiding his involvement. And on the other, his caution of what he reveals reminds her that she is an outsider. Does he not trust her? Or is he prompting her to ask questions? Could he be using the snippets of information, the name dropping, as bait? Hoping she'd bite and join the movement. No, that doesn't seem like him. Though, one never knows. *If he trusts me, if he wants me to join the movement, he should ask me.* She takes a deep breath and lets it out slowly, lets the tension dissipate.

Vaillancourt's fiery demonstration lights up the park, and Liza is glad of the spectacle. She needs something to ease the tension. She claps her hands. "He's pouring the molten iron. It's spectacular!"

In the valley below them, the foundry blazes furiously, as the workers in silhouette tip the giant ladles and pour the glowing metal into the moulds lined up on a

large base. Vaillancourt, in his sleeveless shirt, moves
swiftly about the site, his glistening biceps highlighted by
the inferno around him. Liza is enthralled, as if she were
observing a scene from Greek myth.

Armand—he'd asked her to call him by his first name
—this sparsely built and bearded man takes on Hephaes-
tus' proportions when working at the foundry. His otherwise reserved demeanour and offbeat wit morphs into
unbridled energy and a steely determination no one could
derail. Rumour has it that the name he chose for the
sculpture was rejected by the Symposium Committee and
tensions between the City and the artist are mounting.
David's belief that Armand had not decided on the name
for his piece is not quite correct.

She recalls her conversation with Armand—the way
he said the name of his piece left an imprint on her. *Je me
souviens*. "I remember," he'd said, with such pride and
confidence. *It will be so powerful, it will disturb*, he'd added.
She hardly ever used her high school French she considers
inadequate, but with him she was at ease. *Je me souviens*.
Since then, camaraderie has grown between them, and
each conversation reveals something new to ponder.

Gossip has it that the name he'd given the sculpture
refers to the founding of the Quebec separatist movement
by René Levesque earlier that same year. A few of her colleagues mentioned that Vaillancourt belongs to the Parti
Quebecois—the party that has apparently set out to div-
ide Canada. The idea of using the Symposium which cele-
brates Canada's Centennial as a forum to promote his
separatist views is subversive, to say the least. Yet, one's
art is personal, she reasons. He has the right to name his

artwork in the way it *speaks* to him, and she hopes the City would see it his way.

Eyes glued to the flames that bring into view the groups of onlookers who come and go, Liza sighs. "He has certainly raised expectations."

David motions to the scene. "This foundry's more of a nighttime happening. Putting on this blazing show." He presses his cheek against Liza's. "Ooh la la! You're flushed just at the sight of that Frenchman."

Liza pulls out of David's embrace. "Armand? You for real? What do you think I am?"

"On a first name basis with Vaillancourt, to start."

"So?" She cries out and steps away from him. "Talking to him is my job!"

David slowly moves closer and with the tip of his finger gently lifts her chin. He looks deeply into her eyes. "Just checking, Babe. That it's *me* you love."

Liza's mouth drops open. "With all your secrets, how dare you? What else are you hiding, David?"

"Didn't mean any of that. Didn't know how to tell you, afterwards. But that man down there"—he points to Vaillancourt and makes a goofy face—"with his fire-breathing dragon. How do I compete?"

"Are you implying that I ..."

He presses his lips to hers. After they kiss, David says: "Je t'aime, mon amour."

"What's this about?" she exclaims. "Why in French?"

"Well, if it sounds better. But that's all I know in French. You love me, Liza? In English or in French. I love you in any language."

Liza blushes. "Why are you saying this? Why now?"

David pecks her gently on the lips. "Why not now? Do you love me, Babe?"

Hand over her face, she hides the tears stinging her eyes. Her chest heaves with sudden sobs.

David wraps her into an embrace: "What's this about?"

"It's about you, David. You," she says between sobs.

"What about me? I love you. I told you many times."

"I can't, David. Don't you understand?"

"You can't love me?"

"No, don't say that. Don't ever say that to me."

He whistles sucking in a deep breath. "Oh, Babe. What have I done? I know I was the first. Girls find that hard. Did I pressure you? Oh, Liza, I didn't mean to."

"Girls find *that* hard, you said? I'm not just some girl, you know."

"You better believe you're not just some girl. You and I—we're *real*, Liza. We're for good."

She frees herself from his embrace and inhales deeply. "You did not pressure me, David. You know better than that. I wanted to be with you. I practically threw myself at you. So let's not go there."

He breathes a sigh of relief. "What then? You never said you loved me."

"Don't you get it? I can't say it. I'm afraid something will happen. And I'll never see you again."

"What do you mean?"

"You wouldn't understand. And how could you?"

"Try me. What is it?"

"All right. You asked for it. I've always believed if I fall in love, something horrible would happen. To the man I love. And I'd never see him again. So there it is. You happy now that you know?"

"Oh, Liza, that's illogical."

"No, it isn't. I already told you about my father. My grandfather was also killed. In the First World War. Well, presumed dead. His body was never found. He was twenty one."

"War is a people-eating machine, Babe."

"Oh, yeah? My great grandmother from my mother's side died in childbirth. My grandmother grew up in an orphanage. Should I go on?"

"I thought you said you were worried about me. So I thought the men were the targets. Here it was your great grandmother. In those days, many women died in child-birth."

"All of these tragic deaths happen to the ones who were in love. And I am their direct descendant."

"I see nothing unusual. In the past, people didn't live long."

"My great, great grandfather died of tuberculosis. I can go on."

"Most families experienced what you just told me. You should relax a bit. Live your life. And most of all, love me. Life's a gift, Babe. And so is love."

He draws her into an embrace and gives her a long kiss. Than he looks into her eyes. "Love me, Liza. That's all I ask. If you can't, if you don't feel it, I'll back off."

She frees herself from his embrace. "In my family, love is the killer. I'm trying to cheat fate by ... pretending ... that we're not in love."

He laughs. "How about we make a deal. I'm happy to take my chances and love you. Are you?"

"This isn't funny, David. Why can't we leave it alone? Why do you insist I say those words? You should know how I feel. Don't you know?"

His arm is wrapped around her shoulders as they walk back to Colborne Lodge Drive and turn north toward Bloor Street. The clouds have lifted and the moon illuminates the sidewalk as if it were daylight. David leads Liza to a bench at the edge of the path.

"Perhaps it's me that makes you apprehensive. I'm not easy to get along with."

"Let's not go there, David. It's all your *secrets* that don't help. "

"The antiwar movement? I have to do that, Liza. For my wife."

"Your wife?"

"I was married once. My wife was killed. In Vietnam. She was a nurse."

It takes Liza a few moments to process what he had said. That marker in her brain that filters out the details and distils the essence is enveloped in a migraine that detracts it from its task. She covers her face with her palms and remains silent.

David clears his throat. "Once I got drafted, my wife urged me to leave before being sent off to Vietnam. She was to join me in Canada in a few weeks. She needed time to tie up the loose ends. Her job, her family, her friends. Then she phoned me. She'd volunteered."

He slides his hand up and down his thigh, pressing harder and harder. "She did it to save her brother from being sent to Vietnam. Only one sibling at a time could be in a war zone."

Liza takes his hand and presses it to her face. "I'm sorry, David," she whispers. "For your loss. For not being more understanding."

"No, Liza. I should've explained." His voice croaks as if he has laryngitis. "She called me from Saigon. Told me she was pregnant. Didn't know it until she got there. Said she'd be returning. Joining me in Canada."

"How did she die?"

"A helicopter crash. Near Saigon."

She looks up at him and shudders. His face is a stone mask—grey and cold and lifeless.

CHAPTER 23

November

THE ELEVEN O'CLOCK news is on. Liza reclines on the living room sofa, Benjamin Spock's book on baby care on her lap. Feet resting on the footstool, hand over lower belly, she waits for the baby to stir. Anna is crocheting a white baby bonnet. They sip tea and chat about work — the gossip and curious glances. Although Liza's pregnancy is no secret, not knowing who the father is eats away at some of her female coworkers.

The paternity of Liza's "love child" has become a hot topic. Some in the office believe it could be Armand Vaillancourt. They claim to have seen him devouring Liza with those smouldering eyes during his visits to her office. They blow kisses to each other and feign fainting to demonstrate how irresistible he is. And the mere recollection of his French accent makes them weak at the knees. Others suspect James, the policeman, who has been using his investigation of the missing block of marble as an excuse to continue dropping in on her. Although he does not fit the image of a secret lover, in their words, men in uniform are irresistible to women. Besides, is it not often the unsuspecting quiet ones who should be watched? A few women who came to see the soothsayer at Sculpture Hill think it must be the hippie they saw Liza with on that day. Someone said that, although he looks like a bum, he instructs sculpting at an arts college—Liza would be attracted to an artsy-type. Others said that he is a draft dodger and an antiwar activist, and probably belongs to a socialist party. Liza is a smart girl; she would not be taken in by a communist in disguise. And the most unsettling news about him is that the police have been questioning him about the theft of that block of marble. If Liza's baby ends up with red hair like that man's, the question of fatherhood will be clear, they say.

The freezing rain is icing the window panes. The sticky drizzle seeps into the pores of the city, glazing the streets and sidewalks, the tree branches still clinging to clumps of yellow leaves, and patches of wilted grass.

"Good thing the freezing rain held off until today," Anna says as she slips an orange tea-cozy she crocheted over the tea pot on the coffee table. "The kids had a great Halloween, yesterday evening. Those little ghosts and goblins took over the streets and had a ball. More than a hundred Mars Bars—the dentists will be happy."

Liza is four months pregnant, and is sure the sensation that feels like an air bubble or a flutter of butterfly wings in her stomach has to be the baby's gentle, barely perceptible, movement. She shifts her palm over her stomach. "Feel this, Anna. First a bit of a swish, and now

the little bubbles. These little taps I've come to know."
Anna lays her hand next to Liza's, and their warm laughter fills the room.

The screen door squeaks, followed by the scraping on
the oak door's mail slot. Is someone trying to slip mail
through? The brass slot had been screwed shut and its
function replaced by the mailbox hanging on the porch
wall. Liza gets up to check, but Anna cautions her. It's too
late at night, especially on a soggy and drizzly one such as
this, to open the door to an unknown visitor. The screen
door closes and the mailbox flap drops with a clunk. Anna
walks over to the window and catches a glimpse of a
slight figure in a hooded raincoat walk down the veranda
steps, turn right and continue eastward to High Park subway station.

"Just what we need," Anna says. "More junk mail."

A sense of foreboding settles into Anna's bones, as if
some great calamity is about to befall her. Ever since
Ricky was deported to the U.S., back in September, to face
charges for being AWOL, she has been uneasy. Could FBI
agents be keeping tabs on her? Could her involvement
with the antiwar movement blow up in her face? Could
she even end up losing her job? She had pleaded with
David not to take part in the Pentagon demonstration in
Washington. The situation had become tense and there
would likely be many arrests. It was enough they had
helped to organize it, she had told him.

The blowup over David leaving had been unlike any
of their past disagreements. He took off without a word,
and she had no doubt he was heading to the Pentagon.

To make matters worse, after Ricky's deportation,

the police questioned Anna about a burglary in Yorkville Ricky was accused of. Although she was sure Ricky was innocent, she also knew he was an easy target, especially after being sent back to the States to face the charges as a deserter. She feared being seen as an accomplice, and any knock at the door made her nervous. Soon, her apprehension swelled. She became so tense, as if she were under the mushroom cloud of Hiroshima that was about to engulf her, and forever alter life as she knew it.

Anna has kept her feelings in check by spending much of her free time with Liza and helping around the house. On weekends, she often stays overnight. In Liza's words, Anna's visits offer comfort only David could top.

Last weekend, Anna helped to winterize Liza's roses by mounding peat moss over the bases to protect the grafts from the winter frost. The excitement of Liza's pregnancy has thrown them off schedule, and they made it just before the ground froze. Anna was resolute on protecting the standard Tropicana rose Liza treasures.

The process was tedious. First they dug a shallow ditch along the edge of the perennial bed where a row of impatiens, shaded by the weeping white birch, flourished over the summer. The first frost which singed the impatiens also signalled it was time to winterize the Tropicana. They gently lowered the rose into the trench and covered it with peat moss and soil. In spring, they will dig it out and plant it back in its place to one side of the front steps, where a profusion of blossom welcomes visitors all summer, and often into mid-fall. Neighbours stop to admire the salmon-red blooms and to take in their fruity scent. And unlike other red-hued flowers, which become nearly invisible at night, the Tropicana blooms take on a fluorescent tinge some of the white flowers are featured for in night gardens. Listening to the icy drizzle outside, Anna smiles, pleased the rose has been protected. They could not let this pride-of-the-street freeze the same winter Liza is expecting her baby.

Anna tops off the cups with chamomile tea and sets a plate of Graham crackers on the coffee table. Liza picks up a cookie and dunks it in the tea. With a smile of satisfaction, Anna does the same. "I'll join you and I'm not even eating for two."

Liza laughs. "If I keep going, I soon won't fit through the door."

"You've only gained a few pounds, and it's all water and the baby. If you want a healthy child, you've got to eat. Plenty of time to worry about your figure later."

Liza gets up and straightens out the shirt over her pants. "My appetite's voracious. And since the morning sickness stopped, I feel so energetic. Never thought pregnancy could do that."

On television, the CBC news features the scenes from the Days of the Dead celebrations in Mexico—processions of dancers in skeleton and death masks and floats covered in marigolds, the flower of the dead. The newscaster flashes a footage from Janitzio, a small island in Patzcuaro Lake—the fishermen in their rowboats with torches lighting up the harbour.

Anna props her arms on her hips. "I'd like to see all that pageantry. And all those marigolds. A trip to Mexico. Some day."

"Your Spanish lessons should help. You'd love Mexico.

Not to mention tequila," Liza says and shoots Anna a meaningful stare.

"Tequila? You mean the spirit of Mexico," Anna says laughing. She turns to Liza. "Have you put in the application for maternity leave?"

Liza looks surprised. "No rush."

"Better to plan ahead. Give them time to find a replacement. I'll take a year off after your leave. As soon as you figure out your dates, I'll put in for time off. So the baby will be a bit older before going to daycare."

Liza's eyes widen in amazement. "No way, Anna. I can't let you do that. This baby's my responsibility. And I'm glad of it."

"What are friends for, Liza, if you won't let me in your life? Besides, I'm doing this for myself. I've been at this job forever. With hardly a vacation. I need some time off badly. And what better time?"

Liza makes her way to the bathroom. "I don't know what I'd do without you."

"Without me? What kind of talk is that? And you'd do fine. You'd do fine in any circumstance."

"This bladder's like a regular tap. I've got to pee every minute," Liza murmurs and pulls the bathroom door shut.

"Joys of motherhood," Anna shoots back as she picks up the cups from the table and deposits them into the kitchen sink.

The CBC newscaster's words stop her cold. "United States draft dodger living in Toronto died in prison in ..." Anna's legs turn numb. *Please God, don't let it be him.*

Slowly, as if on crutches, she makes her way back to the living room, eyes glued to the screen.

"It is suspected the complications from the injuries he received during the October 21st Pentagon demonstrations, when 70,000 demonstrators came to Washington to confront the war makers were a factor," the newscaster continues. "What began as a peaceful rally against the Vietnam War turned violent as demonstrators tried to rush the lines of deputy marshals and troops armed with rifles and bayonets. By the end of the protest, 683 people had been arrested. Some demonstrators had been beaten with rifle butts and truncheons."

Anna steps closer to the television anxious for more information on the draft dodger. "Prison press release lists a brain aneurism as the cause of death. The identity of the draft dodger has not been released," the newscaster announces as the bathroom door handle turns. Before Liza walks out of the bathroom, Anna quickly turns the television off and collapses on the sofa.

"My God, Anna, are you alright?" Liza says. "You look like you've seen a ghost."

CHAPTER 24

THE DOOR KNOCKER thumps gently. Anna walks hesitantly to the door, apprehension rising in her chest.

The night before, after Liza went to bed, Anna retrieved the envelope which had been dropped off in the mailbox. It was addressed to Liza, with no indication of who the sender was. She slipped it in the lingerie chest in the guest room she occupies. She had a hunch the two were connected—the draft dodger who had died in the U.S. prison and this brown envelope. When would be the best time to show the envelope to Liza? Should she mention the previous night's news about the draft dodger?

If it is David, at least Liza would be a bit prepared. But if it isn't, wouldn't she be worrying her for no reason? The handwriting on the envelope is not David's. The letters are large and evenly spaced and the "L" has a fancy scroll, as if written by someone trained in calligraphy. David's handwriting is different — uneven angular letters that seen from a distance resemble Egyptian hieroglyphs.

Through the glass door pane, Anna spots a woman on the porch. It's Helena. The gnawing in Anna's stomach intensifies as she turns the deadbolt and opens the door. She is blinded by the morning sun shimmering off the icy glaze on the tree branches and rooftops across the street. Anna squints to adjust her eyes to the glimmer.

Helena steps back. She is pale, with dark circles of sleeplessness beneath her eyes. "Anna? What are you doing here?" she says in a brittle voice.

"Me? You're asking *me* what I'm doing here?"

Helena lowers her eyes. "Didn't know you live here." She turns quickly and begins walking down the icy veranda steps. "I'm looking for someone else."

"Wait," Anna calls out. "And grab on to the railing, girl. It's sheer ice."

Helena stops and rests her hand on the railing. Her blond hair hangs limp under the beret crocheted in stripes of assorted coloured yarn, now matted from wear. Her oversized woollen poncho hangs over a long paisley skirt drooping over moccasin boots.

"I don't actually live here. What on earth are you doing here?"

Helena clears her throat. "I … dropped off an envelope last night. I thought this was the right place. I'd like to take it back."

Helena looks drained, as if she'd been ill for some time, and Anna has a dreadful inkling this visit has something to do with David.

"Who are you looking for?" Anna says softly as if talking to a child.

"For Liza. I was given this address."

She turns and is about to continue down the steps when Anna says: "You're at the right place. Wait here. Let me see what Liza's up to. I'll tell her you're here."

Helena searches Anna's face anxiously. "Does Liza have the envelope? Does she know? I shouldn't have left it."

"Oh, Helena, I sure hope it's not what I think."

Tears burst from Helena's red-rimmed eyes and roll down her waxen cheeks. "I should've talked to her, first. What have I done?"

Anna wraps her arm around Helena's shoulders. "I've got the envelope, Helena. I was afraid of what's in it. I heard the news last night."

Helena grabs Anna's hand. "Thank God she didn't get it. I didn't know what to do. How to tell her ... his letters to her ..."

"It *is* David. Isn't it, Helena?"

Helena lowers her eyes and nods. "What did they say on television? I called every news station while he was in prison. No help. Now finally somebody's listening. But it's too late for him. Too late."

"Are you sure *it is* him? They didn't say so on the news."

"I was there."

"You were with him? Why? Were the two of you ..."

Helena covers her eyes with her palm. "David is my brother."

"Your brother?"

Helena nods.

Anna stares at her. "I never thought …"

"Not his fault. I didn't want to be treated like some-body's little sister. Didn't want to be told what to do."

Anna props her hands on her hips and heaves a sigh: "Helena, why don't you go home and rest for a while? Leave it with me to talk to Liza. I could phone you, and you could come back in a few days when Liza's had some time …"

Helena clutches Anna's arm. "I have to tell her. I prom-ised."

Gently, Anna places her other hand over Helena's. "Do you know Liza's expecting?"

Helena stares blankly. "What do you mean?"

"Expecting a baby. David's baby."

Helena takes a few short breaths. "Oh, my God! David never said anything."

"He didn't know. Liza was looking for the right mo-ment to tell him. Worried how he'd take it. And then he was gone."

Helena looks panicky. "We can't tell her, can we?"

Anna sighs. "If only I knew. Perhaps I could've stopped him from going. I tried. But you know David when he gets something in his head."

"And what if she finds out? You said it was on last night's news."

"They said a draft dodger. Didn't say who."

"But they will. As soon as they confirm with the pris-on. They'll probably announce it any time now. That's why I dropped off the envelope last night. Then I realized, how awful. I need to tell her in person. I promised him. My big brother."

"Oh, Helena. I'm so sorry. I've been so blind. I never thought …"

Helena waves her hand dismissively. "It's all over now. It's Liza I'm worried about. I've got to tell her. But how?"

Anna pulls the wicker chair away from the railing and offers it to Helena. "We'll do it together, you and I. Wait here a minute. I'll go in and see what she's up to."

"I'm glad she has you, Anna," Helena whispers.

A few minutes later Anna returns and asks Helena in.

CHAPTER 25

ELENA BRUSHES BACK the unruly lock of her washed out blond hair from her forehead.

"The riot erupted at the end of the day. Protesters were carted off to prison. I found David in a prison cell, with a bruised and swollen head. I insisted that he get medical care. He was checked by prison medics and taken back to his cell. I hired an attorney who specializes in defending draft dodgers. But the process was slow. A few days later, David was feeling better. The swelling on his head subsided, and we hoped for a speedy recovery. But the next day when I came to visit, he was again bloodied and bruised. He refused to tell me how it happened. A guard said a Hells Angel had discerned the Dead Head logo in David's tattoo and was offended by it being defaced. An inmate said David was defending another inmate, a draft dodger who was attacked by a Hells Angel, and a mob of prisoners descended on them. I insisted he be taken to the hospital. Instead, they took him to the prison infirmary again. The next day, I found him back in his cell, feverish and disoriented. I called the attorney and the local newspapers. A few days later, he was dead."

Liza listens in silence. Every so often, Helena unfolds her arms and smoothes the fabric over her knees, and Liza is reminded that this waif of a woman, who seemed to appear from nowhere, is real. That she is the same smart-mouthed Helena who had waitressed at the Mynah Bird.

She recalls *that* Helena. But *this* woman, this ragdoll propped against the pillow, she does not relate to. And now she finds out that Helena is David's sister? Who had spent the last month near him, with him? While Liza lived in torment of not knowing his whereabouts or his fate.

Since David had vanished from her life, he had remained in the forefront of her thoughts. Her daily chores, her work, conversations with Anna, carried on outside of her, at a plane never as real and immediate as him. She had trained her mind to split itself into two parts where David resided in the more immediate one. And all else was relegated to a distant consciousness.

She will not allow David to fade into a memory and lose him — lose the sound of his voice, the scent of his skin, the feel of his arms around her. No, she cannot lose him, no. And this horrifically fantastic conversation with this pale fairy-like woman with red-rimmed eyes is making her nauseous.

Liza is outside of her own body, observing the three women sitting in her living room and chatting. There is Helena telling her fairy tales. The stone-faced Anna — dear reliable and trustworthy Anna. And there is Liza — *it is*

me, has to be, for the anguish I feel could be no one else's. Liza
is now fascinated with this ability to view herself in conversation with the other two women. Anna gets up and
brings a fresh pot of tea — *dear Anna, always ready to offer
advice and solve problems over a pot of tea.*

How strange it is to observe my own self, Liza thinks. She
sees herself pouring tea into her cup. She is raising the
cup to her lips. She hears Anna cautioning her that the tea
is too hot and she should let it cool. Her lips are now burning, then her throat. The cup falls from her hand and
breaks into two, then three segments that remind her of
the shards David chipped away from the white stone
block he had been carving into a sculpture, the one he
had been working on the day she had surprised him in his
makeshift studio in Parkdale, that abandoned shack overgrown with shrubbery, and chickens-and-hens thriving
on the roof, and blooming goldenrod in the cracks of the
foundation. Liza picks up the shard with a handle still attached and brings it to her lips, eager to taste the warm
tea with honey that would soothe her and reassure her
that the anguish lodged in her chest is a dream, a hallu-
cination, and when she wakes up, David will be there,
next to her, his arms around her. She presses her lips
against the broken china, and the red drops of liquid drip
down her white blouse.

Anna crouches next to Liza. "Please give me that
broken cup, Liza. Please let go of it. You're cutting yourself; you're bleeding."

Liza lays her hand on Anna's and gently pushes it
away. The touch she craves is David's. She has the urge to
caress him, to run her palm along his unshaven cheeks,

to bring her lips to his. She passes her hand along the edge of the shard and the red liquid drips and pools in her palm. Then both women are kneeling next to Liza, unclenching her fingers from the broken china.

Liza sees herself from some distant point above, shielded from the gut-wrenching anguish of missing David.

Anna and Helena exchange looks of alarm. Anna dials the ambulance. Helena wraps her arm around Liza's shoulders. "You've got your baby to think about."

After the phone call Anna wets a napkin and swabs the blood off Liza's lips. She wipes the blood off her jeans. She heads for the washroom, picks up another towel, and resumes cleaning the blood off Liza's clothing.

Liza gazes into the red drops on her blue jeans resembling the purple flowers David had picked at the Center Island and placed on her lap.

Looking into Anna's kind brown eyes as large as ripe sunflower heads, Liza is suddenly grateful. She does not like the slippery feel of the purple stain on her jeans as if she would slide off it into an abyss, into the cold lonely prison cell where David is no longer. If she had only been there, could she have kept him safe? Could she have prevented the beatings?

Helena's silky voice recounting David's death has smudged Liza's reality into a slick red puddle where all is surreal. Why had he left without a word? Her head is spinning and she is drifting into his prison cell to be near him, to hold him and to free him and to escape back to the safety of home, back to Toronto and his great bed with the black wrought iron headboard and the Dutchman's pipe blossoms among the green leaves above. Liza had paid the rent for his apartment so he would have it upon his return and it is as he had left it: his bread maker ready for a fresh loaf; his juicer waiting to concoct piña coladas, the elixirs of life as he called them; and the rattan basket still hanging from the rafter on the patio where she had magically turned into a sunray — the basket now glazed in frost. And it would all come to life upon his re- turn, like the castle cursed by the evil spell and overgrown in thorns waiting to burst into bloom upon the return of the prince who would plant his magic kiss on the charmed princess' lips. And things would be back to the way they were. *You and I, Liza, we're for good. We're real,* his reassur- ing voice whispers in her thoughts. Liza nods in agree- ment. *Yes, David will be back, yes.*

From her purse, Helena takes a small bundle loosely wrapped in a red bandana. She unwraps it slowly to reveal a round blue button with a white dove behind the black wire mesh — a Pentagon Peace Button. She pins it on Liza's white blouse. "David wore this button. It's a symbol of peace, a dove imprisoned in the Pentagon. I wear mine in memory of David. In honour of our soldiers who died in Vietnam. And the Vietnamese who died fighting for their freedom."

Liza caresses the button with her fingertips and feels the bird behind the wire mesh flapping its wings, trying to escape. She wills the dove to soar to freedom, but how? She is as helpless as the dove, her limbs flailing like the bird's wings, red liquid painting the white feathers, and she sees a deputy's baton hitting the dove, again and again, and the dove falls, and lays there on the cold prison floor trashing about, and is finally still.

Anna and Helena exchange worried glances and Anna wishes she could ask Liza to get up from the sofa so she could check for haemorrhaging.

"Best to leave her for now. The ambulance will be here any minute," Helena says, as though some universal women's intuition had kicked in. And the seconds tick on and fill the room with a fog of apprehension.

The doorbell rings. Anna springs up. "Thank goodness they're here."

She opens the door and guides the two paramedics toward Liza. "She's pregnant, four-and-a-half months. She's beside herself with grief. She's cut herself on her hands and lips. Could be haemorrhaging as well."

The paramedics ask Liza a few routine questions to which she is able to answer clearly. When they return to the ambulance for a gurney, Anna helps her to sit up on the sofa—a small puddle of blood is on the cushion and a large wet blotch on Liza's jeans. Anna's jaws clench with fear that Liza could lose the baby.

Anna picks up Liza's purse from the hallway stand. "I'll take your bag. To make sure you have everything on you. Your health card and all your things." She turns to the paramedic. "Can we come with you?"

"There is room for only one more in the ambulance."

Helena picks up her jacket. "You go, Anna. I'll call a cab and be there in no time."

Anna pulls out a hair band from her jean pocket and, while tying Liza's hair into a ponytail, says: "Won't you stay here at the house, Helena? We'll be back shortly. And it would be lovely to spend some time together."

Liza reaches for Helena's hand. "Yes, Helena. If you could."

Helena nods. "I'll find my way around the kitchen. Supper will be on the table." They exchange glances of heartfelt kinship they know would be lifelong.

The paramedics wheel the gurney to the ambulance and, while they make some last minute adjustments, Anna gently brushes Liza's bangs off her forehead. "You're in good hands."

As the ambulance drives off, Helena follows it with her eyes until it turns around the curve and disappears from sight. The fear Liza could lose the baby is making her dizzy. She returns to the house, closes the door, and drops down on her knees. "God, I've been an atheist for as long as I remember, but if you keep Liza and David's child safe, I'll be as devout as a Baptist. Hell, I'll even become a Baptist."

Why would the notion of being Baptist show ultimate devotion to God? She is not sure. But at this moment, it feels right.

In the ambulance, Liza is suddenly sleepy, as if she'd been on a long journey without rest. The siren's wail is a distant lullaby. The paramedic's repetition of the questions she'd already answered is an intrusion on her want of silence. David's words, *You and I, Liza, we're for good,* drift through her thoughts. And the more the paramedic persists on keeping her awake, the more she yearns to succumb to the lull of the siren-lullaby. But before she can submerge into that feathery softness of sleep where the allure of make-believe replaces the harshness of reality, she is slid onto a hospital bed and wheeled down the twisting corridors. Through the flurry of voices, Anna's words — "Everything will be alright, Liza" — guide the way.

CHAPTER 26

THE RINGING OF the phone is a welcome relief from pacing the floor and worrying about Liza's visit to emergency.

"Liza's doing well," Anna says. "They cleaned the cuts and they're not too deep. And the baby's fine. But she'll stay overnight for observation."

The glow of hopefulness in Anna's voice is more telling than the words, and Helena feels it seeping into her core and illuminating her from within. She hangs up and clasps her face in her hands. "God, I'll do anything. I'll trade my life for Liza and the baby." She makes the sign of the cross for the first time since she was a child.

Helena is not accustomed to the ritual of crossing herself—it's for church goers and old relatives, and it makes her feel ancient. She feels worn down. Every joint hurts as if grief has poisoned her blood and infected her flesh. The events of last summer and fall—her mother's death and then David's—this lifetime worth of sorrow weighs on her like a mountain.

She stands by the stove, shoulders slumped, and slowly stirs the stew with a wooden spatula. She found a package of stewing beef in the fridge and is cooking a nourishing meal for Liza and Anna. Outside, the afternoon sun and the quick rise in temperature have melted the ice, and the only evidence of the storm are the shrivelled up impatiens and petunia. She picked a handful of sage in the herb garden just outside the kitchen door and chopped it into the stew. The few leaves left on the cutting board remind her how the suede foliage with pungent fragrance is resilient to early frost—the hardiness against the cold, this determination to survive.

The sunshine is pouring through the window, and the kitchen is infused with the fragrance of stew and sage—and she wonders whether people have ever been able to truly appreciate the precious nature of their ephemeral existence. How simple acts, such as preparing meals or eating dinner, gain significance only when they can no longer be shared with those who matter, with those who give meaning to seemingly routine tasks.

The many arguments she and David had over the years loom large and she regrets the tension they'd gone through—like an arrow pulled back waiting to be shot. She never expected the arrow to be pointed at David instead of her.

Yet, what would David say if he saw her now, despairing in her grief? He would certainly lecture her, or at least she would take it as a lecture, using his authority of an older sibling—she would've seen it that way in the past.

He had insisted that she complete her degree in visual arts. That she quit her menial jobs and focus on her studies. He was particularly cross about her waitressing at Yorkville bars. Money was not the issue. They had a generous inheritance at their disposal.

David had always been the pillar she could lean on, but a strange man in many ways. A loner. He did not see that after their mother's death she needed his support. Feeling abandoned, she drifted between waitressing jobs, took every "street" drug she could get her hands on, and threw herself into the arms of every man she felt even mildly attracted to.

David was furious. She saw it as payback for not sharing the pain of their loss. Now she realizes, the only person she has been hurting is herself.

And she finally sees how wrong she has been about Anna. For a long while, she felt that Anna acted as if she owned David. Helena felt pushed out of David's life. She felt that Anna was possessive of Liza as well. But now Helena sees it differently. She is grateful that Liza has Anna's friendship.

She plugs in the kettle for a cup of tea. A billow of steam begins to rise, and Helena feels something changing in her. Shifting. Expanding. Rearranging. As if a water balloon were rising from her stomach, swishing up through her diaphragm and lodging itself between her lungs. Her heart is pounding against this swelling in her chest. And with each heartbeat, the swelling grows, filling every crevice. Helena is elated about the new arrangement of organs inside of her, about the new life she feels part of her, the new life Liza is carrying, the miraculous new being that is David's child. She is euphoric. Filled with love. Pure, miraculous, ecstatic love.

Helena closes her eyes and in her mind's eye gleans a meandering path, opening up and stretching into infinity. A sense of lightness washes over her as if she were carried on a warm wind high above, observing the future unfold. The insight that all will be well, supplants all else. She had forgotten what it was like to be at peace — and suddenly it happens. She is calm as if David were back in her life. *Everything will be alright. You hear me, David? Listen carefully my bro. You're gonna be a dad! That angel of yours, Liza, is carrying your child!*

After visiting emergency, Liza is advised by the doctor to take some time off work as a precaution for her baby. For the first few days, she remains in bed and welcomes being pampered by Helena's motherly care while Anna is at work. Helena has taken over David's apartment and would stay until the baby's birth.

To Liza, Helena's presence is prophetic, and her likeness to David at once comforting and painful. Comforting, when she glimpses a reflection of his smile in hers, that glimmer of determination in her eyes when she talks about the demonstrations, and the ironic smirk of the upper lip when she condemns the evils of war. Painful when Helena wraps her arms around her in a consoling embrace and Liza inhales a whiff of a cigarette, the same brand as David's, or when Helena reads one of his letters to her.

Unable to sleep and refusing to take the prescribed sedative for fear it might harm the baby, she finds consolation in Helena's talk about David. Helena talks about the letters David had written to Liza while in prison. He had given the letters to a guard for mailing. But the guard had been pro war and resented the draft dodgers. Learning David had worked with the Canadian antiwar groups and had them transported to the demonstrations had inflamed the guard's wounded patriotism. He saw David as a communist traitor, and instead of mailing the letters he threw them in the garbage bin.

Helena had befriended another prison guard who had allowed her extra visitations. He had managed to retrieve some of David's letters and give them to Helena.

Liza passes her fingertips over David's handwriting as if she were reading braille. She lifts the letter to her face and breathes in the aroma of the paper his hands had touched and the faint scent of his cigarettes. She holds the letter against her face for a long while. Then reads it again.

> "Liza, my wild thing,
>   Our love is all that matters. The rest you'll understand, for you and I also share the love of all that's good and just. I will always be with you. If I don't make it, take comfort in Anna's friendship. She, like you, is a great lady. Helena thinks the world of you. And she needs a sister. With all my love, David."

Liza spends her days resting and rereading David's letters. When she closes her eyes in search of David, he is there among the crowds. Marching in the demonstrations. Carrying signs and listening to Dr. Spock whose book she keeps on her night table and reads and rereads.

When the horrid visions of babies napalmed in Vietnam overwhelm her, she cries out in her sleep: "Babies are not for burning." Anna and Helena gently shake her shoulder and call her name to draw her out of the nightmares. Sometimes she averts her eyes from her caring friends in her desire of sleep, happy in her dreams with David.

After several days, Liza leaves her bedroom and resumes her usual routine. Soon, she would return to her job. Leisurely dinners offer time for reminiscing and fulfilling her need to learn all she could about David's work with the protesters and Anna's and Helena's involvement.

CHAPTER 27

THE SCULPTURES HAD been completed by the end of the summer, except for Vaillancourt's piece, now a collection of huge iron cubes scattered over the site. The sculptor had left for San Francisco to design and supervise his new project, the gigantic Vaillancourt Fountain, and the summer months allotted for the construction of the High Park pieces had gone by. His absence had created much controversy. The cost of setting up the colossal foundry, believed to have exceeded two hundred thousand dollars, and doubts about his commitment to complete the piece have been in the forefront of local media. But since he returned in early November, he has been casting more iron cubes with a renewed zeal, and his flaming foundry has been lighting up the hillock night after night as if he were forging a monument of mythical proportions.

The weather has been unusually warm. It is the last day of November, and double-digit temperatures with sunshine have brought crowds to the park. Many people continue to gravitate to the sculpture sites. Liza has not visited the park since she found out about David's death. Taking Helena on a leisurely walk where every tree, bench, and stone, and especially the sculptures, hold fond memories of David will help both face the reality of his absence. Anna agrees to accompany them. They begin with Bernard Schottlander's *November Pyramid* and are surprised to find the smooth brown cubes already scribbled with graffiti. They spot Vaillancourt at his site, preparing moulds for the nightly pouring. He often casts the iron cubes during the evenings, and locals gather for the show of glowing molten iron and muscle power made more spectacular under the cloak of darkness. A tall policeman approaches him and after a brief exchange Vaillancourt's voice rises and he gestures widely.

Anna turns to Liza. "Isn't that the officer who came to your door last week? Asked again about the stolen marble?"

Hand above her eyes to shield against the sun, Liza says: "That's James alright. He's still searching for that stone block."

Anna takes a pack of Luckies from her purse and plucks out a cigarette. "Have to say, I almost accused David of taking that stone. Now I feel horrible about it."

Hands propped on her hips, Helena scans the hill. "It was *not* David," she says and leads the way to Irving Burman's two granite blocks still on the grass. Next to them, the petition which calls for the thief to bring back the marble is still posted.

"How do you know?" Anna says and lights the cigarette. She takes a long drag and lets it out slowly. "I see the volunteers haven't given up. Still collecting those signatures."

Liza nods. "Six thousand signatures so far. And the hype's not letting up."

Anna points to the petition. "Burman's still refusing the quarry's offer to replace it free of charge. No other piece would do. Go figure."

Liza pulls out the petition form from the pouch, looks it over, and slips it back in. She heaves a sigh. "Burman had a breakdown after that stone vanished."

Anna grinds the cigarette on the rim of the garbage bin. "Sure did. And couldn't continue. So there it is, two granite blocks, and nothing else. Taxpayers' money sitting on that grass like a pile of you-know-what."

Helena stands frozen, gazing into the distance. "I know my brother," she whispers.

Down in the valley, Liza glimpses *Midsummer Night's Dream*. It would be a while before she musters up the courage to reveal its source of inspiration to anyone. Many years later, she will tell the story to the child she now carries in her womb. She will tell it in words void of the sorrow she now feels, and it will be the story of their summer together — the summer of love. She will talk about Wessel Couzijn who had been lounging at his site nearby, gazing at the starlit sky, hoping for inspiration for his sculpture. And there they were — she and David — making love under the maple moon-shade. "It's what lovers sometimes do in the park," he had told Liza. But this was not the right day for that story. For now, Couzijn's brain child would remain her secret.

Anna taps out another cigarette and turns to Helena. "We'd like to show you something."

Leading the way to William Koochin's *The Hippy*, Liza feels hot air rising in her chest. She takes a deep breath to release tension. Facing eastward, the dark granite figure on a square pedestal keeps watch over the sculpture sites.

Helena stares at the sculpture for a long while. "It's David."

CHAPTER 28

AT DUSK, LIZA stands by *The Hippy*. *How appropriate the monument is — the likeness of David.* He often stood here — dark shades, hands in pockets — taking in the progress of the installations at Sculpture Hill. Koochin had captured that stance, that casual yet defiant posture: the Love button on David's lapel, his unruly beard, a one-time suit jacket turned casual, and his somewhat stocky build — to Liza a sure giveaway of his gourmet palate and the skill of a well-trained chef — chiselled to the last detail.

The scene replays in her mind. She can hear Koochin's voice: "My piece is a tribute to you, David, my friend. And to your ideology. To freedom in every way. Freedom to love, to create, to live in peace!"

"Some talent, my friend. I'm honoured."

Koochin strokes his bearded chin in satisfaction and says: "I call it *The Hippy*."

David pats Koochin's shoulder. "We're living in the age

of transformation. The name's fitting. I congratulate you, buddy!"

They step back and, circling the figure, examine it from various angles.

Koochin turns to David. "Should've been you, bro. To win this contract. I thought they'd made a mistake."

"No mistake, Bill. It couldn't've gone to a better sculptor. If I were the judge, I would've picked you."

Koochin studies the figure. "David, man, if you had won, what would you have sculpted?"

David takes the Love button off his lapel and pins it on Liza's shirt collar. Arm around her shoulder, he draws her close. "The beautiful woman who's afraid to love me."

Looking into Liza's eyes he gently brushes hair away from her forehead. "I would've sculpted you, Liza — the eyes of Sculpture Hill."

Now, enveloped in long tree shadows swaying in the evening breeze, Liza leans into *The Hippy*. She rests her palm on the cold stone. *If only I could see your eyes behind those shades, David … if I could hear your voice.* Her thoughts wander back to the time she first heard David's voice, she first saw him — eating a burger and wiping his hands on his jeans; to the first time she inhaled his scent and wrote her telephone number on his tattooed bicep; to the first time they made love at the hill not far from where she now stands; to the nights of lovemaking in his colossal creaky bed; to the perpetual coldness lodged in her like permafrost, since he vanished from her life. The child in her womb shifts ever so gently.

Liza scans Sculpture Hill. All about her, dim silhouettes like ominous caves gape in the far angles of the park.

The soaring tree trunks with bare crowns lean one way and the other. She looks up. The stone face is illuminated. Suddenly she feels *love* as if she were in David's arms.

What secrets does the universe hold? What magic? She wonders.

And the next moment the granite is cold and dark and reminiscent of David's face on that night when he told her about his wife who had been killed in Saigon.

Has she been dreaming? She could not describe this to anyone for fear of being thought a madwoman. It's something she felt. Later that night, she will express it in her diary, and it will be many years after her death that her daughter, the child she now carries, will read and understand. She will *know* it in the way Liza feels it now, this flash of at-oneness with the sculpture of David—with David himself—and their unborn child. It will be their family secret—shared with the daughter who will be named Blossom.

PART TWO

CHAPTER 29

Spring, 2008

THE LATE DAY sun is unusually warm for early April. After giving my last lecture of the winter semester, I take a leisurely stroll through the University campus, staying off the paved path. The ground is pregnant with moisture and the air smells of spring.

I glance at my timetable in the folder still in my hand: Blossom Grant, Winter, 2008. My schedule, which during the semester has grown exponentially into prep time, grading, professional development, and faculty meetings, filling up evenings and weekends — each task a metronome mark quantifying the tempo of life as it has been for the past ten years — is winding down. After next week's student exams, I will have a long summer break to use in any way I wish.

As I near Dundas Square, the noise from a heavy metal band assaults my ears. A whiff of frying sesame oil through an open restaurant door draws me to the line-up of students and I join the queue to place my order. Glancing into the broad window next to me, at the reflection of people in the line-up, I am taken aback by the familiar image—the gaunt features with high cheek bones I think of as a gift from my Slavic mother, deep set eyes I know match the turquoise in my dangling earrings, and thick folds of the Irish-red curls hardly subdued by the tinted glass mirage—a willowy figure clad in black in the midst of muted shades. She seems surreal, as if I had not seen her for a while.

The takeout line shuffles along. From the clamorous chatter I soon learn that I am a pesco-vegetarian—a fish eating vegetarian, as oxymoronic as that sounds.

A short subway ride later, I am home on Gothic Avenue, gazing over the ravine to the rooflines of houses silhouetted against the blush of the setting sun. I pick at the tasty seafood morsels and watch a television program about the depletion of oceans due to unethical fishing methods. I turn to the screen and the squiggly sea creatures are struggling in the gigantic fish nets. The narrator's voice goes on about the practice of bottom trawling, dragging the heavy nets along the ocean floor, which he likens to fishing with a bulldozer—everything else is caught in it.

"This coral is a deep-water variety," a bearded man who appears on the screen explains as he pulls a chunk from the net. "It's a slow-growing type, and a single net can snare about a ton and a half every hour."

I point my remote to turn the television off, when the underwater camera zooms in and the screen is filled with the swaying cauliflower-like heads as the voice announces this coral could be thousands of years old. It would take just as long to recover — or may not recover at all. I close the white lid of the Styrofoam container — another enemy — and dump the food into the waste basket. Too late now, but I resolve the word "pesco" would be replaced with "chick peas," at least when it refers to me.

The evening ahead suddenly gapes with unplanned time — the reward I give myself at the end of a busy week or the winding down of a semester, slowly losing its appeal. I am queasy. Is it the seafood? No, it's my work schedule. For the first time in ten years, I chose to take the summer off. I might travel. Or just laze around. Go to the beach, the theatres, art galleries, and museums. Catch up on life. I've been saving for this a long while. I should be excited, not panicky. Perhaps I am simply not used to having free time.

That night, instead of another ritual of sleeplessness, drinking Sleepytime tea and having a staring down contest with the picture on the tea-box — papa-bear dozing in his comfy recliner in front of a roaring fire with a tabby on his lap, I actually go to bed. I sleep and sleep and when I untangle myself from my sheets and dare to open my eyes to a glaring white sunshine unlike any other light I can momentarily recall, I squint at the clock on my dresser and it's ten in the morning.

I am thrilled. I actually jump on my bed and dance and hum, "teddy-bear, teddy-bear, turn around, teddy-bear, teddy-bear, touch the ground." I do the actions as well. I am as carefree as if I were four years old and not forty.

A twinge of nausea suddenly churns in my stomach. I am trapped as if I were a squiggly sea creature caught in

a gigantic fishing net. The room is airless and claustro-
phobic and I run out and down the steps and into the living room now drenched in sunshine. The queasiness is
the aftermath of the dream that has been haunting me for
a while now.

*Among the hills and valleys of the ocean floor and colonies
of coral, a white shadow of a woman shifts, then fades into the
background. I hear my name called. Blossom! I slip behind a tall
clump of coralline, peering through the transparency of the
ocean vastness, then hop, weightless, over a mound, over a
gorge. The shadow comes into focus, her limbs moving naturally as if she is a living being. But she has that white stone look,
and I know it's a sculpture of some kind. She looks familiar, as
if I have seen her somewhere before. She raises her hands, as if
waving to me, but her face is turned away, and I realize she is
trying to catch the clumps of coral floating about, unaware of
my presence.*

The doorbell rings. I gasp for breath as if I had just
surfaced from the bottom of the ocean. It's the paperboy
doing collections.

"It's eleven fifty, Miss Grant," the paperboy grins and
hands me the *Sunday Star.*

My purse is on the hall stand by the door. I hand him
the money and pick up the copy of the Saturday paper
from my porch as well. I stand there, staring at the two
editions of the *Toronto Daily Star*, as if I have never seen a
newspaper before. Did I sleep from Friday evening to Sunday morning? How could this be? I have never done this
before. I am a chronic insomniac, for heaven sake. I sigh
loudly and shake my head and try to make some sense of
this as if it happened to someone else.

What have I missed? The answering machine is flashing. It shows three new messages.

"Hi Blossom. It's Chester. We said we'd meet at five? Our usual? Just thought I'd remind you."

"Hi there. I'm at Marché. The Front Street one. Hope I got the place right."

"Me again ..."

I still cannot believe I slept through two nights and a day. I'm about to call him, but feel nauseous as if seasick, and cannot imagine talking to anyone, especially to Chester. What would I say? Nothing logical comes to mind.

Chester and I met a few semesters ago in the cafeteria line. I smile as the scene unfolds in my thoughts.

"Hello Blossom!" Jane waves at me from the front of the line, and motions me to join her. I am tempted. Then I catch myself. Would students see it as butting into the line?

Jane and I go way back—we have been close friends since childhood. We were roommates at university. Now we share a cubicle and a desk in the faculty office. This is one way the university saves on office space—by having non-tenured and part time faculty share desks. Most of the classes we teach are at different times, so the desk is usually free for one of us. When we are there together, we sit at each end. The good thing is, we chuckle about it. When I was a student I never imagined my professors sharing a desk.

"Come on, Blossom," Jane beckons. "I've been waiting for you." That's our code for butting into lines without it being obvious.

The man in front of me turns: "Blossom?" He pauses for a moment, and smirks as if about to say something.

"Do we know each other?" I ask.

"I just had to see …"

"Yes?" I give him my most serious glare.

"It's your name. I had to see the person with such a name."

By now our eyes are laughing. He is blushing. A guy blushing is very appealing. To me it is. I prop my hands on my hips: "And your name?" I feel juvenile as if in grade school. But I have the upper hand, and it's fun.

He rubs his unshaven chin, black stubble intentional, I can tell. His eyes are periwinkle blue. Guys shouldn't have such eyes. They should be reserved for women.

There is a moment of silence. "You won't laugh?" he asks.

I lift my right hand in a three-finger-salute. "Scout's honour."

He extends his hand to me. "Chester. Chester Cuttail."

I stifle a laugh. "You're putting me on, right?"

"Not at all. You can laugh all you want. But before you do, I've got to tell you. I had a cat named Blossom."

I laugh and it feels good even now, recalling the moment. I wish I could laugh like that more often. What has changed within me? Why?

I pace the floor thinking of a good excuse I could give Chester for missing our dinner. Then I realize, it's just as well. We have been seeing each other so often I am becoming dependent on him. And I am not ready for what that leads to. Commitment. Then a heartbreak. I am not about to replicate Liza's fate. I prefer my life uncomplicated.

Instead, I press Anna's number. She picks up on the first ring.

"Bloss, dear, you must be telepathic. I was about to call you. Have you seen the write-up in today's paper? About the graffiti in High Park."

She fills me in on the week's worth of news since we last spoke and we set a time for our usual Sunday dinner. I am tempted to tell her about my bizarrely long sleep but it would only lead her to worry. She has noticed I haven't been myself lately, and has been insisting I have a thorough checkup. Since Liza died, Anna has been my pillar of strength every step of the way.

We hang up, and I grind some coffee beans the way Liza and Anna used to as a special treat on weekends. As I listen to the spurting of the percolator and inhale the aroma, I flip through the paper in search of the article Anna mentioned. I pour the coffee into the rose china mug—one of Liza's flower collections—and get comfy in my favourite chair overlooking the backyard garden. The trees and shrubs, although still bare, are mantled in secret leaf-buds waiting for the first warm day to burst into their fluorescent hues. As I sip the flavourful brew, I recognize the photo in the paper. The large cubic sculpture in High Park is Bernard Schottlander's *November Pyramid*. Some time ago, someone had painted it a brilliant blue. It had been cleaned of the unwanted "art" and repainted back to a neutral brown. Now it has received a new ambush of graffiti.

The article brings to mind my trip to London, England, in 1999, around the time the sculptor died. I was at a conference when I came across his obituary in the newspaper. It mentioned his contribution to the 1967 Art Symposium in Toronto. I found it strange to be so far away from home and see a reference to sculptures almost in my own backyard.

The obituary had described Schottlander as one of the most stylish, technically accomplished sculptors who worked in Britain after the Second World War, though he received little recognition. He focused on public commissions and held few exhibits, so his work became familiar, but not his name. He had been known to point to an ashtray at a cocktail party or a light fixture on a street corner and say, I made that—say it casually, as a way of informing, without emphasizing his part in it. He had been an ordinary man with an extraordinary talent.

This all reminds me of the sculptures in High Park. Liza had a story on every piece. Many of the artworks are still there—a familiar sight to park visitors. Yet, very few people know much about the artwork and have even less appreciation for it. A few pieces were well used from the day they were completed. Schottlander's large stack of metal cubes had instantly become the children's favourite climbing place. Hubert Dalwood's "Temple," a maze-like construct of stainless steel cylinders, is another popular spot for children and grownups alike. But a number of the artworks appear abandoned. Some are scribbled with graffiti, a few are dilapidated, and some overgrown with vegetation.

For me, they have a certain incongruous flair—original and highly contemporary, and yet seemingly forgotten as if much time had passed. Names such as "pyramid" and "temple" are reminiscent of some ancient epoch. At times, as I stand in front of Bill Koochin's statue of a hippie, now with a broken nose, I imagine him as old as Michelangelo's David.

The Hippy holds a certain mystical power over me. I envision Liza standing in front of it, arms crossed on her chest, head tilted to one side, with this wistful look on her face, eyes penetrating the black granite figure as if staring at it hard enough would bring it to life. I can still hear her voice. *If I could only make him breathe!* I didn't quite understand what she meant. She promised to tell me the secret behind this sculpture. While she was ill, I did not have the heart to ask, although I thought she simply could not find the right words. I catch myself staring at *The Hippy* as she used to, wishing the mystery would reveal itself to me.

A bit farther east where the park is left natural, fewer visitors come — mostly dog walkers who keep to the periphery of this section. I often sit here, on a sunny slope near one of the sculptures and feel right at home. Am I drawn to them *because* they are unappreciated? They seem to exist in a world of their own, mysterious and misunderstood and mostly ignored, except for the complaints about the safety of some of the pieces that had been partially disassembled. In my own quasi-philosophy where all animate and inanimate objects have some form of soul, these artworks, some created by sculptors who have since become world-renowned, seem forlorn.

I decide to spend the day at Sculpture Hill catching up on all the work I should have done yesterday. I roll up my picnic blanket — the handmade quilt Liza bought for my white "princess" bed when I was still in grade school — stuff it in its matching bag, then stash a bundle of student papers waiting to be graded next to it, and head to the park. As I make my way along the path to the sculptures, my eyes follow the trunks of the oaks and maples to the bare crowns, and I envision them lush and green as they will be in another month. To my left, near the Forest School, is Wessel Couzijn's piece, *Midsummer Night's Dream*. The story behind the artist's inspiration Liza told me makes me smile. Behind me is Menashe Kadishman's, "Three Discs." I am amazed that it is free of graffiti considering its inviting circular surfaces—six blank canvasses-in-waiting.

Strange how some places make one feel at home. Here, I feel as if I am in my own living room—but more inspired—as if the air I breathe is infused with an inspiration the artists who created these sculptures instilled into the landscape.

I take my quilt out of its bag and unroll it. I fold it with the flowers inside and the mint green on the outside, as Liza used to, then lay it over the bag so it does not get stained by the grass. A few months ago Chester asked me if I had made it, and I told him how Liza and I, who were not into craft making at all, told everyone we had sewn it, and how we laughed about it afterwards. My first impulse was to stash it safely into the cedar chest, but Liza would want me to use it.

Soon I am sitting on the quilt and marking reports, my back propped against one of the red I-beams—what is left of Mark di Suvero's *Flower Power*. It had been cordoned off as a safety precaution. Yet, I am comforted, as if the space encircled by the yellow tape is reserved for me. Passers-by give me looks of disapproval and walk away, say nothing. Just the way I like it.

CHAPTER 30

THE PHONE RINGS. I am stir-frying tofu and snow peas and cooking brown rice, so I let the answering machine pick up.

"Blossom, dear, I was about to ask you if you could come over for dinner. I called earlier but didn't leave a message. I see you're not home."

I drop everything and grab the phone. "Anna?" She is still on the line. "Come on over. And don't eat dinner. I'm cooking."

After Liza's death, Anna took a year off work. She said she needed to reflect on what mattered in life. She spent most of her time with me. I was twenty-two, certainly old enough to take care of myself. But Anna's friendship got me through some tough times. I know that now.

I continued to live in the house my mother had left me, except I could not think of it as my house. It was always my mother's house. And everything in and around it. But Anna helped me to see things differently. She weeded the flowerbeds with me and reminded me of the stories behind certain perennials.

The pink bleeding heart had been planted as a memento of my first crush on a boy who came to my seventh birthday party. I smile fondly as I recall his chubby cheeks and unruly black hair and especially his mischievous, dark eyes. My girlfriends and I came up with the idea his eyes were smiling from the heart — a rather grown up notion — and we all declared our love for him. He was a bit shorter than other boys his age, and since none of us wished to give him up, we agreed to share him. We held him so he couldn't run away, and took turns kissing him. He squirmed to free himself, and then began shouting until my mother came to his rescue.

The purple Echinacea had been planted one spring when I had whooping cough and was given some Echinacea drops to build up my immune system. The standard Tropicana has been the centrepiece of our front garden for as long as I can remember. It won the prestigious Canadian Rose-Fragrance award the year I was born. The pink peony was David's gift to Liza. And the birdbath with a winged woman was my gift to my mother when she became ill and I wished her to grow wings of strength. Anna reminded me of all the love shared and fond memories infused in every corner of my home.

Soon after returning to work, Anna felt her once exciting job had lost its lustre. Some years later the Department offered an early retirement option and she took it. She was only in her early fifties, and "living life to the fullest" became her mantra. I wondered what that meant.

Most of her time was spent either helping me or taking care of Jane's children. I set a table for two. It would be nice to have company for a change.

"I haven't seen you for a few weeks," I say to her over dinner. "You haven't called."

"It's end-of-semester for you, dear. You have a busy schedule."

I think it a bit odd. We usually have our Sunday evening dinners together, even during the busiest times.

After dinner, we sit with a pot of tea. Anna's hands are wrapped around the steaming mug and only the tips of violet blossoms imprinted on white china peek over her tight grip. This is her favourite cup, matching Liza's.

She reaches into her purse and pulls out a metal flask, the one with her name engraved on the side. She unscrews it and pours some liquor into the cup.

"Rum?" I say.

She nods. "The best. John Watling's Buena Vista. You still have yours?"

"The one you brought me from the Bahamas?" I point to my liquor cabinet. "My collection from your trips is all there. All I have to do is take an inventory of the bottles to recall where you've been."

She laughs and taps the flask with her finger. "They call this the spirit of the Bahamas. I even took a tour of the distillery. They use the water from their own deep well for fermenting."

"Anna," I say gently. "You're diabetic. I thought you gave up *the spirits* long time ago."

She shrugs and sips her tea, then takes the medication from her purse and pops a few pills into her mouth. She looks at me for a long while without a word. Behind her apparently calm façade there is a storm brewing, as if she is mustering the courage to tell me something.

I am tempted to remind her that medication and rum don't exactly go together. I can smell cigarette smoke on her as well. But she seems anxious. No, I better not.

She sets the mug on the coffee table, reaches in her purse, and pulls out an envelope. She gazes at it for a moment, and hands it to me. "Don't open it now. Later. Think about if for a while. Then we'll talk."

I turn the envelope in my hands, tempted to rip it open. It's not like her to be so secretive.

Anna is silent and remote. Her heart shaped face and large brown eyes are void of the usual cheerfulness. The bags under her eyes are puffy and she looks drained as if she has speed-aged over the last couple of weeks. *Has she been crying? No, not Anna. The only time I've seen her cry was when Liza passed away.* Her dark hair, still without grey well into her sixties, is pulled back so tight I can see her skin stretching at the temples.

"Is everything all right with you, Anna? You seem pensive."

She gives me a long intent look. "I don't know how to tell you, dear. But I have to."

My heart is skipping beats. "What is it, Anna?"

"They found a lump. Well, I found it. But you know what I mean."

"No, I don't. I don't know what you mean!" I hear my voice rise to a high pitch. I feel anger welling up in me —anger against Anna. What is she trying to tell me? Why is she doing this to me?

"I'm sorry, dear." She rises and brushes her hands along her pant legs the way she usually does when feeling out of place. Or not knowing what to say.

We stand, staring at each other as the white envelope slides out of my hand and lands softly on the floor.

CHAPTER 31

I TRIED READING IN hopes of getting Anna's lump out of my thoughts, but that didn't work. All I can think about is Anna. How could this be? I cannot imagine her going through what Liza went through. Does Jane know? I need to talk to her about this. But I can't be the one to tell her. It has to be Anna. I am tempted to call Anna just to hear her voice. But how can I? Any conversation that doesn't include the lump is trivial. Perhaps Jane is waiting to hear from me in the same way as I am waiting to hear from her. Perhaps she'll call. Or perhaps she's already called and left a message while I was in the shower. I glance at the answering machine, and there are no messages. Chester! I could talk to him about this, just to get a perspective on the situation, just to get it off my mind. No, I can't call him. He's been cool toward me ever since I missed our dinner. I never did explain, and the more time passes, the harder it is for me to do so. I could ask if he'd go for a late night walk. God knows I am not about to fall asleep. Not after all that's happened today.

I love night walks. Chester knows. He is one of the few people who enjoys them as well. Darkness softens the sharp edges of the world. It soothes the too-harsh colours. The sky recedes, the universe expands and opens possibilities of great adventure: the still air, the coolness, the quietness. Being one of the very few people out on the streets gives me freedom.

Chester and I are buddies. We were getting to be more. We *were* more than that. We used to hold hands and kiss but that was all. Most people we know saw us as a couple. But we were not, not really. I preferred to keep it that way. Sex ruins everything. Now I wonder if I'd been wrong. Perhaps I should've given the relationship a chance. No, I cannot call Chester. Hard to believe how people change — one minute you're a kindred heart, and the next a complete stranger. What would I say to him?

I get out of bed and walk down to the living room. It is close to eleven. I cannot call Jane and wake up her kids. I text her, and the next moment, my phone rings.

"So, you know," Jane says.

"Yes."

A long minute goes by and we remain silent.

Jane clears her throat. "Anna is a tough lady. She'll beat this."

"I don't see how, Jane. After two heart attacks. And she's got diabetes. And high blood pressure."

"She's a fighter, Bloss."

"Sure. So are the soldiers in Afghanistan. And they're dying as we speak."

"That's not fair, Bloss. I want Anna to beat this as much as you. She is in good hands. The Women's Centenary is a great hospital. She has a good doctor. And I don't mean just competent. I mean caring."

"I think she's still smoking. And this evening, she poured a shot of rum in her tea. Then took her pills with it."

Jane sighs. "She's a grown woman. She's always done things her way. You can't change that, now."

After we hang up, I start tiding up, just to keep busy. When I turn on the television, the eleven o'clock news is on, and the National's almost finished. More bombing in Iraq. Eight American soldiers dead. The news moves on to Afghanistan. A Canadian soldier killed by friendly fire. Then on to the Gaza Strip. Hamas fired another missile into Jerusalem. One Israeli dead. Three wounded. Two of them children. Israel retaliated with an onslaught of bombing. A suicide bomber killed six and injured eight people at a girls' religious school in Pishin District of Balochistan. A bomb-laden car exploded in Peshavar killing nine people and injuring three. Death and chaos. Chaos and death. Young lives, wiped out, just like that. Peter Mansbridge announces the upcoming local news. New research on breast cancer is promising. The use of new technology is seen as more effective, less damaging to the immune system.

The local news begins. Another shooting in Toronto. One person dead. Two wounded. It happened at a crowded intersection. No witnesses have come forward. A child missing in the Junction area. An eight-year-old girl. Four days have gone by with no leads. Another announcement of the new research in breast cancer to be revealed during the same news segment is aired. It's illogical — news reporters repeatedly advertising the news they're about to disclose. By the time the news piece is aired, it had been promoted by the newscasters four times. I keep count, fold a finger for each one. It's an old habit I try to overcome. I hide my hands under my sweatshirt just so I could fold my fingers without others noticing. It helps me to keep my hands busy. Now, it helps me to keep my thoughts of Anna at bay.

The feature medical report is finally presented. The reporter explains why the recent method of breast cancer treatment referred to as brachytherapy is becoming more effective. It involves inserting "radioactive seeds" into the affected area of the breast, in the tissue next to the cancerous cells. These implanted "seeds" release medication to the affected area with minimal impact on the immune system. The patient can continue the usual activities, even continue her job while receiving the treatment. The method was being studied along with one of the conventional approaches, "the external beam radiation." The researchers are optimistic — in the case of early detection, brachytherapy could possibly be used as the only treatment.

The new method sounds promising. Anna could be one of the lucky ones. She may be a candidate for the new treatment. No mastectomy for her. No radiation. Not like Liza.

The first time I saw Liza after her breasts had been removed, she told me it didn't matter. The nurse had motioned me to go in. I had opened the door, just a crack. Liza had smiled, just a slant of her eyes and a stretch of her lips, pale as stone. The scene unfolds in my memory.

"It doesn't matter," she whispers.

I nod.

"It doesn't," she says. "I don't need them any more."

It had taken me a few moments to realize what it was that didn't matter and she didn't need.

Next time I walked in she wiped her eyes, quickly, practically scraped her skin off.

"Blossom, dear. It's such a lovely day. Lovely. You look lovely." She was smiling so hard, I thought her skin would crack.

The rash from her chest had spread on to her cheeks and she looked as if she had plastered blush all over her face. It was the turquoise-turban day, the colour of her eyes. Her eyes looked huge. The more weight she lost, the larger they became — reminded me of lagoons we saw some years back when we spent our summer in Pula on the beaches of the Adriatic.

I wished she didn't try so hard to hide her tears. Now I wish I had told her. I wish I could tell Anna it's okay to cry.

I wonder if Anna will try to smile all the time as Liza did. Liza looked so ridiculously cheerful she made me want to scream. So I screamed in my head. Anna may be able to escape the fatigue and diarrhoea and the hair loss. Although, Liza's hair loss hadn't bothered me as much as all else. I think it had to do with turbans. Liza spent so much time choosing the right colour and folding the fabric, she hardly had time for anything else — at least I hoped so.

I hope Anna doesn't have to wear turbans. I turn my attention back to the news.

My body jerks. I open my eyes and realize I had fallen

asleep in my Laz-e-Boy recliner. The television is loud and the commercials are erratic. I wait for them to end. The program I've been watching is most intriguing. I need to see more. But it's David Letterman's face that appears on the screen. The gap between his front teeth is widening with age. Something does not seem right. I flip the channel and go to the next, and the next. I cannot find the program on deep sea fishing.

A quick glance through the TV guide confirms no such program was listed during this time slot. I turn the television off and try to recall the details.

Was it a dream? Yet it was clear, and it was on the same TV screen I am now staring at. I am here in the same chair, and the screen is filled with the cauliflower-like corals. A white statue of a woman is hopping along the ocean floor, from one mound to another. Now fully alert, I remember — it's that stone woman dream that keeps coming back. I glimpsed her breasts in profile, and they reminded me of Benvenuto Cellini's "Cornucopia," the horn of plenty — small pointed breasts of a young woman. I always thought Cellini's title did not fit — the expectation was of a large-breasted, mother-nature type of a female figure — the horn of plenty.

No, I had not seen her face. I am sure of it.

CHAPTER 32

SITTING AT SCULPTURE Hill, my back against *Flower Power*, I take out the tattered scrapbook Liza had put together during the Symposium. I flip through the photos of the sites under construction and try to envision the park as it might have been back then. As the art work grew, it drew crowds from all around.

My mother once said: "When the sculptures were done, they blossomed."

She'd gaze into my eyes with that special motherly look and say: "You were born the spring after the Symposium. I gave you the only name that could come close to doing you justice. First time I laid eyes on you, I felt as if the whole world was in bloom."

From the photos she showed me, and from my memory of the pieces, I knew *Flower Power* did "bloom." And so did *No Shoes*, the same artist's piece, just down the hill. As I sit inside *Flower Power* and gaze into the crisscrossing

I-beams above me, I wonder about the age-old mystery of the healing powers of the pyramids. In ancient Egypt, people who were ill spent the night in a pyramid, in hopes of curing their ailments. A whole new generation of healers focused on alternative medicine has been designing therapeutic tools using pyramidal structures. Could the straddling red girders of the installation I think of as peace symbols also have restorative properties? Hippies used flowers as symbols of peace, as protest against war. What might does *Flower Power* embody? Did the artist hope to heal the nations of violence?

I pass my hand along the gritty surface of the I-beam extending high over me. When I was a child, I spent many afternoons here with my mother. It all comes back to me in a flash. *My name is Blossom*, I hear my own childish voice. *And I can lean my back on "Flower Power" if I want to.* My eyes land on the yellow tape cordoning off the sculpture now for many years deemed unsafe to park users.

"Some rules are made to be broken," Liza would say, smiling mischievously.

I knew what she meant. When I was in grade school and didn't feel like going in, I'd fake a stomach ache.

"Being a civil servant may not be the most exciting job in the world, but it has its advantages. Time to dip into my sick-days account," my mother would say and take a day off work.

We'd go to the museum or the art gallery, or we'd shop and have lunch at a quaint restaurant. Every once in a while she'd ask me if I was feeling better. "Still a little queasy," was my usual reply, as I gulped down delicious morsels prepared by a mysterious chef who knew the magic recipes for Fettuccine Alfredo and Baked Alaska. Many years later I realized just how transparent my act must have been.

At times I wonder what formative value those days instilled in me. Did I grow up as a spoiled brat or an inconsiderate user of other people's good will? And after some soul-searching, I have come to realize there was no harm done. We simply needed a break from everyday routine, and she made it special.

As my mother's illness progressed and she lay in the hospital with a different colour turban each day — she said life was meant to be lived in colours, she tried to impart some of her philosophy on, in her words, that precious commodity called life. She knew she wouldn't be there for me much longer. We both did. Sometimes we pretended she would not only beat the demigod we called Hades, but she would go on forever as if immortal, as immortal as Demeter.

When I was a child, she used to read me stories from Greek myth. Once she was bedridden, I made up my own plots and played out my own scenarios. I played the game of Demeter and Persephone — mother-daughter, Liza and Blossom. I tried to make a deal with Hades.

"Take me, instead," I'd say to him. "I am the daughter, aren't I? You did take Persephone, not Demeter." I guess he wasn't listening. Or perhaps I wasn't convincing enough.

My mother and I used to sit at this very spot, and she would tell me that the sculptures celebrate the hippie era. They instil the notion of the free spirit. I can still hear her words: "They have colour, vitality, life of their own." She used to bring the same scrapbook and explain that di Suvero's installations are painted a vibrant red to symbolize the spilt blood of the soldiers fighting in Vietnam. Now, the red is a bit faded, but the colour is still there.

I flip to the newspaper clipping she had slipped into a clear plastic jacket. "See, *No Shoes* had four free-swinging logs and people used to swing on it. They called it, taking a ride on the sculpture."

She'd go on to explain that this was the sculptor's way of encouraging people to interact with his pieces.

The year before she died, the sculptures were declared unsafe and were cordoned off as a precaution. The paint was peeling and the City received a number of complaints. The top part of *Flower Power* was removed, as well as the swinging logs of *No Shoes*. My mother took it hard—as if a friend was ill—and wrote a poem she pasted in her scrapbook. I open the page and read it, although I almost know it by heart:

Flower Power and No Shoes
by Liza Grant

Born of steel. Rising from the barrel of the gun,
you crown Sculpture Hill. Sentinel to relentless
    strife,
call to peace, end to mindless war.

Your youthful beauty ordained by human toil,
withered by scorching sun. Skin orange-red
as soldier's open wound. As petals of peonies.

Now blistered, the open wound harbours the
     hopes
of the flower child. Not what the jaundiced eye
can see, but the ideals of the just and driven,
chanting their call of freedom.

After my talk with Joan of Arc, who in the
     birthing pains
that gave you life paced the rutted paths of
     napalmed huts,
cradling her sister's child swaddled in ribboned
     flesh and skin,
I paid my visit to you and asked: Why so forlorn?

On this morning of frosty air, crisp with hope, you
     answered:
I am off limits to passers-by, fenced off for safety.
Mothers with strollers, joggers, and dog walkers,
point to the crown removed from my temple,
unlearned of causes that have danced about me.

I'm Mark di Suvero's *Flower Power*, a construct
of steel cables under tension: Interlocking triangles
and orange I-beams — a monument to the hippie
     era,
now affronted as if I were Rochdale.

No Shoes is my barefoot sister, ambling down
the hill. Same orange I-beams, same anchors.
Swinging on steel cables, four wooden logs
lovers once rode on — are no longer there.

Mothers with strollers, joggers and dog walkers,
point to her bare feet calloused from blazing sun
and winter frost, unlearned of the ideals she
    stood for.

You know us. We're two of the standing
seven, atop Sculpture Hill.

One of the people in the photo from the newspaper
clipping looks a bit like Chester. I still have not talked to
him—I have not mustered the courage to explain. Deep
down I think I want him to give up on me. Yet, the little
voice in my head nags and wants him to call me. Hopes
he'd call me.

I drop the last report on the stack of the already graded ones. Within a few hours I have marked one whole
class. An inner glow that goes beyond my satisfaction
with my students' good work fills me. I know it has to do
with my being here, at Sculpture Hill, sitting on my old
quilt, back against the red I-beam of *Flower Power*.

CHAPTER 33

"HELLO, BLOSSOM," CHESTER says, looking at me as if he has something on his mind he is reluctant to tell me.

An image of a lobster being dropped into a pot of boiling water pops in my mind. The lobster is really me, the squealing and all—all inside my head. My face is burning. I turn slowly, as if I were rolled over by a large metal spatula, my nose wrinkled up, shoulders scrunched.

"God, Chester. You'd never believe. No point explaining. Honest. I wouldn't believe me if I didn't know it's true."

He laughs. His white teeth are as perfect as Chiclets. I catch myself looking for the sparkle of a diamond—a scene I recall from an old James Bond movie—but it doesn't happen. Everything about him is handsome as if he has stepped off a movie set. Is he immune to aging? And he is a few years older than me. Hard to believe. It must be some secret male genes.

"All right, all right. Since you feel so bad, you're forgiven," he says, chuckling.

He is behind me in the line-up at the University library waiting to check out a stack of books under his arm. I step up to the counter with my pile of research material. Another station opens up, and Chester is done before me. By the time my books are checked out, he is gone.

I head for the office and keep myself busy for a while. A bit later I walk back to the library hoping to see him there. Then I mosey over to the cafeteria where we often had lunch, and sit at our table. I spread out some old exams and work on compiling a make-up test, at times imagining when I look up, he'd be standing next to me, or looking over my shoulder with that mocking smile that usually makes me laugh. Then I imagine he might walk in by chance, the way we happened to see each other earlier on at the library. I thought he'd show up, somehow.

Another week goes by, and our paths don't cross. When we finally bump into each other on campus, we exchange pleasantries, brief complaints about the end-of-semester deadlines, and that is it. As if the time we did not see each other had turned into a gigantic block of ice that wedged itself between us, cold and impenetrable. Earlier today, I said to Jane: "I really miss those late night walks. Chester's the only one who also enjoys them. Or used to enjoy them."

Jane and I had an early morning meeting and shared our desk for about an hour before it and some time after. Then we thought we might as well have lunch together and share the table at the cafeteria since we're so used to it.

"What are you afraid of, Bloss?" Jane asks, chewing on her roast beef sandwich.

"I don't know what you're talking about," I say and take a bite of my falafel pita.

"He's a nice guy. Unless you don't like him. Then it's different. But if you do, what's stopping you?"

"Just not ready for commitment, I guess. And neither is he." Then I tell Jane about the huge block of ice that has set itself between us. "He really is a very cold person, you know."

She laughs. I know what the laughter means—that twinge of sarcasm. It has to do with being single at my age. And about that same block of ice, or that guy who is in reality a snowman with a candy heart, I've told Jane about a number of times in the years we've known each other. The block of ice that, in Jane's words, sets itself between me and any man who tries to get close.

I want to remind her about the two failed marriages and the three children she's raising all on her own. But I know she has no regrets. She would do it all over again. "Those kids make life worth living," she has told me many times.

"It's end of semester. You and I should take a trip this summer. Bring the kids with us," I say. "Show them the beaches in Pula. The island of Pag. See the beautiful Adriatic. You haven't seen beauty 'til you see the Adriatic."

"Sure, Bloss. Cash their educational fund?"

I blush in embarrassment. How right she is.

"Besides, you're changing the subject, Bloss. Next you'll tell me we should go swim naked with the dolphins. We could do all that. So could you and Chester."

"Chester?"

"That *is* what I just said. Why don't you give him a call? Instead of waiting to *bump* into him."

"I don't really think he's interested in the Adriatic."

"Sure Blossom. You can play your games." She takes a large bite of her sandwich and gives me that look of hers. "Just for the record, I think he is interested. Very interested."

CHAPTER 34

IT IS EARLY morning, the best time for jogging in High Park. The sun has just risen, its rays spilling gently over the treetops. From my home on Gothic Avenue, I pass by a cluster of high-rise condos on the north side of Bloor Street. They are strung along the subway line that links the condo dwellers to the city core. As I cross Bloor Street and proceed southward on Colborne Lodge Drive, the crisp morning air is invigorating and I am peaceful—all tension and schedules left behind. With every stride, the buzz of rush-hour traffic along Bloor behind me subsides, until I veer off the road and enter my refuge under the tall canopy of the park. The farther I run, the more muted the city noise becomes until I will myself to tune it out and listen to the gentle thud of my running shoes on the damp wood chips covering the path along the Spring Creek nature trails that loop through the Black Oak Savannah. I wish the forest would go on and on, but soon I find myself crossing one paved road and then another and looping back toward Sculpture Hill, drawing me like a cathedral draws the pious.

The shade remains deep over Hubert Dalwood's "Temple." I clasp my hands as if I were a praying mantis and bow respectfully before gliding sideways into the sculpture. Weaving among the stainless steel cylinders, I remove the mother-of-pearl barrette holding my ponytail and the open metal clasp is now a baton I tap on the convex surface of each pipe of the installation.

The cylinders, still covered in dew, make faint musical sounds. I wait for the resonance to dissipate. When Glenn Gould was a child, my mother once told me, he liked to strike piano keys and listen to their decay. I draw the clasp along the stainless steel poles as if they were piano keys and wait for the vibration to evolve into thin humming I hear long after it seems to have faded away.

There is just enough room to slowly edge through. I close my eyes and make believe I am in a maze. Not any hedge-maze I have seen in parks and read about. I am in Castlewellan's Peace Maze in Northern Ireland, the largest in the world. I have been hoping to visit it since it opened some ten years ago. Its design resembles the human brain, symbolic of the thought processes in search of peace. It is made up of six thousand yews, trees that can live up to four thousand years. The maze was planted to teach people how to face choices and deal with disillusionments and compromises. If Anna were to find herself in this maze, which way would she turn?

I open my eyes. This is not a maze, I remind myself. This sculpture is, and has been for a long while, my problem-solving place. It is also a favourite spot for children as well as small dogs that seem to play hide-go-seek with their owners. I visit the "Temple" during quiet times.

I place the barrette in my pocket and pass my palms over the dewy metallic surface. Here, among the cylinders I make believe are as high as the sky, time seems to stop. I can pretend to be somewhere else, be someone else. Solutions come to me in this world of my imagining. In this world where the sky is the limit.

If I were Anna, which path would I take? Suddenly, I am faced with choices as rigid as the steel of the pipes surrounding me. Whichever route I consider leads to a dead-end.

The medical terminology I try to expel from my thoughts whizzes through my head and fills every crevice. It leaves no room for imagining. Anna found out that her cancer is more advanced than first thought. Full mastectomy offers a glimmer of hope — this would be part of a local treatment. Anna also needs a systemic treatment. What type would it be, chemotherapy, hormone therapy, immunotherapy? Is there any new research I don't know about, Anna doesn't know about? Which treatment would get to the cancer cells that may have spread beyond the breast? Is there any hope?

Would Anna undergo the systemic treatment before surgery to shrink the tumour? Is this called neoadjuvant therapy? With all the research, not much has changed. Liza was weaving through this maze not long ago. It has been close to two decades, yet it feels like yesterday. I can hear Liza's voice resonating in my thoughts:

"Blossom dear, you need to go home. Get some rest.

You can't spend all you time here with me, in the hospital room.

"Blossom dear, go get some dinner. The cafeteria isn't too bad, I hear. Not too bad for hospital food.

"Blossom dear. There's life outside of this hospital. You need to go out with your friends. It's Saturday night … it's Sunday night …"

But this is now Anna speaking, I say to myself. Yet the words are Liza's. Even Anna's voice is beginning to sound like Liza's. I can no longer tell them apart. Do lifelong friendships do that to people, make them sound alike?

I slip out of the "Temple," out of my make-believe labyrinth, retie my shoe laces, gather my hair back into a ponytail, and resume my morning jog. I survey my surroundings through Chester's eyes. The sun is clambering over the tree crowns, he would've said.

Last Christmas he gave me the *Amazing Book of Mazes*. It seemed odd, as I often think of Chester as a puzzle. For instance, I never told him about my interest in mazes. Yet he gave me a book on the subject. It was signed by the author: "To Blossom by Adrian Fisher." Chester did not include his name anywhere. It seemed impersonal. I wish he had signed his name somewhere in the book. That would've told me he wanted me to think of him each time I open it. But he didn't. So I decided he didn't want me to think about him. Yet I did, still do. For the past six months, we saw each other a few times a week—went for late night walks, early morning walks, had dinners, lunches, saw movies. He has not called since I missed our dinner. It has been two weeks and a day now.

I continue jogging toward the arbour past Grenadier

Restaurant. I hear the peacocks' call and walk down the hill to the park zoo. I recall its symbolism in religion, folk tales, and myth. Buddhists ascribe profound meaning to the bird's ability to feed on poisonous plants with no ill effects—the ability to thrive in the face of peril—and the bird stands for rejuvenation and eternal life. A peacock is fanning its train and strutting around a peahen, and I think it a good omen. They mate for life, and are seen as symbol of eternal love. Feng Shui suggested the peacock's one hundred eyes can protect people from disaster. Could they also protect Anna? Or help with her recovery?

Ever since I found out about Anna's illness, I have been holding a grudge against her as if she wants to die the same death as Liza just so she can feel what Liza had felt and in some absurd way get close to her again. As if they could have been any closer than they already were. As if she is eager to join Liza in eternity. I have been feeling let down by Anna. This sense of betrayal has been creeping into my bones as if Anna has made a secret pact with the angel of death and has already said her last confession.

CHAPTER 35

"OVER HERE, BLOSS!" Jane calls out as she continues to jog in place next to the bench by the water fountain, just down the hill from the administration building in High Park.

I had already jogged through the park all the way down to Queensway, turned north to follow the path along Grenadier Pond, and veered up the hill toward our bench. Up the slope, Jane's grey leggings, her purple shirt with white sleeves, and black hair cropped short, remind me of some rare gigantic orchid that has escaped an eccentric botanist and is running away to freedom, the way Jane has escaped her controlling husbands and boyfriends and has maintained the independence I so much admire.

This is our usual meeting place. The view looking west into the valley encompasses trees and shrubs and rockery gardens, and the maple leaf centrepiece by Grenadier Pond. Across the pond, the steep embankment is capped by a ridge with a row of houses sprouting on it as if they were some exotic mushrooms.

Jane waves and I quicken my pace.

"Bloss, you're late," Jane calls out smiling, and I wonder if Anna is also late, too late for any treatments to be effective.

We hug and head toward Grenadier Restaurant. Jane takes me under the arm and tells me how glad she is we finally managed to get together. Her musical voice blends with the faint ringing of the bells at Saint Joan of Arc on Bloor Street just east of Keele, and we both pause and listen. Jane and I had been attending mass and fundraisers there with Liza and Anna since we could remember, although none of us is Catholic.

We find a table bordering the patio. Jane sits on the wooden bench facing the restaurant and I look over the entrance to the sunken gardens.

A few tables from us in the corner of the patio, some mothers with their babies in strollers are having a cheerful discussion. An assortment of stuffed toys and rattles and baby bottles and blankets in various crayon-colours makes me smile. Jane spots a friend among them and waves to her excitedly. I am drawn in by the view looking south beyond the gardens.

The scene freezes in my mind and I see it as a painting by a child. The motion of Jane's hand leaves a trail I conjure into a rainbow arched above the Gardiner Expressway that streaks just below the horizon and binds Lake Ontario to the sky. Jane's hand waves again and the painting in my mind's eye is smeared, as if it were a splash of raindrops swept aside by a windshield wiper.

Jane's voice brings me back to reality. "I haven't seen

you since the semester ended. It's been three weeks. Where have you been?"

She goes on about the end-of-semester rush. Words flow from her as if they were dandelion seeds scattered by the wind. Her cheerfulness fills the space around us and I nudge my worry away from the present, as if it belongs somewhere outside of this terrace with tables shaded by umbrellas and smiling faces milling about.

I soon realize her exuberance is a put-on. Avoiding the subject we've both thinking about cannot go on forever. Suddenly she is pensive. Her eyebrows gather and her question surprises me, and I think it even surprises her. "Are you gonna teach a summer course?" she asks, and I know she is still trying to avoid talking about Anna.

"No," I sigh. "I need to spend some time …"

"Yes, I know," she cuts in. "You've always taught summer courses. I just thought it'd be good for you. Unless you're planning a trip."

"No trips. Not this summer."

Her words are rattling in my head. Jane, who usually tries to convince me to take the summer off, is now trying to get me to teach summer courses? Although I wish I had committed to at least one class. As much as I wanted the marking finished, the moment the grades were in, I felt a void.

"Old habits die hard," she says good-humouredly as if she's clairvoyant. "I just thought, to keep your mind off things."

A few moments later two tall glasses of ice tea are set on our table. Jane slurps through the straw loudly just to be funny.

"All day breakfast?" the waitress asks.

We always have breakfast for lunch.

I wrap my fingers around the glass and relish the coolness. Jane finally broaches the subject. "I know you're spending every moment with Anna. But you've got to put things in perspective,"

I nod and say nothing. The silence is more telling than all the words, and we both know it.

"Remember Bloss, this is out of your hands."

"I know."

"Anna's had a heart condition all her life. All her life, Bloss. It's not anything new."

"She's in a no-win situation, Jane. She needs a full mastectomy. She needs treatments. Her heart will not withstand surgery." Then I catch myself. Why am I telling Jane what she already knows?

"You can't say that. She's a tough cookie. She'll make it."

"Miracles happen. Right?" I take a deep breath. I cannot keep this in any more: "She still carries the flask with her," I say.

Jane shrugs. "Ah! Is it the spirit of the Bahamas? Or the spirit of Mexico? Or is it just plain, old gin?" She looks at me for a long moment. "Have to hand it to her. I've never seen her even tipsy. She's got her own *spirit*, Bloss. She does what she wants. Always has. Who's to say how life turns out, no matter how carefully you live it?"

Our plates arrive. I lift the three strips of bacon off my plate and place them on hers.

"Bacon doesn't count as meat," she says, chuckling "You should just have it."

After a while Jane balances the last piece of bacon on the tip of her fork. "Sure you don't want it?"

We both laugh, and I am reminded how much I missed her the last few weeks. She is one of the few people with whom I can laugh like that, wholeheartedly.

"Okay," Jane says, "it's early afternoon. I'll come with you to Anna's house for a bit. Check if there are any chores to get done. And after, we'll do a bit of shopping, get some dinner, then catch a movie."

We find Anna in her garden, in the midst of purple summer phlox and white alyssum and bees and butterflies. She tells us that her surgery has already been scheduled —it took only a month after her diagnosis.

The gate squeaks and a tall elderly man pokes his head over the black wrought iron scrolls, his bushy white hair billowing in the breeze. "Is this a good time?" he says.

After a long moment, Anna says: "Well, I'll be. If it isn't James."

"Am I interrupting?" he says.

Anna gets up and walks halfway toward the gate, and Jane and I follow. He looks familiar. I recall that name. Then it all comes back to me in a flash—he is the cop who used to investigate the missing marble. I recall him dropping in on Liza a few times. Anna did not like him much.

"You come as a friend or a foe?" Anna says. "As a friend, you're welcome."

"Always a friend," he says with a crooked smile.

"In that case, what are you waiting for? Come on in!"

He pushes the gate and clambers along the path,

supporting himself with a cane and limping on one leg, as if he were pulling great weight behind him. He shakes Anna's hand.

"You haven't aged a day," he says.

"Neither have you," she says and they break out in laughter.

Anna arches her eyebrows. "It's been, what, twenty years? Since Liza's funeral. What happened to your leg?"

"Got shot in the hip. Long time ago. I'm retired now."

"That's good news. Now we can all breathe easier," she says with a smirk. "Take the load off. Have a seat."

"Correct me if I'm wrong," he says, looking at Jane and me. "Blossom and Jane. Right? You were in your teens when I used to visit Liza. You've grown up."

"We saw you at Liza's funeral," Jane and I say in unison. "We were in our twenties, then."

He nods and stares into the distance. "I meant, I remember you ... when you were still very young."

He looks up into the towering crowns of the white pines in Anna's yard. "I always remembered this part of Toronto. This urban forest. When my wife passed away, I sold the house and decided to move to a condo. This is the first place I came to look. And here I am."

"So, you're a neighbour, now?" Anna says.

He nods. "Just around the corner. That new building on Quebec."

Jane asks Anna to join us for a dinner and a movie, but she declines and insists that Jane and I go on with our plans.

"Would you like to watch the sunset with me?" Anna says to James. "It drops magically into the valley below."

CHAPTER 36

O VER THE NEXT few weeks, Anna has her house cleaned from top to bottom and her garden weeded, and her windows washed, and each time Jane and I offer to help, she has already arranged a maintenance crew to ensure that every corner of her home is as tidy as it could be.

A few days before her surgery, as we sit in her living room and sip tea, I ask her about James. Why did he come to see her?

She ho-hums and says: "He was fond of Liza. But he's a cop. Retired or not. It's in his blood. Sniffing for clues. He was suspecting David, then."

"I know that much," I say. "But why now? Why did he come to see you?"

"I'm still trying to figure that out. He's been going for walks around here, enjoying the best tree canopy in Toronto, he says. That's why he moved to the area. And when he saw us in the garden, he thought he'd drop by.

He and I didn't see eye to eye back then. I didn't like him dropping in on Liza for any excuse he could find. Looking for leads. Now, I see no harm. It's kinda nice to chat about the old times."

"Did anyone find out what happened to that marble?"

She shoots me a pensive look. "Blossom, my girl. Leave the past in the past."

"Anna, the way you say that makes me think you know something."

"It wasn't David."

The evening before surgery, when Jane and I walk into Anna's room, she sits up in bed, wraps the housecoat around her shoulders and says: "Everything will be as it should."

She goes over a list of things for us — and tells us that she also left all these instructions written down. She has the maintenance company taking care of the house, and all we need to do is pick up the mail and keep an eye out that everything is in order.

Jane and I exchange looks but say nothing. *How long is she planning on staying here?*

"Don't forget to take the rose, Bloss, when you leave tonight," Anna reminds me, although we just arrived.

I have been keeping up Liza and Anna's tradition of planting spent miniature roses in a corner of my garden and have been rewarded by a profusion of colour year after year.

Anna takes Jane's hand and holds it in hers. "You

should get back so the sitter can go home. Kiss the children for me, will you, dear?"

Jane kisses Anna on both cheeks and they hug for a long while. "I'll see you in the morning. You're the greatest. And those kids of mine adore you."

Jane's voice sounds as if she is speaking under water and her eyes are misty but she keeps her emotions in. With her palm, Anna caresses Jane's cheek. Her lips begin to move as if she is about to say something she has held in for a very long time. Then she starts taking short breaths. Jane and I reach for the call button but Anna stops us. "No nurse, my dears. I'm perfectly fine." Anna reminds Jane again about the three children waiting at home and urges her to leave.

"Give the kids a hug for me," I say to Jane. "I'll stay for a while."

Anna's eyes remain glued to the open door as Jane's footsteps fade down the hall. Her lips are moving but the words are silent. I think she is saying, "My sweet, sweet darling girl," but I am not sure. I take her hand in mine, and we sit in silence.

The nurse comes in to take Anna's blood pressure and temperature. She is chatting incessantly as if being chirpy is a prescription she dispenses liberally to her patients. She has light brown eyes, an upturned nose, and her short blond hair is flipped up in back. Her smile creases etched into the thickly powdered face cause to her to appear ageless — she could be Anna's age or mine or somewhere in between — and I wonder what she would look like if she stopped smiling. She hands Anna a small paper cup with pills, and she pops them in her mouth, all at once. Then she takes a few sips of water. The nurse coaxes her to down the rest of the water. She fusses over Anna, plumps the pillow around her, and pats her on the shoulder. "I won't be here in the morning. Another nurse will check in on you. Remember, nothing to eat or drink after ten tonight."

I prop my hand against my head like a visor to block out the smiling. When I look up, the nurse has left. Anna removes her housecoat. Her pink hospital gown makes her cheeks glow and sets off her dark hair pulled in a low bun. Her eyes are deep and she reminds me of a religious icon.

"I've never seen you wearing pink," I say. "That shade looks amazing on you."

She laughs. "Hospitals do that to you. Make you fashionable."

She gets out of bed, tiptoes to the open door, looks down the hallway to one side and the other, then comes back in. She opens the drawer of her night table and grabs her purse, then tiptoes toward the bathroom, all-the-while glancing at me conspiratorially, as if I am part of her secret plot.

"No, Anna ...," I start to say, but she disappears into the bathroom.

Before closing the door, she says: "If anybody comes, just tell them I'll be out in a minute."

I wring my hands, then drop them in my lap and try to look calm.

A few minutes later she opens the door, and the scent of air freshener and cigarette smoke escapes into the room. She leaves the fan on, shuts the bathroom door, and sits on the bed.

"I can smell the cigarette, Anna."

She shrugs. "What are they gonna do to me? Send me home?"

I take mental snapshots of her. Not remembering her every gesture would mean I was letting go of her. Or is it the other way around? Why am I doting on her every move, every word? Jane said Anna is going to make it. Anna is a survivor.

Anna rubs her face with her palms and, when she removes her hands, she is suddenly cheerful as if she has wiped off some ancient worry. Then she says: "End of the Long Day." A mischievous smile dances on her face. She waggles her head from side to side, challenging me. We both know the game — we have been playing it most of our lives. The title, "End of the Long Day," is familiar. I just have to place it, link it to the appropriate piece of art. Then the images surface: the setting sun glinting through the branches as if igniting the forest on fire, burning bush in the foreground, contrasted by the deep blue reflections of the water.

I play along. "We saw it together ... A few years back. Opening night, Gallery 1313, right here in Toronto." I pause. She knows I guessed. I can tell by the pleased look on her face, pleased with herself for infusing me with a love of art.

"Shinya Kumazawa," I say, taking on the voice of an art critic. "His unassuming, bashful demeanour a disguise for such an outburst of primordial images in his art. His paintings encompassing the turbulence of van Gogh, the ruggedness of Tom Thomson. His stomping ground that of young James MacDonald."

She nods. "I regretted not purchasing it. Remember? I took time to decide and it was sold."

"I never forgot that painting either, Anna."

"And why am I telling you this, Bloss?"

Now she catches me off guard, and I see a lecture coming.

"Carpe diem," Anna says. "Carpe diem, amore mia."

She loves Latin phrases and often combines them with a few words she knows in Italian or other languages she has learned from tourist guide books and classes she has been taking for as long as I can recall. She is radiating wisdom, loving every moment of spreading her sermon, thickly and generously, especially for me. I raise my eyebrows, prop my chin with my elbow, and give her the look. I used to give Liza that same look when she lectured.

My role in the game of guessing I inherited from Liza. Except, Anna and Liza used to play these games with the enthusiasm of an inventor — guessing the titles of paintings, moments they shared from art exhibits, characters in movies or books or plays. I never could fully take Liza's place. And when it came to lectures, I could only play the part I have always played. The lectures have always been given for my benefit. They still are, although I am middle age. My only defense now is a look of dismay.

"Don't let life pass you by, Bloss," Anna says.

I roll my eyes and sigh. I've heard this same advice from Anna ever since my mother died.

"You need to live a little, my girl."

Looking exasperated is all I can do under the circumstances.

"Don't get trapped into that superstitious fable about the lovers in your family. Dying. Everybody dies. We get to be born. And we get to die. Simple as that. Liza lived life to the fullest. And so have I. Some things are beyond our control."

I wish she were not trying to console me, when I should be the one comforting her. But I am at a loss for words. Everything I do is somehow measured against Liza's death. The events are timed as before and after. The lessons I should draw from them. As every other time, I'm speechless. Even now, the evening before Anna's surgery, I seem unable to offer solace.

I am about to say, "This is not a fair game, Anna." But I can't say it. Instead, I plaster on one of those smiles that can absorb just about anything.

"You were a happy child, Bloss. But after your friend died, the young boy, you changed."

"He wasn't a boy. He was sixteen."

"Liza and I tried everything. Including counselling. But you lost your happiness. Your innocence. You've got to find it again, my girl."

"And he didn't just die. He committed suicide."

"And you think it had something to do with you?"

"I should've been there for him. Should've seen it coming."

"Are you being fair, Bloss? Do you really believe that?"

I shrug. "I don't know. All I know is that I can never look at a bleeding heart without thinking of him."

"You were just being children, Bloss. Funny — I never realized the bleeding heart had that effect on you. Maybe you should take it out of your garden and give it to someone if you can't throw it out. Put it behind you. And this whole thing about being unlucky in love makes no sense.

He was a friend, not a boyfriend. Sweet kid. But troubled. Got into drugs. That is such a difficult age."

"I can't do that, Anna. I can't give the bleeding heart away."

"Ok, ok," she says. "But you've got to take things in stride. Some things are out of your control. Promise me you'll do that."

I know she is right. I feel trapped in some gloom and I can't figure out why. I wish I could free myself. "I promise," I say.

"And that young man of yours, Chester. Why not give the relationship a chance?"

"He's an artist. I said I'd never date an artist." The words slip out before I can stop myself.

"Here we go again. I thought we just dealt with that. Your friend wanted *to become* an artist. His death was not your fault. You need to accept that. Besides, I thought Chester was a colleague at the university."

"He is."

"I don't recall you saying you'd never date an artist."

"It was a long time ago."

"Let go of the past, Bloss." She gives me that motherly look.

I get up from my chair and move to her bedside. I am still the child in this family, what is left of it. Anna is all that is left. And Jane.

Anna says: "What kind of artist? You never told me Chester's an artist."

"A painter. He paints reptiles. Mostly turtles and crocodiles."

"Oh!" is all she says. Triumph flashes across her face.

Her eyes twinkle and I know she is glad. Glad he is a paint-er of reptiles? But I am not surprised.

"You remember my favourite song?" she says.

"Who could forget it? *Superstition*."

She nods. "Stevie Wonder. The one and only. If you won't listen to me, listen to Stevie."

It's my turn to ask questions.

"What is your favourite tree?" I say.

Anna perks up, smoothes her hair and straightens out her housecoat, and I know she's up for the game.

"Ginkgo biloba, of course," she says.

We both knew what the answer would be. Over the years we have observed the ginkgo biloba saplings in High Park grow into majestic specimens. We have a men-tal map of all the ginkgos in the park and are thrilled they have become widely used for city landscaping in the past few decades. Not that we do not appreciate other species. We love the oaks and the maples that endow the city with a cooling shade, and are saddened to see them replaced with dwarf specimens which do not contribute to the tree canopy Toronto is so fortunate to have.

But this is a game, and when I ask why ginkgo is her favourite, she rhymes off the reasons. "Because it's a living fossil, dating back two hundred and seventy million years, and, of course, predating the Jurassic age, the era of the dinosaurs, but then you know that."

I nod, smugly — she loves the ritual.

Then I come down with the punch line. "Did you know six ginkgo trees survived the atomic bomb in Hiro-shima? They were in the epicentre, and still returned to budding shortly after the blast. They're alive today."

Her eyes widen. "You got me. You really got me, Bloss. That is what I call a golden nugget of knowledge."

I spread out the photos of the surviving trees. I printed them in colour. She traces her fingers over each crown and smiles. Her cheeks are flushed. She is happy. And I am thrilled I could make her happy at least for a moment.

"I'll leave them here next to you. And tomorrow morning before the surgery, we'll look at them again, together."

I pull a handful of ginkgo leaves out of a zip lock bag in my purse, lay them in her hand, and press my palm to hers. The leaves are cool and supple and seem alive between our palms. "Hold them in your hands tonight." She smiles with wonderment.

"You're a ginkgo biloba, Anna. Tomorrow, when you're in the epicentre, I want you to remember that. You're a ginkgo biloba."

She studies my features and says, quietly: "Non quo sed quomodo. Not what we do but how."

I know this phrase well. Mother Teresa used it as a reminder of what matters in life — everything you do, you do it with love. It has been a motto Anna and Liza had lived by. It is also a guiding principle of this hospital, engraved in the plaque of the tall white marble sculpture *Femina*, gracing the lobby.

We hug tightly and the room is silent, and only the ticking of the wall clock is a reminder for me to leave and for Anna to embrace sleep before her big day.

I exit through the front entrance so I can pass by *Femina*. Her serenity always puts me at ease. I wave an inconspicuous goodbye to her and will her to take care of Anna.

CHAPTER 37

I TURN THE lights off in my bedroom and saunter down to the living room. There is no point in going to bed. It's the evening before Anna's surgery and I will not sleep. I lie on the sofa and find myself watching an old black and white movie on television. To my surprise, one of the characters is named Blossom. She is a teenage girl in a frilly dress and curls, all prim and proper, talking wisely with, oh my and such, as if she were a matron already. It *is* boring, but there is nothing else on. I need to sort out my thoughts about Anna.

I hear my name being called. "I'm here," I answer. My voice is slurred, still asleep, as my mind begins to stir. I jump up and the screen is all snowy, making a shushing noise. I press the "off" button on the remote control. It's five in the morning. I got some sleep and have plenty of time for breakfast before getting to the hospital. The surgery is scheduled for eight.

I am light-hearted. The dread that's been weighing me down has lifted as if the sun has burned through the fog. And then I remember the dream.

Drifting below the ocean surface, I peer through a transparent vastness filled with dead whitish coral floating about—ripped out of the seabed by fishing nets bottom trawling. I am weightless, breathing freely and coasting down to the ocean floor. My bare foot touches rock and I spring up as if I were made of rubber, and as I bounce among the hills and valleys of the seabed carpeted by colonies of swaying, living coral, my vision is sharp, far reaching as if I am looking through binoculars. I wish to remain here, among the living coral, far below the graveyard of dead ones hovering above me. Behind a tall clump of coralline, a woman, white as if made of stone, appears. She is gliding from one mound to another, like me, propelled by the buoyancy of the sea. In my dream, I know this woman.

A clump of dead coral is descending, until it lands on the rocky bottom. Another follows. And another. They are now settling all around us, like mini parachutes. The stone woman reaches out with her white hand and catches one. She sets the clump back into the ocean floor and the coral turns a brilliant pink. She grasps another piece of dead coral and plants it, then catches another one, and yet another, her flips, dives, and leaps a graceful dance. She pushes each stem back into the sea bed, and each piece changes into shades of crimson, blue and purple, radiating under the water. It's spectacular. And each time the coral glows I know it has taken root. I try to see her face, but she does not turn toward me. She does not see me. I try to call, but my voice is silent—a subdued gurgling of the bubbles displaces speech.

As I stand over the stove looking into the boiling water in a stainless steel pot, I drop a handful of organic oatmeal and some chunks of apples and the mush bubbles just like my silenced words in the ocean. The dream replays in my thoughts, scenes as vivid as if segments of a movie.

I realize it's six fifteen. I gulp down my oatmeal and rush to the subway, hoping to arrive at the hospital by seven the latest. The June air is fragrant with spring bloom and my short walk along Gothic Avenue is invigorating.

Scenes from my dream play on, the colours of transplanted corals unseen by anyone but me. They must be a good omen.

Life is meant to be lived in colours, Liza's voice surfaces in my thoughts. I pick up my pace, inhale the morning air. *Anna will make it. Anna will be fine.*

CHAPTER 38

IN ONE HAND, Chester is holding a cardboard tray with three cups, and in the other, a paper bag of baked goods with a cranberry muffin perched at the top. His back is turned to the Starbucks counter, tucked in the south corner of the University Avenue entrance to Women's Centenary Hospital. Our eyes lock, and we stare at each other in silence.

He nods. "Blossom."

His voice is croaky and his eyes are solemn. He is frozen in the concourse between the two sets of doors, one leading to the street and the other to the hospital. The doors open and close as passers-by hold them for each other and people glide in and out as if seven in the morning is happy hour at the hospital.

With his back, he pushes open the door to the hospital and holds it for me. "Here, Bloss," he murmurs and clears his throat and his second, "Here, Bloss," is just as hoarse.

I take the paper bag out of his hand, and as we enter, he motions to the muffins. "The cranberry one's for you. And I have cranberry tea for you here."

A string of questions — what is he doing here, and how did he know I would be here — gel in my head but I cannot bring myself to ask him. We walk side by side, quietly, and I realize he knows the way to Anna's room.

Jane is leaning against the wall, next to Anna's closed door. She rushes towards me and enfolds me in an embrace. *Jane is not a 'huggy' type.* I give her a puzzled look and head for the door.

She steps in front of me. "No, Bloss."

"Is she being prepped already? I thought they'd start at eight."

Jane takes my hand in hers and I think it strange. She is usually not a touchy-feely person either. She's a talker, a cheerful one, an optimist. Seeing her looking sombre makes me queasy.

Chester sets the cardboard tray with cups on a chair. He and Jane exchange knowing looks. *What are they hiding from me?*

Chester shuffles his feet. "I think you should tell her, Jane."

"Where have you been?" Jane asks me. "Your phone's off the hook. We called the operator when we couldn't reach you. I was about to come over."

"Pardon?" I say. "Worried about me? I was asleep on the sofa." *Did I leave the phone off the hook?* Then I realize — I most likely didn't put the receiver back on properly last night. I was about to call Anna, and then decided not to, thinking she must be asleep. Then I was going to call Jane and decided not to for the same reason.

"So you don't know? The hospital didn't reach you?"

"Know what?"

"They tried. They've been trying to call you all morning. I tried your cell phone. No answer. Chester came here for you. He asked me and I agreed."

Chester places his arm around me. "Hope it's okay."

"She passed away, Bloss. In her sleep. They found her just after five this morning. Minutes after it happened." Jane's voice is serene.

My head is swimming and all sounds seem muffled as if I were deep down in the ocean.

Chester says: "Peacefully. She passed away peacefully."

"No surgery?" I hear myself say. The words seem illogical, but they slip out. They sound far away as if somebody else is speaking.

Jane smiles. "They found ginkgo leaves in her hand. She was a grand lady, wasn't she, Bloss?"

CHAPTER 39

W OODY ALLEN's "I don't mind dying, I just don't want to be there when it happens," was one of Anna's favourite lines, and all who come to pay their last respects agree that she would have liked to be at her own funeral.

Before the coffin is closed, I place a ginkgo leaf on her chest.

Jane sets a marigold next to the leaf.

She does not need to tell me why. Although I was only in grade one and Jane in grade five, our trip to Mexico with Anna, Liza, and Helena, to take part in the Days of the Dead Festival as a way of remembering David, is etched in my memory. The festival which first was linked with David's death, which occurred only a few days before, became linked to everyone's death. When Anna said that somebody went to Mexico for the marigold festival, we knew it meant that the person died.

Anna had not been the sentimental type. Witty and

warm-hearted, the only tears she let loose, as she put it, were those of happiness. And Jane and I make sure that Grand Lady Anna, as many of her friends call her, is sent on her journey in a manner as gracious as her life had been.

Helena, who has joined the Baptist church since she moved to Florida, several years after David's death, suggests a Baptist service. Not that Anna was a Baptist. Anna had her own view on spirituality — a mixture of Christianity and paganism sprinkled with the collected wisdom of everyday life. During Helena's visits to Toronto, we got to know the minister at the Baptist church in our neighbourhood. The minister is a friend of the local jazz trio, regular performers at the bar Anna frequented, and we thought him most appropriate for the service. So a traditional Baptist funeral with the church choir and the jazz trio seems fitting.

We march the procession through High Park, playing Louis Armstrong's "When the Saints Go Marching In," the saxophone resonating through the valleys and along the trails, and the walkers pause and swing to the tune.

We stop at the majestic ginkgo on the west side of the maintenance building — the tree Anna saw as sacred. She often marvelled at its lyre-shaped limbs, and called these branches the Portals to Heaven, the hidden gateway between worlds. Here, Jane and I recall how Mother Teresa's devotion to helping those in need had been Anna's lifelong guiding principle.

James the policeman approaches the coffin — I had not seen him until now. He was not part of the procession. He kisses the tip of his finger, places it gently on the lid, and holds it there for a long moment. His large frame in a black suit, topped with a black fedora, evokes an apparition from another epoch. He bows and backs out of the gathering, awkwardly leaning on his cane, his polished black shoes squeaking each time he rests his weight on his injured leg. He stands rigidly behind the group, as if on guard duty. Our eyes meet and he nods to Jane and me — a twitch of a smile. Helena walks over and they shake hands. He bows to her, then slowly walks away. Jane and I exchange looks of consent — it's a glorious send-off, one Anna would have approved of. Everyone agrees she might have even shed a few tears of happiness for having such thoughtful friends.

That evening, I invite Chester to stay the night.

CHAPTER 40

April, 2009

I T IS LATE afternoon on a windy first day of April, and I take a walk to Sculpture Hill, to my thinking place by *Flower Power*. Another school year is winding down and I need to make some decisions about the summer.

Blossom dear, you should take some time off and travel. I hear Anna's voice in my thoughts. I enjoy teaching summer courses, but Chester has suggested we plan a trip together. He has a long list of places. His idea is to travel to Belgrade, then on to Holland to search for my grandparents' distant relatives. Visit Nuenen. Who knows, I could find myself related to Vincent, the famous painter. He has suggested that we visit Ireland and Scotland and search for David's roots. Chester's family is as Canadian as could be — French, English, and First Nations — and everyone accounted for going back a few hundred years. We've also talked to Jane about driving together to Florida to see

Helena. Chester tells me I haven't been myself since Anna died. A visit with Helena would do me good.

Walking through the park, I am fascinated by how changeable this time of year is. One moment the sun is shining hot as if it were July, and just as I take off my jacket, a gust of wind whips across the clearing, and a flurry of snowflakes scatters over my face. They are not soft and fluffy, but sharp and icy, grazing my cheeks and clumping on my eyelashes, coming down from the heavens since there are no clouds in sight. Suddenly, the snow thickens, and the sun's rays turn pale and cold, as if cast by an abandoned fridge light. I waltz full circle, bewildered. This place I know well, this landscape with tall bare oaks and maples and triangles of red I-beams of Mark di Suvero's sculptures silhouetted against the sky, feels surreal.

It *is* surreal. Empty. Missing a fragment of itself. Wide-eyed, I scan my surroundings. *Flower Power* is not there. The sky which held the red I-beams ever since I can remember is gaping. On the brown grass, the gargantuan body of an uprooted sculpture is heaved on its side, its cement-clad roots jutting into the air. I hear rumbling close behind, and as I turn, a large truck advances along the rutted path gouged in the grass, toward the upturned structure. A portion of the sculpture has already been removed. I feel as if something has been upturned in me as well, part of me severed.

I make my way down the hill, where an attractive young woman with a tripod and camera is filming the scene. A few workers are milling about. I greet the woman and soon discover the sculpture is being shipped to the artist in New Jersey for refurbishing. It will be brought back to Toronto and reinstalled at another location, a more prominent one near the CN Tower.

The second piece, *No Shoes*, has already been disassembled and stored on the truck.

I am happy Mark di Suvero's sculptures are being refurbished. But having them reinstalled somewhere else?

The image of my mother sitting on the grass, her back pressed against the red I-beam, surfaces in my thoughts. Am I about to lose that vision, and with it, to lose my mother all over again?

"There have been a lot of complaints over the years," the photographer says. "About safety. And about how unsightly they are."

Why did people see them as an eye-sore? Could they not see beyond the peeling paint?

"They'll be restored. Placed where people will be able to appreciate them."

I nod and she continues: "I heard the artist has become well known. Apparently, he was just a beginner when these pieces were commissioned. It was way back …"

Her voice blends with the wind whistling through the bare trees, and I feel it entering my bones.

The disparity of our experience of these sculptures stuns me. This young woman is learning about them only now, as they are being removed. How different she and I are, and how at this moment our lives are intersecting — for her, the removal just a job that leads to mild amusement by these structures. She is unmoved by them, by what they stood for — what they stand for — and especially by the fact that they were envisioned, designed, and constructed for *this* park, and this is where they belong.

How could I tell her that these sculptures are a link to my mother, a link no one could ever conceive of? How could I tell her that *Flower Power* has been my thinking place since childhood?

When I get home, I take out Liza's scrapbook and read her poem about di Suvero's sculptures.

Below the poem, I add the following lines:

> Dear *Flower Power* and *No Shoes*:
>
> I paid my visit to Sculpture Hill as I often do
> And found you — departed.
>
> Six half-bolts, two braces, a quarter inch thick
> palm-sized steel plate, all with flaking
> orange-red paint is what you left behind.
> What new cause, or old, has captured you?

The next morning, as I pick up the newspaper from my porch, I am faced with the front page photo of the up-turned *Flower Power*, a write-up about its removal, and a reference to the article about the sculptures created during the 1967 Art Symposium that still remain in the park. I flip to the article. It includes photos of the remaining five sculptures: *Midsummer Night's Dream*, *The Temple*, *Three Disks*, *November Pyramid*, and *The Hippy*. It also features Burman's incomplete one — comprising of the two granite blocks set on a base, with a subheading: *The unsolved mystery of the missing Carrara marble.* My heart beat quickens. I scan the article and spot the lines that refer to David Gould, a draft dodger who was a sculptor and a lecturer at the Toronto Arts College … and a suspected marble thief. The piece goes on. And I cannot believe my eyes. It talks about Liza Grant, who was the project coordinator for the 1967 Art Symposium in High Park, and whose "love child," sources claim, was fathered by David. It is believed that David and Liza's offspring, who is now a woman in her forties, still lives in the High Park area of Toronto, and is currently a lecturer at a local university. The article concludes with: "David's sister, who currently resides in Florida, is suspected of being an accomplice in the theft, but no proof of any of the allegations has been found, and no charges have ever been laid."

I call Chester, and while I wait for his arrival, I call Helena.

"Don't you worry about a thing," she reassures me. "It's that hound that used to badger Liza when she worked for the Ministry. He tried to question Anna, but she put him in his place. And me when he could find me. He's a real paparazzo, that one. What the heck is he looking for, beats me. Back then, he said he was determined to find the truth. But I don't buy it. I think he's obsessed with that case because he couldn't dig anything up. Liza even filed a complaint against him. He was banned from entering the building where she worked. And he never gave up. I thought he retired some time ago. Is there anything some of those reporters won't do for a story?"

Chester arrives and begins a Google search for a lawyer. Helena suggests that we contact Anna's attorney who is a friend and an activist from the sixties, and has been familiar with the case of the missing marble. He is handling Anna's estate which is being contested by her relatives.

"Our lawyer-friend has bailed out many a protester in the sixties," Helena says. "He *knows* that reporter."

She fills me in on the status of Anna's will. Anna has left her house and all her possessions to Jane. But these relatives Anna had seen only a few times in her life, while her parents were still alive, claim that Jane had coerced Anna into leaving the property to her alone. They insist that Anna's illness caused her to be emotionally unstable toward the end of her life.

"Anna was never unstable in anything, least of all her will. She was the most organized person I've ever known," Helena says. "I'll call the lawyer first thing Monday morning. He's semi-retired, but he'll help. He'll know what to do. He'll make that reporter eat his words."

A few days later, the newspaper issues a retraction of the article and an apology from the editor. Unfortunately, this type of info does not make it to the front page, but rather in the section only those who have been wronged like me look, hoping to find justice. I am satisfied that this will not reoccur. Hopefully.

A couple of days after the retraction, *The Villager*, a small neighbourhood weekly paper publishes an article about a fortune-teller who proclaimed the stolen Carrara marble cursed. The write-up provides a brief retelling of the Sculpture Symposium, and the theft that shocked the Toronto community. It includes a photo of the fortune-teller—standing by the two blocks of granite still in crates —her arms raised in the air. She is surrounded by a large gathering. I peer closely, hoping that I *don't* recognize Liza. And I don't. The photo is of poor quality, and for once I am grateful for inadequate technology.

Over the next week, a sense of dread sets in me. I wonder if my colleagues at work know about the articles. What do they think of me? Do they think that I am the illegitimate daughter of a criminal? That I come from a family of thieves? My mind conjures up assumptions and speculations and accusations—and pure malice. When I see them talking, I think they are gossiping about me.

"Chances are not many people read the articles," Chester says. "And if they did, how would they make the connection?"

"My last name. How difficult is it to make a connection?"

"There are many people with that last name, Bloss. Besides, that was the sixties. It's rather cool to be the daughter of a hippie. Don't you think?"

"David wasn't a hippie. And Liza wasn't even close to a hippie."

"What's the worst case scenario, Bloss? Let's say, somebody does make a connection. So what? There is nothing there. Not even an arrest. Nothing!"

"I have a feeling somebody knows something. Somebody *always* knows something."

I telephone Helena. "I think you know more than you're letting on. I'm part of this. You owe me an explanation. I need to know."

"Nothing to know, my girl. And that reporter won't bother you anymore. Believe me."

"I wish I could believe you, Helena."

"Don't worry about the piece in *The Villager*. That's harmless. But the other reporter, the hound? Our lawyer-friend will take care of him. Trust me."

CHAPTER 41

November, 2009

THIS PAST SUMMER, Chester and I cancelled our travel plans. I was not feeling well. I was unusually tired and unfocused, and my doctor insisted on some tests.

More tests followed and each time I spoke with Jane, I found myself evading her questions about the results. Not telling her has been my way of escaping the truth. The more messages she left, the more I tried to dodge the phone calls—as if revealing to her that I have been diagnosed with leukemia would make it that much more real. When my doctor booked me at the hospital for more tests I was glad—glad I would not be home to dodge Jane's calls.

I've been at the hospital for a week now, and have not checked my answering machine. This way, I don't have to feel guilty about not returning her calls. It's not like me to be so inconsiderate, but this game has helped to keep the reality of my illness at bay.

Not long after Anna died, Jane accepted a tenured position as Associate Professor at Carleton University's School of Journalism in Ottawa. After the move, the responsibilities of the new job combined with raising her three teenaged children filled her days, with hardly a minute to spare. We kept close contact for a while, with phone calls or brief visits between Toronto and Ottawa. This past summer, however, Jane had been immersed in professional development, and in the fall, in addition to teaching, she had taken on the position of acting coordinator for the Communications program, and has been busier than ever.

We agreed to keep in touch by phoning and visiting, and not through email or Facebook or Linkedin. Electronic communication is too impersonal. Yet, she sent an email asking me why I have not returned her calls. She said that we are not in the dark ages and she should be able to reach me. I have not replied. I *am* in the dark ages. I don't know what the future brings.

It is past ten on a Thursday night, and Jane is likely at home. I long to hear her voice. To bare my fears.

I used to think how unlucky Jane has been with her three failed marriages and the responsibilities of a single mother. But now I see it differently. Now I think how fortunate she has been and what a fulfilling life she has had. Securing a tenured position was a dream-come-true. The competition had been fierce. Many of her colleagues, including me, have been teaching our whole life on contract. And here she is, already holding the position of an acting coordinator in her department. And although she sees herself as unlucky in love, her three wonderful children, now teenagers, have been her anchor. She's always had supportive friends.

The National news is on television, and the meteorologist features Wellington Street on Parliament Hill in Ottawa, not far from where Jane lives, glazed in icy rain. On an evening such as this, I imagine Jane snuggled on the sofa in her twelfth storey condo, the view illuminated by the city lights stretching beyond to Hull and the Gatineaus across the River. I picture her marking student essays and listening to the rain frosting the window panes. The job security has changed so many aspects of her life. She received mortgage approval for her condominium. And her concerns about her three teenagers living within the confines of a high-rise were quickly put at ease — they love the central location and would not give up the downtown and move to the desolate suburbia for any amount of space. In the past, the only savings she could put aside were for her children's education. But last time we spoke she was going through the automobile ads that offer incentives on a van she could now afford. She's always wanted to take her children on a road trip across Canada while they were still young enough and enjoyed travelling with her. Next summer is a possibility. She had asked me to plan ahead and join her. She also hopes Helena would come along, for although she now lives in her Florida trailer, she has kept David's apartment where she has spent many summers. In Helena's words, her heart remains with us in Toronto. And although money is not a problem, as she has inherited her parents' and David's estate, the superintendent — a lifelong friend and a pacifist — has kept the rent frozen in the sixties, and she does not have the heart to let the place go.

All these wonderful plans. Sure I'll take the summer off next year — whether I want to or not. Not only did I have to cancel my travel plans for the summer, I had to give up teaching the fall semester as well. What hope do I have of returning to work?

An urgent need to talk to Jane tenses every nerve in my body. I pick up the hospital phone on my night table and begin to dial. If I used my cell phone, I'd press the icon with her name and would not get the chance to change my mind. I hang up before the last digit.

My cell phone rings and it's Chester. I am relieved. My temptation to call Jane has passed.

In a silver frame on the night table sits a photograph of Jane and me as little girls. Next to it is a photo taken about the same time with Anna, Liza, and Helena. Chester brought the pictures from my house to make me feel better. We look like a happy family — we were a happy family — still are. Liza used to say, death does not end the love we feel — love is eternal.

A patient from the next room, sporting a flowery turban and hot-pink lipstick matching her housecoat, is leaning against the footboard of my bed. She is chatting about the luncheon menu, and the new chef who is determined to turn bland hospital fare into gourmet cuisine, and the nurses who make up excuses to visit the kitchen and get a glimpse of the gorgeous new "culinary hunk." She rhymes off the colours of, in her words, the "designer" hospital gowns, and encourages me to try the "new fashion" rather that cling to my own. She lists the names of patients who prefer one colour over the other. I am grateful for the cheery monologue as it breaks up the boredom of the hospital routine. She slips out of the room just as impetuously as she came in, fluttering her hot-pink fingernails in a friendly wave, and flip-flops down the terrazzo hallway.

I stare at the empty doorway, her Barbie-doll pink imprinted in my vision. Another person appears in the doorway and for a moment I wonder if I am hallucinating. Do I miss Jane so much, I conjure up her image at my hospital room? It *is* Jane. Long strands of her dark hair have escaped her ponytail and are framing her flushed cheeks. She is dripping wet as if she'd just risen out of a swimming pool. She looks as stunned as I am.

Something feral, defensive, yet frightened in me stirs. Why is Jane here? To find the truth about me? The truth I don't want her to know? *As long as she remains in the hallway, as long as she doesn't cross the threshold, I am not in this hospital bed. I am somewhere else — lecturing in a classroom, riding my bike, or jogging in High Park.* If Jane enters the room, she will confirm the woman in this bed is in fact me. Oddly, I think of myself in third person. *No. Blossom isn't here, no.* I will Jane to turn and walk away. But she enters the room.

She hugs me and the fear dissipates. Her wet face is feverish against mine as if she'd been jogging. I am taken aback. *It is I who is feverish.* She takes her coat off, drapes it around the chair, and sits on the edge of my bed.

I temper my voice into calmness. "Is it raining out there?"

"Buckets," she says.

Her eyes are glued to my face, and I am transported to our childhood, to her role of the older sister when she guided and protected me. And made me happy.

I am seven years old again, waiting with Anna at the Bay Street bus terminal. Jane steps off the bus, wiggles her hand out of her mother's, and runs toward me. We hug. She slips the knapsack off her back, pulls out a box wrapped in Barbie paper, and tells me to open it. I hesitate. She reminds me that I am allowed to open one early birthday present and it should be hers. I tear the paper off. Through the clear cellophane wrap of the packaging, an Olympic Barbie in her red ski suit is looking back at me.

Jane knows this doll is at the top of my birthday wish-list. We hold hands and jump up and down and scream with joy, and the sparkle in Jane's eyes, her thrill at making me happy, is forever etched in my memory.

I reach for her hand. "Jane, will you ever forgive me? I couldn't talk about it. You understand, don't you?"

"Nothing to forgive. But promise me you'll never keep me out of your life again."

I ask Jane about her children's art classes and ballet lessons and about her new job. I keep firing questions to avoid talking about myself simply because there would be only one thing to talk about, and it is not pleasant.

Finally I give in to what I have been avoiding. "How did you find me here?"

She shrugs. "I haven't been able to reach you. But I guess you know that. So I called the university and found out you took the semester off. I knew something had to be wrong. I took the first bus from Ottawa this morning. Then the subway to your house. Your neighbour told me you've been readmitted to the Women's Centenary for more tests. She was surprised I didn't know."

I discern a twinge of blame and avert my eyes. "Some type of escapism, I suppose."

She looks so sad, I feel guilty for hiding my illness. What was I afraid of? I tell her how I've been diagnosed with an aggressive form of leukemia. And of the search for a donor.

She brushes my hair away from my face then hugs me again.

The wayward patient with hot-pink fingernails walks back into my room and shrieks in delight. "Ah, a visitor! And it's only morning! I fetched a turquoise gown for you before they're all gone. To match your beautiful eyes."

She turns to Jane. "Blossom is our princess in an enchanted castle," she says jovially with a broad sweep of her hand as if I were a piece of furniture in a showroom, and not a patient at a cancer ward. She holds the gown against my chest. "Good contrast against your flaming red tresses." She points to her turban and winces. "Hope it grows back soon." She leans close to me and whispers, excitedly. "Rumour has it the hunk, you know, the new chef, is coming around at lunch to see what we think of the new menu." She scrunches up her nose and chuckles mischievously, lays the gown on my bed, and waltzes out.

Jane looks even more crushed. She can see right through this put-on cheerfulness.

I wish I could tell Jane this is all a big mistake, a misdiagnosis, and all will be cleared up, and I'll be back home this evening, and we'll have a lovely dinner and herbal tea with lemon and honey, and tomorrow we'll take the subway to the opera house where we'll admire its awe-inspiring architecture and superb acoustics and grumble about how some of the opera company's recent productions lack the pageantry and flourish we both enjoy—and this whole notion of my illness will be but a bad dream.

Jane passes her hand along her forehead as if to wipe away her worry. Out of her bag, she pulls out a yellowed paper scroll bound with a purple ribbon in which she had tied a small bouquet of fresh lavender. She places the scroll in my hand. "Bloss, I have some very exciting news. And some exhilarating news."

A mischievous smirk on Jane's face tells me she recalls the word game Anna and I used to play—a game Jane, who prefers more straightforward talk, never took part in. But now, she prompts the game.

It's a strange way to present flowers—in an aged paper scroll. So I hold the bouquet in both hands as if it were a bottle with a genie in it. "Two sets of news—one exciting and one exhilarating, ha?"

Jane nods keenly. "Open it up. And read the letter."

"The letter?"

I untie the ribbon and unfurl the pages—pages tightly hand-written. I hold the lavender bouquet and recall this was Anna's favourite herb—a numinous cure-all—for chasing the blahs away and lifting the spirit.

Jane is unable to hold back the excitement. "Let's read it together. I've already read it over and over. But I'd like to hear it again." She arches her eyebrows. "Even better. Could you read it out loud for both of us?"

CHAPTER 42

JANE AND I lean the pillows against the headboard and settle in. The pages of the scroll are curled from being rolled tightly, and when I flatten them with my palms, a few dry bits of lavender spill on my lap. I take in the hay-like sweetness of this fragrant herb that has been in documented use for over three thousand years and recall its many qualities. The Egyptians made perfume from it; the Romans used it for bathing and cooking and scenting the air; French and English royalty demanded lavender filled pillows; and over the years, Anna and Liza had tucked lavender sachets in dresser drawers and armoires to repel moths. *This is a good omen.*

Jane gets up and begins to pace the floor.

I start to read.

The date at the top is, Ottawa 1969, and it begins with, "My Sweetest Love."

What is it about the magic of love?

I know the answer. The magic—all that wizardry love conjures up—is in the enchantment of loving you.

I spent the evening in a room filled with men in business suits, women in cocktail dresses—some of the handsomest human specimens. Yet, I was lonely.

After exchanging a few pleasantries with colleagues, I stepped onto the patio for some fresh air and a cigarette. Oxymoronic, I know, marching out for fresh air and inhaling smoke, but what the hell, I needed it—and as I lit up and drew in the nicotine, you were in my thoughts. You, Liza, are all that matters.

How fortunate we are to have found love—the true meaning of life—love for each other, love for our darling daughters, Bloss and Janey. I feel warm inside just repeating their names.

I bought matching dresses for our girls today— the two little sisters. I was so happy to find the sizes. I'm so sentimental tonight, my love, and I can't help but reminisce about you and me and David. My darling Liza, isn't it prophetic he is the father of our daughters?

All those years I felt guilty for not telling him about Janey. Now, I see it all as providence. The way the universe itself had lined up events and made you and me and our girls a family. This isn't gin talking, my love. The gin may loosen the tongue, yes. But the feelings are genuine.

Oh, how I long for you Liza my love. It's two weeks until I see you, two long, boring weeks of meetings and business suits and cocktail dresses. I'm off to bed now, alone but no longer lonely, radiant with thoughts of you.

My love for you is eternal.

Your Anna

I drop the letter in my lap and cup my face in my hands. I can hear my heart beating. I pick it up again and run my fingertips over the signature, as if I was reading braille. I was not wrong. *Your Anna.*

Jane is still pacing the floor. I stare at her. How this single letter must have transformed her life. Yet she is composed, focused on her even steps as if hypnotized.

"David is your father," I whisper and she nods, smiling.

"I've had a couple of days to mull it over," she whispers.

I pick up the letter again. Fingering the paper reassures me it *is* real. My thoughts are imploding like a dynamited high-rise. *Jane is my sister!* I get out of bed and pace the floor with her. Jane takes my hand. We stop and look at each other — and laugh, laugh happily.

She kisses me on the cheek. "I felt my life upturning. Transforming me into someone else. Someone I tried to see from this new perspective. Someone I hardly know. And yet know as well as my own heartbeat."

She arches her eyebrows and looks at me, intently, wide eyed. "Then I asked myself, what has changed? How am I different?" She continues. "I'd never imagined Anna and Liza as lovers. They'd always been my aunts. Liza the same way as Anna. They'd been inseparable. Whenever I came, on weekends … summertime … I used to spend my whole summers with you guys! And loved it!"

"Neither dated anyone else," I say. "To me this didn't seem unusual, though. It all seemed … routine."

I think back to Liza and Anna going about the daily tasks, chatting and laughing. And the notion they were a couple is heart-warming. They were content together. Now I realize they were more than that. They were happy. They were in love. And knowing Anna is Jane's biological mother makes me warm all over as if I am lit up from within.

Jane takes my hands in hers. "Bloss, you know what this means, don't you? We're sisters! Sisters!!!"

When I look up, I am met with that gleam in Jane's eyes I have not seen for over thirty years.

She hugs me, tear-stained cheeks against mine. "I've been hearing about him for as long as I can remember. Hearing about *your* father. While all along he was *my* father as well. Imagine! And the father I grew up with is my uncle. And my mother is my aunt. And my aunt my real mother. Who would've thought?"

Jane wipes her tears. "Now for the exhilarating news. Since we're sisters, I have a much better chance of being a donor. This could all be behind us very soon."

Jane spends the night at my house and comes to the hospital early in the morning. She sits on my bed and takes my hand in hers. "Bloss, I've been thinking. You didn't seem surprised." She pauses. "Well, not as surprised as I expected. You know, about David being my father."

I shrug. "I've always seen you as my sister."

She laughs her warmest laugh, the one that rolls out mellifluous and genuinely mirthful. "And I you. But I thought you'd be astonished. Shocked."

"I'm whole. Justice has been done. The truth revealed."

"Not surprised? That David is *my* father as well?"

"A little. But I'm just so happy! And that's all that matters."

I untangle my feet from under the sheets, get out of the bed, wrap the housecoat around my shoulders, and slowly pace the room. "You never did fit in with your parents, Jane. You always belonged with us. *We* were family. And after your visit, each time you went back to Ottawa, I thought it unfair."

She is genuinely thrown by this. She presses her fingers to her temples and closes her eyes. "And Liza and Anna being lovers? Did you have any idea?"

"They'd been together for as long as I can remember. As a child, I never thought about … the *nature* of their relationship."

Jane laughs. "No? Not at all?"

"When I was in grade school, they worked flex-hours. One walked me to school in the morning and the other picked me up after school. Come to think of it — I had two mothers."

Jane makes a funny-frog face, as in our childhood, and says with emphasis: "So you *did* suspect something?"

"On weekends, Anna often stayed at our house. In the morning, I'd run to their bedroom and jump on their bed and snuggle in between them and they'd talk about my school, my friends …"

Jane pipes in. "And which ingredient made the best oatmeal-raisin cookies."

"I liked walnuts. You wanted coconut."

Jane claps her hands and laughs. "And Anna insisted on using butter. But Liza usually snuck the olive oil into the batter, instead. To make the cookies more healthful. Except Anna could taste the difference. Hilarious."

"And the breakfasts? Who could forget those? Crepes with berries and whipped cream. Heavenly."

"You still have that whipping crème dispenser? We'll get some cartridges and do the crepes. And waffles. Soon as you get home."

"You bet," I say. "Then we'll go to the park and visit our old friend, Mr. Peacock."

A shadow of sadness passes over her face. "Remember, Bloss? You thought his magical eyes could see into the human soul."

"I've always had this need to glimpse into other people's thoughts. My mother's, primarily. I wondered if my mother had been lonely. Whether she'd sacrificed her own happiness for me. Not wanting to subject me to having a strange man in my life."

"It never crossed my mind," Jane says.

"That small measure of guilt? Now, all dissipated. Liza and Anna had each other."

CHAPTER 43

CHESTER IS PERFECTLY at home in my kitchen. He had prepared our favourite dinner — stir-fried tofu with broccoli and snow peas and toasted slivered almonds. A bottle of Châteauneuf-du-Pape Grenache is breathing on the table. He is enthusing about the pastoral landscapes of Provence he'd visited during his university days, and the ruins of the fortress-like-palace of Châteauneuf-du-Pape — a historic village in France's southern Rhone Valley famous for full-bodied red wines — places on our must-visit list.

His optimism is contagious. I underwent a series of tests at the hospital, and was approved for an experimental drug. I am responding well to the new medication. My energy level is close to normal, and the doctor has given me the green light to return to my usual activities as long I don't exert myself. I am even allowed to have a bit of wine with dinner. The professional development workshops I had committed to at the university are now exciting, and I hope to return to teaching in January.

Chester pours the wine. As he raises a glass to offer a toast, someone knocks on the door. He sets the glass on the table and opens the oak-panel entry. From the dining room, over the living room sofa and the wingback chair and through the vigorous Ficus benjamina thriving in a tall ceramic pot, through the glass of the screen door, I glimpse the woman on the porch. My heart begins to race. I run to the door.

I open the screen and scream in delight: "Helena!"

Helena has an irrepressible golden tan, and her shoulder-length white hair is bound by a turquoise scarf. We hug for a long while.

She turns to Chester and gathers him into an affectionate hug. "How wonderful to see you!"

"Helena, what a surprise! You're like some exotic bird from a botanical garden in Florida. Blown in by the wind."

Chester shrinks into the embrace of fairy-like Helena. They hug in a side-to-side rhythm, and as she pats his shoulders, the long corners of her scarf sway along her back like peacock tail feathers. She is dressed for July, although it's December. She releases Chester and signals to the cab in the driveway and he backs up and leaves.

She slips off her running shoes and shrugs the knitted white cape off her shoulders. Her white cotton dress splashed with scarlet peonies flutters about her.

"Blossom, darling, how could you keep this from me? You're my little girl, don't you know?" Helena kisses my cheeks tenderly and her love, like perfume, infuses the space she carries with her.

Chester takes off to the kitchen. He busies himself at the sink and leaves us to our catching up. He does so as much for himself as for us. I've gotten to know that tension in his face. Although he puts on an air of optimism, his fear for me is deep-seated, like some ancient curse he is unable to dispel. He has sequestered this worry in some corner of his mind. Every once in a while it scores through his defenses like sharp claws, and I glimpse it in his face when he is unaware of being observed. Then he sets another plate, pours another glass of wine, and announces that dinner is ready.

Helena claps her hands in awe and tells us good-humouredly that she planned it all and arrived just in time — dinner, wine — stir-fry is her favourite meal, and Châteauneuf-du-Pape Grenache? She's always wondered what that burgundy elixir, in that wind-blown, sand-pitted bottle tastes like. She vouches to make it to Provence some day and see the vineyards for herself.

"The secret to that whole region is in its poor soil," she says. "Dry and rocky, like gravel. Forces the grape vine to grow deep and seek nutrients for sustenance. The limestone in the soil absorbs the sun and keeps the vine warm at night. And the wind beats it day in, day out. Dries the mold and saves the grapes."

Chester gives a nod of approval: "You've done your homework, Helena."

"Took a wine tasting class. And would you believe my luck, that bottle got finished before it got to me. Never happened before, or after. Go figure."

We clink glasses and sample.

Helena raises her glass against the light and admires

the colour: "It's the vine stress that causes high quality grape. And best wines." She gives us a meaningful look. "It's the struggle that creates some of the best people in the world. Makes survivors out of us."

Our dinner conversation is about Helena's morning flight from Miami and how quickly she made it to Toronto. And the miraculous discovery David is Jane's father as well. Her enthusiasm about having two nieces is thrilling! But she scolds Jane and me for hiding my illness from her. I remind her that Jane is not to blame, that I am the culprit. Jane is the one who called Helena. She waited for the test results, hoping she was the right match. This way, she could give Helena some good news as well. After finding out she could not be my donor, she thought we had to let Helena know. We could not keep her in the dark. She also hopes Helena might have some ideas on how to widen the search.

"We won't let that happen again," Helena declares. "It's been over a year since we last saw each other. Way too long."

After dinner, Chester puts the kettle on and clears the dishes. He insists on taking care of it all, himself. The kettle trips off and he pours the boiling water into the tea pot. He sets the cups on the coffee table and soon we're settled into the comfort of the sofa cushions and tea and almond graham cookies Helena brought with her.

Helena asks Chester to update her on everything, to keep nothing hidden. I dread the thought of putting him through it. But who could refuse Helena? So I offer to tell the story. I tell her about friends and colleagues who had been tested as possible donors, and how crushed Jane was when she found out she was not the right match. She thought it inevitable she would be. In her mind, the cosmos itself had lined up the events in such a way that we'd find out about being half-sisters, and that Jane was the right donor. And like in the movies, there would be a happy ending.

I talk about feeling better since taking the experimental drug, and about my hopes to return to teaching in the winter semester. Chester is tense. I can hear his thoughts. Each time I take on the all-will-be-well outlook, as if I've come down with a stubborn flu that is about to run its course, he sees it as denial. He believes that I have lost hope. That I am overcompensating—all this optimism and cheerfulness, a put-on. That I've given up.

Have I?

Jane used to tell me that I am afraid of commitment. She was right. Only when I became ill did I realize how unfounded my fears have been. Does it take death to feel free to live? The irony of such a notion is hard for me to bear.

Jane takes the bus from Ottawa and comes to visit while Helena is still in Toronto, and I am grateful. Jane's discovery that David is her biological father gives new meaning to her relationship with Helena, and they have much catching up to do. But I am also grateful for Jane's visit for another reason—I need her to take Helena's mind off my illness.

A Toronto clinic refuses to test Helena for a suitable donor—she is past the acceptable age. Covering the cost for testing is not an option as the clinics are forbidden from charging for services. Helena's fury is like a hurricane. She is reminded of her long-ago efforts to have David admitted to the hospital after he was beaten, and instead of receiving medical care, was dumped into a prison cell, only to be subjected to other beatings that quickly led to his death.

Helena rejects being trapped in yet another bureaucratic web. The right match has not been found and something must be done — perhaps relaxing the age restriction could be considered?

Although she enjoys spending time with me, finding a suitable donor is the overriding concern and she is frazzled from fear the right match would not be found. The constant unrest she discerns in Chester amplifies her worries, and any hope based on the all-will-be-well mantra is to her delusional. She fears that my immune system could weaken to the point where my body would not be able to withstand the stress of the transplant. She is disheartened by the discovery that Jane's sixteen-year-old daughter has been turned down for testing as she is under age. Teenagers are issued driver's licenses at sixteen but disqualified from saving a life, although the threat to their own health would be minimal? She finds it difficult to accept family members are not able to help in certain circumstances — one is either too old or too young. On Sunday, after Jane returns to Ottawa, Helena takes the last flight of the day back to Miami. She will be visiting her own doctor to explore other options. In her words, there must be an alternative. She cannot fail David once again. She believes she is failing me — the daughter she's never had. As much as I love seeing Helena, I am relieved she's gone back home. I could now stop pretending to be cheerful. I could go back to being myself.

Helena calls me from Miami. She has undergone the testing. She is the right match.

She is exhilarated and disheartened at the same time — she is the right match, but her age still prevents her from being a donor. We talk about the risks and we all agree waiting any longer may not be the best tactic. Am I willing to take the chance with Helena as donor? I know I am. Helena suggests we approach American clinics. Perhaps a private clinic would agree to the procedure. She begins the search.

CHAPTER 44

February, 2010

I SIT UP IN my hospital bed and open Margaret Atwood's hand-bound booklet, *Double Persephone*. It's signed to Liza, 1967, Bohemian Embassy. I came across it recently while cleaning out a bookshelf. I remember this poetry book well. I Googled it and discovered two hundred copies had been sewn into a booklet by the poetess herself. She distributed them to local bookstores in 1961, and they sold at fifty cents a copy. Although I adore the author, I gain new admiration for her. My mother used to recite the stanzas from it by heart, instead of a bedtime story.

Now, as I read "Formal Garden," I recall how at once excited and frightened it made me feel. In my childhood imagination, I fantasized about marble sculptures with rose garlands turning into white ghosts. "Pastoral" was my favourite. I recall making up scenes from the stanzas, also not knowing what the poem meant, but I liked the way they rhymed and flowed and I envisioned the fields

during the hay rides we took in the fall when apple picking at a farm in the countryside. And it always lulled me
to sleep, an uplifting and calming sleep.

How the memory of my mother always comforts me.

I place the book on my night table, and a white envelope slips out of it. I have been searching for it for almost
two years, since Anna died.

Don't open it now. Wait a while, Anna's voice echoes in
my thoughts. I realize the time to open it is right.

The envelope reveals two faded photographs and two
letters. Going by the washed-out quality of the photos,
the images only ghostly shadows of the original, they
must have been taken by a Polaroid camera. The man in
the photo is tall and burly. He has an unruly head of
shoulder-length hair, and a bushy beard. His hair ob-
scures much of his face; the photo must have been taken
on a gusty day, with the wind at his back; his loose jacket
is puffed up. Although the picture is pale, the redness of
his hair and beard stand out.

The second photo is of my mother and the same man
taking a ride on Mark di Suvero's *No Shoes*.

They are swinging on a log suspended from the I-
beams of the sculpture, high in the air. It is just like the
picture of those people I do not recognize my mother had
cut out of the newspaper and pasted in her scrapbook. He
sits behind her, holding her around the waist, her long
dark hair draped over his shoulder. She is wearing beige
shorts and a white T-shirt. He is in blue jeans and a bluish
T-shirt. It strikes me that his hair is almost as red as the
I-beam—red like mine—and his build is a bit more slen-
der than in the first photo. A closer look assures me it is

the same man. The lush tree crowns drenched in sunshine tell me this photo must have been taken on a summer day. My mother looks carefree with this man who must be David.

I have seen very few photos of David — a passport shot and a few black-and-white ones. Perhaps he didn't like being photographed. This is the only picture I have seen of my mother and David. I cannot think of him as my father. He is simply David. My mother looks happier than I have ever seen her. And this makes me very sad. She always seemed content, but never really happy. At least I don't remember her that way.

I try to recall her looking like this, young and playful with her hair flowing in the wind, as if she has no cares in the world, as if all things are just the way they should be. But I cannot.

This photo would always remind me of the side of her I never got to know — my mother caught up in laughter. It would be my favourite photo.

I move on to the letters.

> *Toronto, June, 1989.*
> *My darling Blossom,*
>
> *There are different kinds of love each person experiences in a lifetime — the love of a child, a friend, a parent, a sibling. Then there is romantic love for a man or a woman in one's life.*
>
> *You, my fragrant flower, have always been the love of my life. You gave meaning to my existence, purpose to everything I did and did not do. For that — for having you in my life — I am the luckiest person in the world.*

I've been blessed in many ways. I've had two other loves in my life — the love of a man and the love of a woman. And what a happy life it's been.

I won't apologize for being sentimental. Sentimentality is a feeling, and apologizing for one's emotions has no place in human relations. To love, to mourn, to fear, to hope, is to be alive.

I am not sure I'll have the heart to give you these letters, but I believe they will come to you when you most need them.

All things happen for a reason; all is transient, ever evolving, and nothing ever stays the same. And if today or tomorrow, or whatever time I have left does not give me the courage to tell you what must be told, I know all will be known to you when the time is right, because the universe is alive and all powerful, and the closer I come to that other state of being, the more convinced I am it is real, just as real as you are to me and I am to you today and every day we are gifted to be together.

I wish you'd had the chance to know David. Although he died far too soon — I mean physical death — the one that leaves sorrow and emptiness in the hearts of those who love him, his spirit is alive, and will remain with me until I join him in that other existence.

The night before you were born he came to me — in a dream of course — the type of dream that is a vision. We sat inside di Suvero's Flower Power as we often used to, and he said our daughter is the blossom of our life and our love, and as the bloom is the magic of every flower, you are that magic.

You see, I was not completely truthful when I said I named you after the sculpture. We chose your name, my sweet Blossom, together, and I know his love for you is eternal.

And here's something rather neat. Just before you were born, when my labour pains became unbearable, I closed my eyes and in my mind's eye, there he was, David, next to me. He placed his palm on my forehead and all pain vanished, and in its place an orgasmic joy spread through me. The doctor and the nurses were urging me to push, then telling me to hold, not push, and then again to push … I kept my eyes closed as that was the sure way to keep David next to me. The exuberant voices of the doctor and the nurses announced, "It's a girl," but I already knew it had to be a girl. It had to be Blossom. I heard your cry—the most beautiful sound in the world—and a new life was born not only for you my darling, but for me as well. I was reborn, and it was the most sublime feeling of all.

When I opened my eyes, Anna was next to me, her palm on my forehead, where all along I thought David had been. And this was another awakening. But that's another story, my love.

I'll go to sleep now. David is calling to me—sleep my love, sleep, and I'll be with you as always, in your dreams.

I fold the letter carefully and slide it back into the envelope. There is also a poem in gilded letters. I love Liza's poems. They allow me a glimpse into her most intimate thoughts. It reads:

William Koochin's *The Hippy*
by Liza Grant

Suited colossus.
Sentinel to rebellion.

Dark shades.
Hands in pockets.
Peace branded in lapel.

With an air of indifference
blankly surveying remnants of your realm.

A guru?
A mentor?
    An anarchist?

The answer
masked by a bearded stare
in stony silence.

The rest of the page is about the inspiration for *The Hippy* and now I understand why my mother wished she could bring it to life. I realize how wrong I've been. My mother had lived a happy life. And with this knowledge, the pieces of a puzzle that represent who I am are brought together into one meaningful whole.

I wrap my housecoat around my shoulders and take a walk along the corridors. Soon I am sitting on a bench in the main lobby, near the sculpture, *Femina*. Outside, the last glow of sunset envelopes the city and soft twilight

flows into the foyer, unusually empty for the main entrance of a busy downtown hospital. A sense of tranquil-
ity envelops me as if *Femina* can hear my thoughts—I am
part of this infinite, living universe, where order reigns,
and there is a reason for everything.

CHAPTER 45

B*LOSSOM, MY GIRL, what good would it be to find the right match at some point in the future, if it's too late for you, and your chances of recovery are minimized or lost altogether?* Helena's voice whispers in my head.

I am in and out of the hospital—home for a few weeks at a time when I feel better. I replenish the toiletries in my overnight bag to have it ready. My oncologist is strongly opposed to Helena as donor as the risk of failure is too great. The stem cells obtained from a younger donor, preferably between the age of eighteen and thirty-five, have a much better chance of survival once transplanted. And although potential donors are able to register up to the age of fifty in Canada, some countries, such as Britain, accept only those below forty.

Helena is sixty-two, and although she is healthy and energetic, her stem cells would have a much lower chance of developing into oxygen-carrying red blood cells, infection-fighting white blood cells, or clot-forming platelets, after being transplanted. My doctor also hopes the increase in young moms' donations of their new-born infants' umbilical cords would soon lead to a suitable match. The cord blood stem cells do not need to be as closely matched as bone marrow or peripheral blood stem cells.

The waiting game continues. Days turn into weeks and weeks into months. It is now mid-winter and still no news of a potential donor. I had not returned to teaching in winter. I am feverish and tire at the slightest effort and Helena's daily phone calls are a constant reminder that proceeding with her as donor may be worth the risk. This morning Helena calls with some good news. A highly regarded oncologist at a private clinic in Miami has agreed to perform the procedure, and although he has warned of the potential risks, he is optimistic.

I walk into The Bay store on Queen Street, head to the fifth floor where the designer labels reside, and stroll between the display boutiques. The mannequins have changed since I last paid attention to their wardrobe, some years back. They've grown taller and slimmer and more expressive, more opinionated. The blond model, hand over mouth, examines her brunette companion's face, as if whispering secrets. One figure has the look of discontent, another of envy, yet another of dismay, pride. I stroll through the aisles and study each one, as if they were living beings. I admire the flowery silk dress on one, the casually draped linen blazer on another, the chunky bracelet of tarnished silver on yet another. In the change room, I slide on the chosen items and the transformation takes place. The effigy in the mirror smirks ironically and removes the items slowly, one at a time, as if she were a dispossessed crow that has ornamented herself with found trinkets, only to realize she has no use for them. I am not likely to return to work. In a hospital, I have no use for fancy clothes.

I proceed to the casual clothing section and pick a T-shirt in every colour on the rack. My collection is a rainbow I cart home. I lay them out on my bed and the assortment reminds me of Liza's turbans. Her voice whispers in my thoughts—life is meant to be lived in colours.

I call my oncologist at the Women's Centenary Hospital as if expecting a miracle. I wish she would agree to the surgery with Helena as a donor here in Toronto. I would be more at ease with my own specialist and the hospital staff I've gotten to know during my treatment.

To my surprise, my doctor tells me she is wrapping up the final details which would make the surgery possible. She has brought my case before the hospital ethics committee and the surgery has just been approved.

Helena is so elated she would fly from Miami on her own wings if a flight is not available in the next few days. She plans it all out in no time. She'll stay in Toronto at David's apartment while I wait for the surgery, and for at least a few months after to help with my recovery. And before I have the chance to tell her I might be waiting for quite a while, she's already set herself up as my personal chef and nurse, after being my donor. Her excitement is catching and I feel it stirring in me like the late winter breeze that in its earthy scent hints of spring.

Over the years, David's apartment has been the place of refuge where Liza and I spent many afternoons while she told stories about David. Having Helena stay for a while is reassuring. In her company, I often feel as if Liza and Anna were still with me.

The oncologist informs me she has found an opening for the surgery only weeks away. Excitement tempts me, but I remain reserved. After months of uncertainty, suddenly the arrangements become immediate — decisions made, dates set, pre-surgery treatments scheduled. Helena's arrival makes the preparations that much more real. She is so hopeful she is buoyant, and I find myself worrying. If anything goes wrong, she will be inconsolable. I cannot share my concerns with Chester. I have a similar fear for him as well.

When Chester and I arrive at the apartment to get it ready for Helena, we are pleasantly surprised. The landlord has kept it in tip-top shape. He has left a box of supplies — batteries, fuses, light bulbs — and all we need to do is make sure everything is in running order.

We replace the battery in the sun-burst clock that was one of David's prized possessions. Chester is charmed by the clock's audible ticking that emanates from the round face with gleaming brass spears branching out. Over the diamond-shaped hour markers, the sweeping seconds-hand shifts erratically.

I tell Chester how Jane and I used to imagine that a sleeping genie resided in the clock and was having a fitful nightmare. Chester gives his take on what's really the cause — Peter Pan's crocodile is trapped in it. He struts along the parquet floor singing "Never Smile at a Crocodile," and recites the words, "tick-tock the croc," to the clock's ticking, as he pretends to chase me while tapping his teeth together, and my heart expands with love for the boy in this man.

I wish I could tell him the ticking has a different message for me. I have come to accept fate, accept death, and the sudden news about my surgery has left me numb with apprehension and doubt. Should I hope for recovery, only to be let down? I put on an air of optimism for those I love, but my heart is empty. I have lost faith. And so I am left with my betraying heart that dissolves hope as soon as it discerns the ruse, before hope has the chance to germinate. How could I tell him that deep inside I am like an iceberg, frozen in despondence?

We dust the brown leather sofa and accent it with large burnt orange pillows. We set a pot of flowering freesia on the teak dining table — now seen as retro and fashionable — and imagine Helena delighting in the sweet fragrance floating through the angular space of this third-storey apartment. Chester replaces the light bulbs in the drape-chain hanging lamp with six hammered glass panels, two each in blue, amber, and amethyst, and we bask in the ambiance emanating from the coloured panes.

That night, Chester and I sleep in David's large wrought iron bed. The tea-light candles cast a flickering glow on the ceiling mural, and we search for the red

hummingbirds among the green leaves and orange blossoms of the trumpet vine painted in the mural, and he tells
a story he's never told me before.

Chester places my palm on his chest. "You feel it? You
feel the tick-tock the croc in my chest?"

"Sure do," I say, giggling.

"Once upon a time, there was a five-year-old boy,"
Chester says in his storytelling voice, husky and warm.

"And his name was Chester," I say.

"Ah, you know this boy," he says, chuckling. "One
day, he was at the Fairchild Botanic Garden in Miami.
Through the tangle of the mangrove swamp, a sparkle of
sun in the green bog catches the boy's eye. He approaches,
stealthily, through the undergrowth, footsteps soft on the
mossy earth. An alligator is sunning on a muddy bank.
Silent. Large and grey like a submarine."

He kisses my cheek and lowers his voice to a whisper.
"The boy crouches beside it, the palm of his hand on its
scaly, steely hide. He glides his hand along the roughness
of its ossified scutum. The boy's temples are pulsating. His
small hand presses tightly against the alligator many times
his size."

I feign a frightened look. Chester raises himself on his
elbow and looks deeply into my eyes. "The boy's heart beat
pounds in rhythm with the alligator's. And the moment is
an eternity. He's at one with the life force of the massive
animal—the boy and the alligator, one life, one heart."

"Grooowl!" Chester roars.

I scream, laughing.

"It's not the alligator. It's the boy's parents!" He chortles.
"They snatch him away and run. The boy had wandered

off, and they'd been looking for him. He glimpses his
mother's cried-out face, pale like raw fish. His father's
grimness. Why the worry? The boy never felt threatened.
Exhilarated! But not fearful. The alligator wasn't about to
harm him. Or was it?"

Chester's hand on mine, he runs my palm along his
chest. "Feel it?" he says. "You feel my clandestine heart?
The alligator beat in my bosom?"

"I had the pleasure of meeting your alligator," I say.
"At the same garden."

"You've been to the Fairchild Garden?"

"A few years back. Helena and I went to see Mark di
Suvero's exhibit. Five of his installations. We took a ride
on his famous 'She'."

"Did you sit on the swing?"

"We sure did. That's the largest swing I've ever seen.
A suspended platform," I say, and promise to show him
the photos.

"That sculpture has magical powers," he exclaims and
gathers me into an embrace. "And you saw my alligator?"

In candlelight, Chester looks enthralled. "Was he
huge? Was he fierce? My alligator?" He is laughing and his
put-on voice quavers, but I wonder if a small part of him
actually believes it could be the same alligator—the small,
adventurous five-year-old boy.

I savour the moment. "The *hugest* I've ever imagined.
It just lay there on the bank of a pond. They're a common
sight. But this one was humongous. Helena and I stayed
far away, though. We were amazed the alligators live in
those ponds in the midst of the garden and the visitors
simply wander around. Small children, as well."

"Must be well fed in those bogs—frogs, snakes, turtles, wandering small childr ..." He stops, eyes wide in the dancing shadows.

He props himself on his elbow, leans his ear to my chest, and listens to the beating in my breast. He tells me my covert heart is also thumping to the tick-tock the croc rhythm and he thanks the alligator for sharing its heart and tells me he and I and the alligator are as one. Invincible. And for the first time in a long while hope again takes root in me. And we dream.

CHAPTER 46

September, 2010

I INHALE THE fragrance of the lavender bouquet Chester brought this morning. A tiny card hanging on a purple ribbon reads: "To Blossom with love. Your alligator." He leaves love notes throughout my house to keep my spirits high, and to me he is Hansel from the fairy tale who sprinkles bread crumbs to help him find his way home —his way to me.

It has been several months since the stem cell transplant. I still think of the first critical hundred days in the hospital as a century in exile, an interlude between my previous life and my new one. Like the princess who pricks herself on a spindle and instead of dying is cursed into a century-long sleep—my hundred days, a hundred years of fading in and out of fever. And it is hope infused by love and teeming encouragement that sustained me and propelled me through the rough times. I am a new person in so many ways, I find myself trying to remember

the other Blossom, the weary, listless, feverish and fearful—fearful not just of dying but of living as well. Those
days are behind me now.

After the exile, I was able to return home and continue with medication under the transplant team's close
observation. The last couple of months have been almost
free of complications, and my medical tests show dramatic improvements. In the past few weeks, as if a miracle
had occurred, my energy level has been soaring. Each day
I wake up, I find myself believing Helena's stem cells have
magical properties that have infused me with her zeal for
life. Helena is like a winged fairy. She disseminates joy
among us as if she were the spring rain and we the flowers
in her garden. She is in a festive mood and David's old
apartment, which for decades has been the place to reminisce, and in Helena's words, the place to laugh and cry
and pray and be grateful, is still our refuge. We've cele-
brated birthdays, anniversaries, and Jane's official welcome to the family she'd always belonged to. Chester's
new name for Helena is Mother-Humming-Bird-Wing
and he utters it shortened, and it sounds like, *Muing*. She
adores her new moniker and claims it has brought her
mystical powers from some ancient civilizations of the
Orient. He tells us it's a take on the common Chinese
name *Ming*, which literally means "enlightenment." He
settles on her name being Mother-Muing and she wears it
proudly as she flutters about and hovers over us, her children—she, our communal mother. Chester teases her
that she is at once Tinker Bell and Wendy—spreading
pixie-dust infused with love.

This weekend Jane is visiting, and Helena and Chester

are preparing dinner at David's place, and although no words are spoken as we all know I still have a long way to go before I am out of the dark wood, I know it's to celebrate my recovery.

I waited at my house for Jane's arrival from Ottawa so we could drive to the apartment. When we get there, David's retro kitchen has been roused back into action. The aroma of baking bread wafts from the stainless steel bread maker on the counter, and the appliances are buzzing like bees in a clover field. Chester is blending fruit shakes in the red blender. Helena is whipping egg whites. And the mint-green Kaidette stand mixer Chester had rewired is kneading cookie dough and humming laboriously.

Jane and I retrieve the vintage Pyrex bowls and platters from the cupboards. We place the mixed greens in the gold butterfly bowl, the lentil salad in the spring blossom one, and the asparagus in the two-tone orange pudding basin. Chester serves the fruit blend in the stemmed plastic glasses in an array of misty colours—yellow, pink, purple, and lime green—with matching reusable straws washed with a miniature bottle brush kept especially for that purpose. It's a balmy summer day, and even the bees and butterflies seem lazy.

Chester has washed the patio furniture and replaced the chain on the rattan swing chair which, although bleached from the many summers, remains sturdy. Jane beats me to the rattan chair and climbs in, and after a few minutes of swaying, drink in hand, she bounds out and guiding me by the shoulders, plants me in it as if I were a cat.

I curl up in it and sip the fruit blend and recall that this was Liza's favourite seat. *Liza's swing.* And my memory of her materializes. She is snuggled at this same spot, the Queen Mother special in hand. Her dark hair with auburn highlights painted by the sun is spilling over her shoulders, and I am reminded of the transience of life and the importance of living in the moment.

I still do live in the moment, and yet, hope has rooted itself in me and is sprouting fast, like the green sapling stretching out of the avocado pit I suspended with toothpicks over a tumbler of water and placed on my window sill. The sunshine beating down on my hair and shoulders warms the invincible alligator heart beating in my chest. My eyes meet Chester's and I can read his thoughts. *Human body is guided by a purpose of its own — to heal itself.*

Helena sets the black wrought-iron patio table with David's mismatched flow blue china and his mismatched sterling silver cutlery. Jane lights the candles planted in the Chianti bottles that seem cemented to the chipped milk-glass plates by decades of use — by old wax that had sculpted rutted paths along the sides of the bulbous purple bottle glass and glazed the straw wrapping.

Chester has taken on the role of chef and the dinner is scrumptious — baked salmon topped with lemon wedges, roasted sweet potatoes, steamed asparagus, and a tossed green salad with red radicchio and avocado and Jane's homemade sundried tomato dressing. As we make up our plates Helena tells Chester that even David could not have prepared a more perfect meal. We know being compared with David is the best praise anyone could receive from Helena. Chester raises a toast to us, the family with alligator hearts — and we chime in with "tick-tock the croc."

For dessert, we have fresh berries. We pass the whipped

cream dispenser from one person to the next, and as we pile up the frothy topping, Jane and I reminisce about those decadent Sunday breakfasts from our childhood.

After we clean up and dusk sets in, the mosquitoes move onto the deck and we retreat into the living room and sit on the sofa in front of the Silvertone Suburbanite slim-angle TV. The newscaster appears and fades into the static-filled screen as if he were Omar Sharif in *Doctor Zhivago* — Anna's and Liza's all-time favourite movie — marching through the blizzard-ridden Siberian landscape. We strain to get the gist of the news on this snowy channel, the only one with some reception, as the cable service has never been connected.

The following day, after Jane leaves for Ottawa, Helena and I sit in my rose garden. It's a sunny Sunday afternoon, and as we sip lemonade, I say to her: "I miss you already, and you haven't left yet."

"I changed my flight. Staying for another week. Not leaving tomorrow. The following Monday."

I jump up in excitement. "That's fantastic! You're staying for the unveiling!"

The long anticipated reinstallation of *Flower Power* has finally begun. Mark di Suvero is in Toronto overseeing the reassembly of the refurbished sculpture. The official ceremony will take place on the weekend. Jane will be returning to Toronto for it as well.

"Lucky I could change my flight," Helena says. "Especially now that I don't have to worry about last night's storm. That little maintenance company's a dream. The one that takes care of my trailer. Those two women look after everything. They took all the precautions, covered the windows and all the rest. The storm did no damage. When I get back, it'll be as if I never left."

"You're lucky to have them," I say.

"Learned everything there's to know about maintaining a place from Anna. Pity her will hasn't been settled yet."

"The lawyer says it should be any day, now."

On the morning of the unveiling, Chester insists on driving instead of the four of us taking the subway, and Jane is glad. She came in the night before and the long bus ride, after a busy week of classes, left her drained. We arrive at the sculpture's new site, a prominent platform among high rises with clear visibility from the Queen Elizabeth Way and the railway lands, at a courtyard just south of Front Street on the West side of Spadina. I am not disappointed with the sculpture's new home — it will have many admirers. Although I cannot help but wish it were back at the place of its creation where I could visit more often.

Helena says: "I've seen *Flower Power's* birth in High Park. Seen it get run down. And now I see it rise again. It's spectacular."

Mark di Suvero, although aged, is tall and energetic as Liza used to describe him, and beaming with enthusiasm. He announces that *Flower Power* blooms again. He talks about the importance of the sculptures he created in Toronto, back in 1967. This was the first time he had the opportunity to work on a project of massive scale and to create pieces with steel I-beams, which became the focus of his career.

"In 1967," di Suvero says, "I was very dedicated to an idea, as I am now, that the world can exist in peace."

Helena whispers: "That's all we ever wanted. Peace. That's what David died for."

After a few speeches, the gathering begins to disperse. We walk over to di Suvero and introduce ourselves. He shakes our hands, and I can hardly believe that we're talking to this great man, to this world-renowned artist. He recalls Liza with much fondness and tells us how she kept the project moving smoothly and made sure the sculptors' supplies and equipment were plentiful and timely. He tells us that the Symposium provided a springboard to his career and how glad he is to be back in Toronto and to have his sculpture refurbished and reinstalled. I have heard so much about di Suvero and have spent so much time by his sculptures, I feel as if I have known him most of my life.

We say our goodbyes, and I have a strange feeling that Liza is with us.

di Suvero's conviction about peace is etched in my thoughts. *I was named after Flower Power—it gives me certain rights—I dedicate the new Flower Power to the world in peace.*

Chester leaves to pick up the car, and we make our way toward the street to meet him.

Suddenly, a young man wearing a baseball cap blocks my way and shoves a microphone in my face. "You're Blossom Grant, aren't you?"

I freeze. Helena places her palm over the mike. "Take a hike, young man," she says firmly.

"Excuse me," I say, and try to get by him.

"Excuse us, young man," Helena echoes. But he stands in front of us, with an elderly man holding a camera next to him.

"I know who *you* are," Helena cries out looking at the camera man. "Out of the way, you hound! Or you'll be hearing from my lawyer!"

Jane steps in front of us and spreads her arms out. "Step aside, or I'll call the police," she says to the reporters.

The young man slips under her arm and, pushing the microphone to my mouth, shouts: "You're Liza Grant and David Gould's 'love child' aren't you? David was accused of stealing that block of Carrara ..." I step back, away from him. He moves closer and reaches for my arm, and as I try to free myself from his grasp, I stagger and fall, landing on my knees and my palms. Jane rushes to my aid, and Helena screams, "Police!" and pulls the cell phone out of her purse. I close my eyes and wait a moment to let the pain in my knees dissipate.

I hear an irregular tapping on the cement accompanied by heavy footsteps and a sound of something dragging. When I look up, James the policeman is leaning over me. He and Jane are calling out: "You all right?" Jane slips her arms under mine and tries to lift me.

"Give me a moment," I say. "I'm fine." I get off my knees and sit on the cement pad. I hear a siren. James says: "I saw them. Called the police." He walks toward the approaching vehicle. Two officers step out. James talks with them briefly, and the next minute they are handcuffing the reporters and guiding them into the back of the cruiser.

CHAPTER 47

ELENA CHANGES HER flight again. She will stay until after the Christmas holidays.

"What's the point of flying back and forth," she says. "My maintenance crew is so good, the place is better taken care of than when I'm there. Those women should be cloned."

The more I try to convince her that I am perfectly all right, the more set she is on staying. Jane is thrilled. She has been visiting every few weeks since she broke up with her *new man*.

"After all these breakups, shouldn't you give up?" I say to Jane.

"Not a chance," she says. "I know *he* is out there somewhere. Just have to find him."

When Jane comes to Toronto again the following weekend, Helena and I suspect that she *found him* and wants to tell us in person.

As we sit in my rose garden on a sunny Saturday morning that feels more like July than late September, Jane pulls out the letter from Anna's lawyer and announces that Anna's will has been resolved. Jane is the owner of Anna's house on Pine Crest Road, a short walk from mine.

That afternoon, with Jane in the lead, we head to the stately arts and crafts house, which had been Anna's life-long pride and joy. We walk toward the front door along the cobblestone driveway under the mottled shade of a large oak—walk slowly, ritualistically—and this drive-way we know so well feels new. No longer Anna's. It is now Jane's driveway.

Helena wraps her arm around my shoulders. "Bloss, let's check out the backyard." She calls out to Jane. "We'll meet you down by the old garage."

Jane pulls out a set of keys from her purse. "Come with me. I can't do this on my own."

"You go on in. It's a big moment for you," Helena says softly, her eyebrows raised in an encouraging slant.

Jane walks to the front door and Helena and I take the winding path along the side of the house that leads to the backyard. Although two years have gone by since Anna's death, every corner of the house is clean and tidy as it always had been. The maintenance company Anna arranged before her death has been taking care of the place, but while the court case went on, we did not feel comfortable visiting Anna's house. Now, it all feels new somehow. I am reminded how Anna's garden receives more sunshine than mine, and her flowers bloom longer in the fall. The summer phlox, in shades of pink and

purple, is still in full bloom. The butterfly bushes are ha-
loed by flitting monarchs stockpiling on pollen before
their journey to oyamel fir forests of Mexico. And the
sweetly-scented breeze rising from the slope leading to
the valley below is intoxicating.

Some of the backyards of the houses on this side of
Pine Crest Road slope down a couple of stories to the street
in the valley below, where they have their garages and
coach-houses — many left overgrown. When we were
children, Jane and I played house at the patches we cleared
among the goldenrod and queen's lace and the dense
shrubbery. We called it our enchanted garden — the bees
and the butterflies were our fairies.

"I'll go see how Jane's doing," I call out to Helena. I'd
like to walk down those overgrown steps with her, as we
have done many times before.

I return to the front entrance of the house. Jane is still
there, hesitant. She raises the brass ring beneath the lion-
head knocker, then gently lowers it back onto its groove.
She peers through the light yellow tulip in the stained
glass pane of the door. Then she slowly unlocks the door
and steps into the hallway. She waves me in, signals me to
follow. I cross the threshold — the oak grain of the step is
still gleaming. Jane and I had stripped the old varnish and
had refinished the wood not long before Anna died. I take
Jane's hand and we inhale the familiar scent of furniture
polish.

"I almost expect Anna to welcome us with open

arms," Jane murmurs. Then she wrinkles up her nose and makes her wet-kitten face. "I mean *my mother ...*" She stops mid-sentence and shrugs.

I wrap my arm around her shoulder. "You've always called her Anna. You can't expect to change things now."

She nods and walks over to the kitchen window and opens it to let in fresh air. Then she rushes out through the side door into the backyard. *She will not allow tears to ruin the moment, no.*

I follow, and we pause quietly on the back porch before returning to the kitchen.

On the counter is a yellow envelope with Jane's name and "open me" written in capital letters. I pick it up and hand it to her. She shrugs, pulls a kitchen knife out of a drawer, and slides it in. She pulls out a handwritten page, and I step back out onto the porch. A few minutes later I hear crying. I rush back in. Jane is holding the letter in her hand, tears streaming down her cheeks—but she is smiling and snivelling at the same time while her shoulders are rising and falling with sobs. I've never seen Jane cry. This is the first. And she is smiling? She hands the letter to me and nods to me to read it.

> *My dearest Janey,*
>
> *My regret, my only regret is—not being a proper mother to you.*
>
> *You gave meaning to my life. And whatever mistakes I've made, hope you can forgive me.*
>
> *I've carried my gargantuan secret for so long, I could not let go—could not release it out into the world not knowing what damage it could cause. The*

universe does not like secrets. It conspires to reveal the truth. Yet I kept it. Kept the miracle that shaped my private life — out of my public one.

I have been tempted and driven and often obsessed to the point of madness with the desire to call you Daughter, my sweet Janey, my love. To tell you how you are my reason for living. You have the right to know.

But the thought frightened me. Revealing it would be like throwing the book that is my life — the book I carefully arranged page by page, event by event, with no gaps left in the plot — into the wind and all the loose sheets blown into disarray that could never be put back together to tell the same story. What if you could not forgive me? What if you decided never to see me again? What then?

No, don't go there, I told myself. Things have been going well. Don't open this Pandora box. It could lead to consequences much worse than living with my secret — this division into two lives. It has worked well so far. I must curb the desire to open up to you, I convinced myself. Even if you are part of it.

Sweet Janey, will you ever find it in your heart to forgive me?

Your mother

Jane and I hug and gaze into each other's eyes for a long while, silently — and we both know this is one of those moments when words are obsolete.

We walk down the winding steps to the naturalized lower part of the yard overgrown by grass and sweet alyssum that seeds itself year after year. The stairway leads to the stone-rubble garage, and we step back in time. The disparity between the orderliness above and the wilderness below is accentuated by the dilapidated structure shrouded by trees and shrubbery.

Jane's girlish smile tells me we're thinking the same — about playing hide-go-seek with neighbourhood children. I can still hear Anna's warning to stay away from the rundown building, the same one we're about to enter.

This had been one place left to itself — we'd never seen anyone enter or leave. We've always called it a garage, although at one time it was a coach house. Weeds, like hanging flower baskets, bow from wall cracks. Shrubbery pokes out of the crevices in the stone rubble foundation like swords wedged in by some ancient soldiers. I peek through the small rectangular window, but the frosted glass insert allows only a multi-coloured blur.

Jane turns the tarnished brass handle of the weathered door, but it does not budge. She jangles an assortment of cast iron skeleton keys suspended on a metal ring as if she were a prison guard. She picks the one with a yellow tag, inserts it in the keyhole, joggles it until it catches, and the wooden door gives with an ominous groan. We step into the dusky interior and it takes a few moments for our eyes to adjust. The open rafters give airiness to the space, which is incongruous to the squat appearance from outside.

Helena has been inspecting Anna's garden figures — a stone dragon the colour of seaweed, a Buddhist temple, a girl with an umbrella. As she approaches, her new running shoes make squishing sounds as if she is walking on wet grass. She steps into the garage, glances around the room, and shakes her head. "When David was alive, this place was stuffed with supplies for making demonstration signs."

Jane props her hands on her hips. "This sure isn't what I expected. Somebody's cleaned it up. It couldn't have been like this for the last forty years."

The whole interior is covered with a light coating of dust, but otherwise, the place is uncluttered. The outside walls are lined with metal shelves filled with plastic storage boxes, some with tools and all kinds of do-jiggers poking out. A rocking chair, a wicker cradle, a carved wooden hope chest—the type brides brought with them on a ship from some European country—and a stack of blue metal trunks take cover under a small green tarp folded and laid over top.

In the middle of the room, under a drop sheet, is a square object that hints at a low coffee table. Jane and I exchange puzzled looks and step closer. Jane lifts the cover to reveal a block of dark granite about a yard square. The top is chipped and bruised. Its weight has sunken the cobble stones beneath it and the frost of many winters has heaved it so it appears lopsided. And like a mosaic, the gaps between the pavers around it are filled with white marble chips.

Helena kneels next to the granite and passes her palm over the battered surface. She rests her forehead on her folded arms. Jane and I rush to her side, but the wave of her hand tells us that she needs this moment to herself.

CHAPTER 48

August 2017

JANE AND I sport the sixties garb we've gathered searching through Anna's and Liza's cedar chests and scavenging used clothing stores. In a gold mini-skirt and a mod sequined tank top, Jane looks glamorous. She's kept up her jogging and is as fit in her fifties as she was in her thirties. A large copper tree-of-life pendant suspended on a leather string sits on her chest. Her shiny white go-go boots and a pair of enormous rhinestone sunglasses complete the look, and I think it a pity she did not live in the sixties.

She is equally impressed with my transformation—a creamy peasant blouse with a long, flowing paisley skirt in earth tones, a seashell necklace and a multi-strand bracelet, a wide suede belt and matching ankle booties that could double as house slippers. And a multi-coloured scarf tied as a headband.

Helena is her usual self. She picked out one of her

frumpy skirts and Indian cotton blouses. With a permanently creased beige cotton vest and Birkenstocks, long silvery locks flowing over her shoulders, and a daisy behind her ear, she looks the part. We admire our reflections in the hallway mirror as we wait for Chester to pick us up.

This is the first day of Toronto's weekend-long Art-of-the-Sixties Festival. Over two days and nights, non-stop art exhibits, concerts, and literary readings will take place at various venues throughout the city. The Art Gallery of Ontario and the Toronto Arts College are featuring displays which will remain open around the clock.

Chester has taken on the task of driving and planning for parking spots along the way in hopes of covering more ground than going in and out of the subway. Helena has set out an itinerary. We were able to cross off a visit to the restored *Flower Power* and *No Shoes* as we had attended the earlier reinstallation ceremonies.

As we wait for Chester, we peruse the Festival agenda. Canadian musicians and authors, many with humble beginnings in the sixties, are featured at concerts and readings with proceeds going to charities and non-profit organizations.

Jane does not want to miss the Neil Young concert. She tells us it's because it will fund a program that builds green affordable housing in the inner city. But Helena and I know it's because she gets weak in the knees every time she hears that cracked falsetto voice of his. Though I understand. I don't want to miss Gordon Lightfoot's performance. Not only because it will raise funds to add three hundred beds to shelters for the homeless, but also because hearing him sing his "Canadian Railroad Trilogy," or "Couchiching, Couchiching," inspired by the lake at Orillia, his home town, where I spent many summer vacations, would be thrilling. Also, this would be the first of the series of concerts in support of Canada-wide social justice issues — a collaborative venture with David Suzuki and First Nations people — and I'll do all I can to support it.

Helena is determined to hear Joni Mitchell's poetry reading at Massey Hall which will fund a tree-planting initiative for city parks and open spaces. During her recent show in Toronto, Joni stayed at the Chelsea Hotel and was awed by Lake Ontario and the expanse of greenery of Toronto Islands. When she passed by Dundas Square across from Eaton's Centre, the grey pavement reminded her of a parking lot. She managed to convince the city to designate the eastern wedge of the Square as a parkette, and to plant trees and install flower beds and benches.

And we've all marked Margaret Atwood's evening of readings at Hart House as a must. It would be followed by an open mic, and would raise funds for a women's shelter for victims of domestic violence.

We certainly cannot miss Leonard Cohen's concert — the funds are designated toward the purchase of musical instruments for children from low income families. Besides, we've been life-long fans. And here's another must-do — a Ricky James tribute concert in support of a drug rehabilitation centre. Knowing about Ricky's and Anna's passionate love affair gives us the right to call him Uncle Ricky — how could we possibly miss this event? In all, the Festival offers over fifty concerts, readings, and art exhibits. And we'll be riding on caffeine if need be, to cover as much as possible.

The highlight of the Festival will be the unveiling of the installation at Nathan Phillips Square to honour Alice Munro. It's a tower of books about ten metres high, formed by a stack of fluorescent lights with titles of her short stories for which she became the first Canadian to win the Nobel Prize in literature. Next to the tower is a "read-in shack" — a gazebo that will accommodate non-stop readings by authors. The donations will support the city's literacy programs for disadvantaged children.

The Festival also includes a self-guided tour of Art-of-the-Sixties that runs through city parks and galleries. Some of the major exhibits such as the sculptures installed during the 1967 Art Symposium in High Park are listed as a must-see and include the audio tour which had been installed at selected locations over the past year.

Chester swings his Honda into my driveway and steps out of the car. We hardly recognize him — he is sporting a shoulder-length black wig, mirrored shades with round lenses, a tie-died purple tunic, and a fringed suede vest over it. And bell-bottom jeans. A large Love button is pinned to his breast pocket. As he approaches the front door he raises the fingers of both hands in a peace sign. We laugh so hard our stomachs hurt.

Chester enfolds Helena into a hug. "Gorgeous as always, Mother-Muing."

And we're off.

We voted Helena the group's official guide, as she had lived the sixties. She suggests we begin the tour at *Femina*, which had been reinstalled in the newly completed atrium at Women's Centenary Hospital. We enter the atrium and are dwarfed by the voluminous space. The white marble sculpture about two metres high, for decades relegated to a corner of the hospital's old lobby, is now the centrepiece of the new atrium. The familiar figure — an abstract, elongated shape of a woman — is set in a reflecting pool about five metres wide. Every so often, jets of water rise from the pool's rim and cup the figure as if in a lotus flower.

This is the first time I see the figure since it has been moved from the old lobby. While at the hospital, I had spent much time near *Femina*, as it offered me comfort I could not explain to anyone — not Chester or Helena, and not even Jane. I have shared my white sculpture dream with them, but have not told them this marble figure is *as in my dream*. Perhaps they would've understood. Yet, this sublime emotion I submerge in each time the white figure comes to me in a dream is too personal. I fix my eyes on the sculpture's face and feel a presence. Otherworldly. Who could possibly relate to my vision?

The sculpture stands on a round marble base that elevates it above the water. The plaque on the pool's rim reads: "*Femina* was a collaborative project of the Toronto Arts College students. In 1971, it was donated to the hospital to commemorate its founders. She symbolizes the strength of all women, and embodies the commitment to women's progress in arts and sciences."

As the water spouts erupt, the still surface of the pool shatters, and the marble figure sways in the reflection of the azure tiled bottom of the pool as if it were a deep blue ocean. She bends and shifts fitfully, like some mythical stone woman brought to life.

I am spellbound. "In my dream, she's just like this. Except she's planting coral. And last night, I saw her face."

Jane lifts her rhinestone sunglasses to the top of her head. She puts on a cheerful look. "What are you saying, Bloss? Did you have your sculpture dream again last night? You know, Cellini's 'Cornucopia.' Botticelli's 'Birth of Venus'."

Jane the pragmatist, a non-believer in signs and dreams.

I walk over to the sitting area and settle into a brown leather sofa. Helena and Jane join me, and Chester leans against the window ledge, each silent in thought. The morning sun clambering over the high-rises casts shattered-glass wedges throughout the atrium. The few who come and go tread gently without a word on this Saturday morning, as if they'd all taken a vow of silence.

Chester glances at his watch. "Got to feed the parking meter. How 'bout some muffins and coffee, ladies? There's a place across the street."

"Let's meet there in a few minutes," Jane says getting up from the bench and approaching the pool. Chester jingles the keys as he heads to the door, and we gather around *Femina*.

Jane studies the figure. "Some people believe she symbolizes a nurse. Or a nun. It's her mantel and head piece. Her veiled face."

"There's a lot more to this stone woman than meets the eye," Helena says proudly, as if she's talking about a close friend. "She's a champion for women. To do their best. So she's here. Encouraging. Inspiring."

Jane places her arm under mine. "So, you saw her face, Bloss? In your dream last night."

I nod. "It's funny. I never thought I'd get to see it. And last night, in that surreal world at the ocean floor, the figure turned. Our eyes met—for only a moment. It was eerie. Now, when I close my eyes, she's there. And this sculpture ... there's something about this piece."

Jane tilts her head and squints an eye as if she's observing me through a microscope. "Did she resemble anyone you know, Bloss?"

"It's Liza," I say quietly.

"Liza?"

"Not the way I knew her. She's different, somehow. Strange."

Helena brushes the front of her skirt with her palms as if she's removing lint—the way Anna used to when feeling out of place. "We honoured our code of secrecy—in memory of David and what he stood for." She heaves a sigh. "But now it's time for unveiling. Those muffins and coffee Chester suggested? We better get going. He might be there by now."

We approach the door, and it slides open. On the other side, coming in, is James. Helena props her arms on her hips: "What on earth are you doing here?"

He is leaning on his cane, awkwardly. He raises his bushy eyebrows. "The new home. For *Femina*. Gotta see it for myself," he says. "It's a festival, isn't it? I lived the sixties too, remember?"

We exchange brief pleasantries as we always do when we see James taking his walks through the neighbourhood. After the incident at the reinstallation of *Flower Power*, I invited him over for tea a few times as a way of thanking him, but he used one type of excuse or another until I gave up. He encouraged me to press charges against the reporters, which I did, and he offered to serve as a witness, along with Helena, Chester and Jane. But the case was settled out of court, and I am glad that I have not been accosted by them since.

Helena stares at him, puzzled. He shifts his weight and his shoes squeak and remind me of Anna's funeral. He looks a bit haggard, as if he has been ill, and seems to have aged since I last saw him, a few months back. He gestures with his eyes toward the sofa and says to Helena: "Wanna chat? For a bit?"

She continues staring at him, then turns to us. "You go on. I'll be there in a flash."

CHAPTER 49

T STARBUCKS, WE huddle around the square granite-topped table overlooking the street. Jane and I sip tea and Chester holds a mug of hot chocolate. Helena arrives about forty minutes later. She looks anxious. Distracted. Perplexed.

"What was that about?" Jane says. "Why was James there? Why is he interested in that sculpture? And what did you two talk about?"

"Give me a minute, dears, will you?" Helena says.

Her coffee arrives. She scoops a teaspoon of cappuccino froth and savours the cinnamon laced topping. She folds her arms across her chest and leans back into the chair. "We swore an oath of secrecy, Anna, Liza and I. We knew some day the truth would be told. What I had done. And why. What David and I stood for."

She gazes pensively through the window. Silence encapsulates us and blocks out the cacophony of chattering customers as if they exist in another realm. The stories about David have been told and retold so often, I imagine him as a guru who, even in death, carries on his struggle for peace.

Helena scans the crowd in the coffee shop—medical staff, hospital volunteers, and visitors. A group of young Festival goers—bell-bottoms and tie-dye shirts and over-sized sunglasses. "On the outside, we're just like them," she says. "But on the inside, I'm alone. With memories not shared."

Helena takes a deep breath. "David needed to realize his vision. If in this whole mayhem of existence I could make it come true, then I would. If I were to do it all over again, I wouldn't change a thing. The first time he laid eyes on that block of marble, he sensed a form only he could bring to life. Then he realized it was not just any figure. It was of Liza. His want of that stone turned into an obsession. And moral agony.

"I told David he should steal it. He laughed.

"David and I had a huge argument over my missing classes. I told him he had no control over me. Never to treat me like his little sister. If he told anyone I was his sister, I would move back to the states and enlist in the war.

"I told a few of our protest organizers—how David fell in love with that block of marble. I was angry at him —it felt good to make fun of him. One guy worked for a construction company and had access to a flatbed truck. 'Let's steal it,' he said, 'and give it to your bro as a gift.'

"We were high most of the time and thought it hilari-ous. Stealing a block of stone from a park. It became an in-joke. For a few weeks. One evening our friend said: 'It's now or never. Got it all arranged. Me and a few guys.'

"He was not joking. 'Where do you want it?' he said. He had the keys to the truck and a fork lift already loaded and a few friends who wanted in on the excitement.

"We covered the license plates, drove into the park shortly after midnight, and took it. It was ridiculously easy.

"We didn't know what to do with it. We drove it around Roncesvalles for a while, covered under a tarp. One guy knew of a dilapidated shed in Parkdale. It was once a car-repair shop. When we got there, it looked abandoned. And had a huge wooden door. The guys managed to get the fork lift right through it.

"Afterwards, we returned the truck and piled into our friend's car and drove back to the park. We drank some beer and smoked a few joints, and it was dawn by the time we dragged ourselves home.

"We heard all the commotion, and about a week later went back to the shed at night to see that the stone was still there. We couldn't believe no one saw us. We thought we'd be thrown in jail. I almost wished it just to spite David. I wondered if I'd ever get the courage to tell him.

"A few weeks later, David and I had another argument. He found out I dropped out of school. And he saw me with some Vagabonds. When I reminded him he was friends with the Angels, he said that was different. He did it for a reason. And I had none. I was a girl, and it was not safe for me. He told me that sooner or later things would get rough for me. Seriously rough. And I would regret it.

"Then I told him I had a gift for him. I took him to

the shed. He became so angry I thought he'd have a heart attack. I'd never seen him that enraged.

"After several days, he told me he'd arrange for the stone to be returned to the park. I freaked out. I was convinced he'd get caught. And returned to the States. And sent to the war. And got killed.

"I begged him to reconsider. Promised to do anything he wanted of me. Promised to go back to school. To stay away from Vags. To stop dating 'losers' — I was tired of all that anyway.

"He said he would think about it.

"One night, I rode my bike to that shed. It was past midnight. The place was deserted. I waked in and there he was. David. Sleeping next to that stone.

"That night, for the first time since we were children, we had a real heart-to-heart. About his wife who was killed. About my fiancé who met a similar fate in Vietnam. About the horrors of war and why he and I do what we do. Why we organize the demonstrations. And how in spite of everything, we believe peace could happen without war.

"I told him he should keep that stone and turn it into his vision. For his dead wife. For me. For Liza with whom he was in love. It should become an inspiration to all the women, past, present and future. It was meant for him.

"*Femina*, he said. We could call it *Femina*. But he couldn't do that, he said. He was an artist. He couldn't take another man's stone.

"Then he gave in. A figure of the woman he loved was trapped in that block of marble, and he had to give it life. He began to work on it. He'd go all night with no sleep."

Helena props her chin in her palms and remains quiet for a long while. "After the second beating in the prison, David knew he wasn't going to make it. While I tried to get him into the hospital, he wrote letters to Liza. He went on and on about failing her. She was all that mattered. He made me promise I would finish the sculpture. He gave me a letter for a colleague at Toronto Arts College. She was one of the movement leaders. He told me to tell her everything—to hide nothing. She guided us every step of the way. One thing about the movement is how it brought us together—friends from diverse backgrounds—ethnic, religious, educational. We made a pact to continue our work with the antiwar movement. And to realize David's vision. David had done much work on *Femina*. 'Make it count, Helena, use it for a good cause,' he'd told me. He'd gone on about the importance of not getting caught. Of making sure none of us could in any way be linked to it. I returned to my studies. I enrolled at Toronto Arts College. The program was hands-on, and I dove in with a zeal I never knew I had. I was told I had a talent for sculpting, a good eye for scale, shape, and dimension. What started out as a promise to David became my calling. The dilapidated storage shed in Parkdale where the sculpture had been stored was slated for demolition. A condominium complex would be built. We moved the figure to Anna's garage—Anna insisted—where I could work on it. After losing David, all my thoughts ran into sorrow. Once I took on his project, my grief drove me to sculpt. He'd done a lot of work on it, and I followed a copy in plaster he'd cast as a model. Made sure it would be as he'd envisioned it. I fell in love with *Femina*. Shaped her as if the chisel in my hand was guided by some invisible spirit. We let the hype over the stolen marble in High Park settle down."

Helena clears her throat, nervously. "Liza was worried about the curse. She told us about her family legacy — that she was not meant for love. That she was to blame for David's death. That the stolen marble would bring the curse on to her child. So we found the fortune teller. Asked her how to remove the curse. She said she couldn't help. Then she told us, if the stolen marble was used for a good cause, the curse might dissipate on its own. It's the all-seeing eye, the higher power, the good and the evil forces at battle. At the end, the good always wins over, she'd said. Anna and I couldn't believe — that did it for Liza. We ordered another block of white marble for the Toronto Arts College. It took a year for it to arrive from the mountains of Carrara. This way, the college had a piece to work on — as well as a record of a purchase with an agreement of anonymity by a private benefactor, while the cost was covered by David's estate. It took a few years, one step at a time. When we felt safe, we brought *Femina* to a warehouse which served as a work area and storage for the students. In the meantime, we donated the new block of marble to another arts school with an agreement of anonymity. We engaged a number of students in putting the final touches to the figure, then had it donated to the Women's Centenary Hospital. And the rest is history as you know it. *Femina* has been an inspiration to women to be the best they could be. She's doing good work."

Helena shrugs and smiles. "And I kept my promise to myself as well. I resolved to create for the common folk.

My pieces would be affordable. I didn't go after large commissions. Nor prestigious ones. That little shack by my trailer in Coral Gables is what it's about for me. Carving small pieces. Selling at art festivals and beach stands. I've done some garden figures. I love working with white marble. Reminds me of David."

My head is exploding from all this. I would like to ask how Liza could have kept this from me. How could they do this to me? But I cannot. Somehow, in some deep chamber of my mind, it all makes sense.

I try to say something, but the words don't form. I am tongue-tied. I gaze at Chester and Jane — they are silent and still. *As if we've all been turned to stone.*

After a long pause Helena gets up. "One more thing," she says. "I'll be right back."

She walks to the far corner of the coffee shop where James sits at the table, reading the newspaper. Jane, Chester and I exchange dubious glances. Jane says: "Didn't I just ask Helena what she and James talked about? And there he is."

Helena picks up James' coffee and walks toward us. James gets up and leaning on his cane, follows. Chester pulls up another chair.

We sit quietly for a few long moments. Helena looks at James. "This is it. All cards on the table."

He shrugs. "Not much to tell. Except I know."

Jane shakes her head. "Everything?"

His eyebrows gather. "No, not everything. But enough. I found out a couple of years later, when the sculpture was moved to Anna's garage. I went in … broke in … was determined to solve that case … and I couldn't bring myself to report it. As Liza used to say, it was only a chunk of stone that was stolen, like a lump of clay, and not a piece of art."

"Liza kept it all in. Never said a word," Helena murmurs.

James shrugs. "Liza and I thought that was best. For all of us."

"All these years. We thought you were still looking for that stone," Jane says.

He laughs and gives Helena a meaningful stare. "Never did find that stone. Found a sculpture, instead."

Helena claps her hands, her face beaming. "And now, *we* have a pact. Lift your cup, James, my friend."

Chester nods. "Sure do. We're the family with alligator hearts."

We clink our cups. "Tick-tock the croc." And our secret is etched in stone — literally.

EPILOGUE

T THE ART Gallery of Ontario, we study the wall of photographs with "significant" motifs of the sixties that capture the spirit of innovation and socio-cultural awakening—antiwar demonstrations, scenes of Yorkville, of Paint-ins and Love-ins and Be-ins—that draws waves of enthusiasts.

We proceed to the special collection of sculptures acquired by the Gallery. Helena pauses at a piece displayed on a column that positions it at eye-level. The figure cast in bronze is about thirty centimetres high. It features a young woman with a garland of daises on her head, waist long hair evoking an image of being blown by the wind, and a skirt swished in a twirl-like pose. In her hand, she is holding a disproportionately large daisy and fitting it in the barrel of a gun pointed at her by a teenage soldier.

Helena stands motionless. She grabs my hand with

an iron grip. "Blossom, my girl! The exhibit in Boston. David's exhibit."

Jane and Chester huddle closer. Helena continues. "This was David's prized bronze. It was the centrepiece of the show. And it disappeared during the event. We never found out what happened to it."

She covers her eyes with her hands. "I can't look. I don't want to know. This is David's piece. No one else's. All these years. And now, someone's claiming it as their own?"

Helena stands still and takes shallow breaths.

I read the inscription first to myself, and then out loud:

"Child Soldier, by David Gould (1934-1967), a sculptor born in Boson, USA. He immigrated to Canada as a draft dodger and was one of the leaders of the antiwar move-ment … Child Soldier, donated to AGO by a gallery in Boston, on behalf on an anonymous donor, is part of the AGO's collection of significant art of the sixties."

Helena claps her hands, her luminous smile rejuven-ating her face into blissfulness, the way I remember her as a child, which tells me all is well. She enfolds us into a hug and whispers: "Everything David did was for love."

Non quo sed quomodo, Not what we do but how.

ACKNOWLEDGEMENTS

In the process of researching and writing this novel, I have encountered so many wonderful people who have provided valuable information, who have read and critiqued excerpts or the whole piece, and most of all, who have inspired this novel along the way, that I feel indebted to all.

My immense gratitude to my editor and publisher Michael Mirolla for his insightful and meticulous editing of this novel and for entering the lives of its characters with compassion and editorial rigor that helped bring it to life on the page, to Connie McParland for her guidance and inspiration, to both for their continuous support, and to all at Guernica Editions — a staunch proponent of multicultural voices for over 35 years.

To David Moratto for the quirky book cover I love; Gabriel Quigley for a whimsical book trailer; Anna Geisler for her tireless advocacy on behalf of the writers.

Special thanks to Bethany Gibson for peering deeply into the shadows of the earlier draft of this novel and for offering detailed and constructive feedback.

My gracious thanks to Frances Gage, a true Canadian icon, for sharing with me her wisdom and knowledge as a sculptor and what it took—her joys and sacrifices—to follow her calling as an artist. Frances revealed to me that *Woman* is her favourite piece: "To me, *Woman* is all women," —our conversation of Feb. 20, 2016.

My special thanks to Karen Yukich from Friends of High Park for providing valuable insights on High Park history, art, and natural habitat, and for her ongoing support and encouragement as well as her kindness and patience with my endless questions over the years.

Kind thanks to David DePoe for sharing his experiences of the 1960s and 1970s Yorkville, and for providing valuable insight into the challenges draft dodgers and deserters faced during that time. During the 1960s, David was the leader of the community activist group known as The Diggers. The group helped provide food, shelter, and employment for the youth living on the streets as well as newcomers and the Village residents. Under DePoe's leadership, the group also organized a number of protests such as the Sit-in—an attempt to deal with traffic gridlock on Yorkville Avenue; the Love-in at Queen's Park; and the Talk-in with Toronto City Council.

Thanks to Lloyd DeWitt, Curator of European Art at the Art Gallery of Ontario, for providing tips and leads on researching works of art, and sculpture in particular, and for facilitating access to the AGO library.

My gratitude to Women's College Hospital for providing access to *Woman,* for its leadership and mission to "advance and advocate for the health of women and improve health care options for all by developing, researching, teaching and delivering new treatments and models of integrated care"—and for inspiration.

Thanks to the numerous libraries and their efficient and knowledgeable librarians: Toronto Public Libraries — City of Toronto Archives Library; Toronto Reference Library — among others; University of Toronto Libraries; York University Libraries; Art Gallery of Ontario Library, among others.

Thanks to Toronto Police Service, Division 11, 22, and 14 for providing advice on police procedures.

The following works provided inspiration and the info on the period: Margaret Atwood, *Double Persephone*, a collection of poetry she had self-published in 1961 inspired certain scenes. Story has it that after having the poems printed, Atwood had the pages hand-sewn into booklets which sold at Yorkville stores and coffee houses at 50 cents a copy. Stuart Robert Henderson, *Making the Scene: Yorkville and Hip Toronto*, 1960-1970, a Doctorate thesis, Queen's U, Kingston, ON, 2007; Nicholas Jennings, *Before the Gold Rush: Peace, Love, and the Dawn of Canadian Sound*, Viking, 1998; John Warkentin, *Creating Memory: A Guide to Outdoor Public Sculpture in Toronto*, Becker Associates, York U, 2010; David Burnett and Marilyn Schiff, *Contemporary Canadian Art*, Hurtig Publishers with The Art Gallery of Ontario, 1983; Sidney Lens, *Vietnam: A War on Two Fronts*, Lodestar Books, 1990; Don Lawson, *An Album of the Vietnam War*, Franklin Watts, 1986; Katie Daynes, *The Vietnam War*, Usborne Publishing, 2008; Denise Chong, *The Girl in the Picture: The Story of Kim Phuc, The Photograph, and The Vietnam War*, Penguin, 2001; Michael H. Hunt, *The Vietnam War Reader: American and Vietnamese Perspective*, Penguin, 2010; Dave Bidini, *Writing Gordon Lightfoot: The Man, The Music, And The World In 1972*,

McClelland & Stewart, 2012; Lela M. Wilson, *York Wilson, His Life and Work 1907-1984*, York University Press & Carleton University Gallery, 1997; Henry Mietkiewicz and Bob Mackowycz, *Dream Tower: The Life and Legacy of Rochdale College*, McGraw-Hill Ryerson Ltd., 1988; Gino Gaudio, essay, "Vietnam War Draft Dodgers North of the Border: The Impress of the Dividing Line," York U; Anita Aarons, "An Absent Minded Attitude and Events," *Architecture Canada*, October, 1967; Arnaud Maggs fonds, 1967, City of Toronto Archives Library; "Look at What's Happening in High Park," *Toronto Daily Star*, July 3, 1967; "Sculptor's 700 Ton Torture," *The Globe and Mail*, Oct. 2, 1967; Anita Aarons, Urjo Kareda, "Sculpt-in: the hectic background," *The Globe and Mail*, Sep. 2, 1967; "What the Dickens or a Tale of Two Cities," *Arts*, 3, 1967; "Yes, Virginia (and New York) there is a 'Canadian' art," Barry Lord, 1967; Hugh Garner, "A Sculpt-in comes to Toronto," *Toronto Life*, July 1967; "The artists and Expo," Norman Alexander Armstrong, *Architecture Canada*, 1967; Barbara Fischer, "Sculpture in the Garden," Toronto Sculpture Garden, 2008; Paul King, "Urban Pose," *The Canadian*, Oct. 1971; "Toronto International Sculpture Symposium 1967," a pamphlet, Toronto Reference Library. Numerous other books, essays, journals, lectures, radio and TV programs, movies, magazine and newspaper articles and columns, conversations, and websites, were also very helpful.

I would also like to thank my colleagues at various writers associations and critiquing groups: Bloorwestwriters who were the first to critique the very early chapters way back in 2007; Toronto Writers Co-op members who read excerpts and offered feedback; Wasaga Beach

Writers for helping tweak excerpts from the most recent drafts of the novel; Algonquin Square Table at U of T, at the time led by Albert Moritz, for critiquing some of the stanzas in their early stages, back in 2007-9; to Mirko for listening to my many permutations of the plot and for providing feedback on early chapters; to Shellina for sharing details on emergency procedures; to Jake Hogeterp and Liisa Hypponen (board members during my presidency at the Canadian Authors Association, Toronto) for pondering the plot when the novel was only in its infancy. To friends and colleagues who offered suggestions and shared expertise.

An excerpt from Chapter 31 was published in an anthology, *Gathered Streams*, 2010, under the working title of the novel which at the time was *Flower Power*.

My heartfelt thanks to my family for their love and unwavering support. To Sierra Sunrise, Austin Robert, Sarah, Michelle, Marijan, Adrian, and Mirko.

For a map of High Park and its sculptures, please see: http://www.highparktoronto.com/map.php

Frances Gage's *Woman* is housed at Women's College Hospital in Toronto.

About the Author

Bianca Lakoseljac is an author and educator with special interest in women's issues, the environment, and social justice. She holds a BA and MA in English from York University, and is the recipient of the Matthew Ahern Memorial Award in Literature. Bianca taught communication at Ryerson University and Humber College.

She has judged literary contests such as the National Capital Writing Contest, the Dr. Drummond Poetry Contest, the Canadian Aid Literary Award Contest, and served on panels for the League of Canadian Poets and the Writers Union of Canada.

Bianca is a liaison with the National Reading Campaign on behalf of The Writers Union of Canada, and sat on the TWUC National Council; she is past president of the Canadian Authors Association, Toronto Branch; served as a board member of the Book and Periodical Council; and sat on the Freedom of Expression Committee for a number of years. She is a member of the C.G. Jung Foundation of Ontario. She is also a member of the Writers Union of Canada, PEN, CWILA, and the League of Canadian Poets, among others.

Other Publications

Summer of the Dancing Bear
A novel exploring the rite of passage of a
fourteen-year-old girl befriended by a gypsy clan,
set in the countryside near Belgrade.
Guernica Editions, Toronto, 2012.

Bridge in the Rain
A collection of stories linked by an inscription
on a bench in Toronto's High Park.
Guernica Editions, Toronto, 2010.

Memoirs of a Praying Mantis
A collection of poetry addressing environmental
issues, horrors of war, and legends of High Park.
Turtle Moons Press, Ottawa, 2009.

Work in progress: another novel set in Toronto.

Her short stories and poems have been published in journals
and anthologies such as: *Canadian Woman Studies,* Inanna
Publications and Education, York University, 2007; *Canadian
Voices,* BookLand Press, 2009; *Migrating Memories: Central
Europe in Canada*, Central European Association for Can-
adian Studies, 2010; and *50+ Poems for Gordon Lightfoot*, The
Old Brewery Bay Press, Stephen Leacock Museum, 2014.

Bianca divides her time between Toronto and Woodland
Beach on Georgian Bay.

Bianca Lakoseljac
www.biancalakoseljac.ca

Printed in July 2016
by Gauvin Press,
Gatineau, Québec